An Erotic Compilation

A collection of nine erotic stories

By Lonely Woman

Lonely Woman

About the Author:

Follow me on twitter @RealLonelyWoman or on facebook.com/LonelyWomanAuthor
You can find my other works on amazon.
If you read this book, please leave a review.
I enjoy writing sex as much as I enjoy having it. Every day, sometimes three or four times a day. I hope people enjoy reading my stories as much as I enjoyed writing them. If you ever need inspiration for your life and bedroom, feel free to check out my amazon wish list for some sexy ideas. Stay horny my friends, and enjoy your own happy ending.
kisses
https://www.amazon.com/Lonely-Woman/e/B071HK542R/ref=dp_byline_cont_ebooks_1
www.twitter.com/RealLonelyWoman
www.facebook.com/LonelyWomanAuthor

Special thanks to Krysi Foster for the affordable formatting. She can be found at AuthorKrysiFoster@yahoo.com
And I wish the happiest of endings for all my readers. I hope these stories keep you 'cumming' back for more!

Contents

Naughty Neighbor

By Lonely Woman

Lonely Woman

Chapter One:

Michael pulled over to the side of the road and waited as the girl walking along the side of the road approached the car. It was Tina, he was sure of it. Rolling down his window, he stuck his head out and called to her. "Tina?"

She was walking a crooked line, her motions exaggerated. Her young, barely eighteen-year-old body was clad in only her string bikini top and a tiny skirt, so small he'd noticed the bottom of her ass hanging out before he pulled over in front of her.

Raising her head, she looked at him, as if she'd been unaware of him pulling over. Her dirty blonde hair hung in damp strands around her face, and her eyes were glassy and unfocused. "Oh. Hey Mr., uh, Mr. Jones."

"Hey. Do you need a ride?"

She bit her lip, and blinked twice, as if responding to his question took an inordinate amount of effort. "Yeah. I guess."

"Get in." He leaned over and opened the passenger door for her.

9

She plopped onto the seat and groaned as she put her hand to her forehead. "Thanks. I wasn't looking forward to walking the whole way."

"What happened?"

She shrugged. "I was at a party down the road, back that way. Got into an argument with the guy I was with."

He nodded. "You were drinking." It wasn't a question; he could tell by the way she was staggering along the side of the road.

She dropped her hand and turned her blue eyes to him. Her hair hung in her face, the dishevelled strands sexy in their disarray. She held his eyes a moment before she grinned. "Yeah."

"Don't worry. I'm not going to tell your parents. Let's get you home."

She chuckled, a deep, throaty sound. "There's nobody to tattle to. I have the house to myself this weekend."

"Really? Where are your parents?"

"I don't know. Vegas maybe?"

"You're staying by yourself?"

She looked at him again, her eyes glassy from the alcohol, the lids slightly lowered. She smiled again. "I told you. I had a fight with the guy I was with. He won't be coming home."

"Oh." Michael didn't know what else to say. Her firm, pert breasts looked ready to pop out of her bikini top, and he was fighting to keep his eyes on the road, and not her.

But she noticed where his eyes were straying. She smiled again.

He took a shuddering breath. "A little cold for a bikini."

"I was getting cold. Like, really cold. Here, feel." She grabbed his hand, which had been resting between the seats, and before he could pull it away she'd placed it on her thigh.

With a nervous laugh, he pulled his hand away. "Heh, seems cold to me. Want me to turn the heater on?"

"Ugh. I'm too drunk for a heater." She slid down in the seat and moaned.

"You're not going to be sick or anything, are you?"

"No." She smiled as she said it.

The drove in silence, and after a short time she heaved a sigh, closed her eyes, and slid even further down the seat. Her skirt, already dangerously short, rode higher, only barely covering her pussy.

He looked up at her face, and saw her smiling at him with her hooded eyes.

He looked away hastily and cleared his throat. "You shouldn't, uh, drink so much." The car suddenly seemed warmer than it had been moments before, and without the aid of the heater.

He shot her another glance, and she was still smiling at him, her full, plump lips slightly parted.

She leaned closer to him and said, "I like to have fun."

He cleared his throat again, and avoided looking her breasts. Breasts that practically begged to be touched.

He reached the end of the cul de sac. Her house was across from his, with a house between them. He parked and turned off the car. The roar of the ocean behind their homes could be heard in the night's silence. He risked a final look at her golden tanned legs.

"Can I come to your house for a bit?"

"I'm not sure…" he said, his brain not working as it should.

"Will you help me to my door?"

He climbed from the car and hurried around to open her door. Offering his hand, she took it. As she stepped from the car, he caught a flash of her nether regions; she wasn't wearing panties.

She leaned heavily against him and wrapped her arm around his waist, giggling quietly in the calm night.

He cleared his throat again. "Maybe you should come in. Have some coffee or something before you go home."

She leaned more on him, her firm breasts pressed into his side.

He slid his arm around her bare waist, his pants growing uncomfortable. He was aware of every move her body made, his own waking up in response. A jiggle of her breasts, her breath on his neck, and her skin warming under his arm. He led her into his house.

Chapter Two:

He didn't bother with the lights, the light from the back patio was sufficient to see by. He didn't have curtains on the large glass patio door, preferring his view of the beach and the ocean to be unhindered.

Letting go of him, she staggered into the dim living room and flopped onto the couch. She'd been here several times before, but she's always been with her family.

From the kitchen he asked, "Black?"

"Huh?" She turned her eyes to him and he almost forgot what he'd been saying.

He cleared his throat again. "Want your coffee black?"

"Whisky's better." She was looking at his golf trophies and not paying much attention to him.

He started to speak, but thought better of it. She was already drunk. What harm would another drink do? He poured two whisky doubles, neat, and made his way to the living room, careful not to spill their drinks. He handed her the drink he'd made her before taking a seat next to her, pressing his back into the opposite arm rest, creating some distance between them.

"Thanks," she said, then took a sip. She moaned, and slowly ran her tongue along her bottom lip. "This is good. Do you still play?" She indicated his trophies with a nod of her head.

"Not anymore. Bad ankle."

"Too bad. Thought we could... play... sometime." She chuckled.

He wondered if she was aware of the innuendo. She was so beautiful, almost delicate, in the poorly lit room. She was a tiny thing, except for her breasts.

"You're divorced?"

"Yeah."

She smiled, and finished her drink. "That's a shame. She was sexy."

He laughed. "Yeah, she was that."

Tina gave a small, half smile. "She was a bitch, but she was hot. I used to hide in the bedroom next to my step dad's and listen as they fucked."

His mouth open and closed a few times. Not sure what to say, he finished his own drink instead.

"Did you know I'm eighteen now?"

"Yeah, I knew that."

"How old are you?" she scooted closer.

He chuckled, but couldn't get any further away without standing. "Older than you."

She swatted playfully at the air in front of him. "No, for real though. You look like, really young. And I don't know how old you are."

He sighed. "Almost thirty-seven. Old enough to know better. You're drunk."

She giggled like the teenaged girl she was. "Yeah. And you like looking at my legs."

He grinned, and looked down. "Yeah I do. Did you go out in just that or did you lose the rest of your clothes at the party."

She shrugged. "I had a wrap cover thing but I lost it."

"How did you lose it?"

She smiled, and looked up at him through her thick dark lashes. "I was making out with someone out on the beach."

"Not the same guy you went to the party with, I'm guessing."

"Nope. Different guy."

"How naughty of you."

She bit her lower lip. "Yeah. I am."

He took a deep breath.

She kept looking at him, her eyes still hooded, and she spread her legs slightly. Brushing her fingertips over her smooth thigh, she gripped the hem of the bit of fabric that barely qualified as a skirt, and moaned softly before saying, "I lost my panties, too."

"I saw." His waited with baited breath, wondering what she would say or do next.

"I saw you peek when you helped me outta the car."

His eyes roamed her body. From her plump lips, to her firm breasts, and down to her long legs.

"Wanna look again?" She slowly pulled her skirt up.

He swallowed hard. "You're drunk."

"It's a yes or no question."

"Yes," he said, his voice hoarse.

She pulled her skirt to her waist, but kept her legs crossed. Her pussy was mostly hidden, and what he could see was completely smooth.

His mouth and lips were suddenly dry.

"You like that? Give me another whisky." There was a raspy quality to her own voice. It made her even sexier, if that was possible.

"Tina…"

"Now."

He stood and made his way to the kitchen. His hands were shaking as he poured the drink, and he spilled a little on the counter. By the time he sat back down next to her, the skirt was back where it should be.

Chapter Three:

"Wanna know what happened to my panties?"
"Lost them at the beach, right?"
"Mhm." She sipped her drink.
"Were you guys fucking?" Michael wondered aloud.
She chuckled. "Of course not. We'd just met."
"What were you guys doing?"
"He put his fingers inside me," she whispered.
"Did you like it?"
"Meh. It wasn't bad, but he wasn't good either."
"I'm guessing you aren't a virgin then."
She laughed. "Hell no. I like to have fun."
"Why weren't you with the guy who took you to the party?"
She snorted and sipped her drink. "He was lame."
"No wonder you got with someone else."
She finished her drink and uncrossed her legs. "I like being touched. That's natural, right?"
"Uh, yeah."
"I like to drink, and have fun. Dancing, kissing, rubbing against them."

He cleared his throat. "Sounds good."

"Put your arm around me," she whispered.

He scooted closer and put one arm around her waist, the other on the inside of her warm thigh, warmed from the whisky.

She scooted closer still, and pressed her perky tits against him.

He gasped with pleasure.

She turned her face to him and he could smell the whisky on her breath. She put her hand on his, and pressed harder into her thigh.

"Did he get to touch your tits?" he rasped.

"Nuh-uh." Her breath was warm on his face. She moved his hand from her thigh and put in on her breast, and moved his hand. They both inhaled sharply, enjoying the pleasurable sensations.

He kneaded her breast through the small bikini top, her hand on his, guiding him. She moved his hand to her other breast and she moaned, her body writhing under his hands.

She leaned in to kiss him, but he turned his face away, smiled, and nuzzled her neck instead. "Why would I kiss a naughty girl like you," he breathed into her ear before nipping it with his teeth.

She moaned. "That feels so good."

"You want it soft and gentle, or hard and rough," he asked, his hands enacting his words.

"I like it hard, and rough," she whispered.

He squeezed hard, and twisted slightly. Her nipple was poking through the cheap spandex. Taking it between his fingers, he pinched.

She moaned, and arched her back slightly, then grabbed his head and kissed him hard on the mouth.

He could taste the whisky, and the other alcohol from the night as he hungrily met her kiss, matching her passion as their tongues danced.

Soon, she was squirming under him, and he backed off. Releasing her, thinking she'd changed her mind, he leaned back to give her space.

She stood, swayed a bit, and untied her bikini top. There was almost no shake or wiggle in her breasts. They sat proud and high on her chest, the hard nipples pointing at his as he cupped her tits in his hands.

16

She smiled then, and slid her skirt down to her knees. Swaying, she almost fell before managing to remove her skirt completely.

Straddling him on the couch with her young, tight, slim body, he could feel her moist pussy hot against his cock. Her round, perfect tits were in his face and she grabbed the back of his head, pulling him to them. Her skin smelled of suntan oil and salt.

"Suck," she moaned.

He made a guttural groan as he licked her hard nipples, moving from one to the other before opening his mouth to see how much he could suck at once, massaging the nipples with his tongue.

She threw her head back and moaned as she wrapped her arms around his head, pinning him.

Reaching between her legs, he slid a finger into her wet pussy. It was like fingering a warm peach.

She cried out and spread her legs farther apart, bouncing on his lap as he slid another finger inside her.

Her moans were loud in the silent house as she rocked her hips, bouncing and sliding her hot pussy on his slick fingers.

"Oh, god, don't stop," she moaned, shaking.

Reaching down, she opened his pants quickly, her fingers fumbling in her haste.

His hard cock sprang free, and she grabbed it, gripping it in her soft hand. Looking down at it she said, "Oh god. Fuck me!"

Breathless, he lifted his hands to her tits as she guided his hard cock. It slid inside, and she gasped.

His breath caught as her pussy covered his cock. He pinched her nipples, hard, and she cried out with pleasure. Grabbing her waist, he forced himself to go slow. But she was on fire. Her breathing quickened and she writhed with uncontainable pleasure on his lap, his cock sliding in and out with the motion.

He reached down and stroked her clit with his thumb.

She growled, a desperate sound from deep in her throat and grabbed her own tits, pinching her nipples and sliding her long nails across them.

He was breathless. "You feel so fucking good," he moaned, watching her body flush with pleasure.

17

"Don't stop," she cried, moving her hips faster on his cock, "I'm gonna cum!" Her body trembled, and she threw her head back with a loud cry as she came, her pussy clenching on his cock.

He clenched his teeth, not wanting to cum yet.

She was still shaking and trembling, moaning softly with her eyes closed.

He couldn't take it. He pulled her from his lap and set her next to him on the couch, stroking his throbbing cock. "Suck it," he murmured.

Obediently, she scooted to the edge of the couch, one hand between her legs. She stroked her clit and opened wide, taking his hard cock into her wet mouth while looking up at him.

He thrust his hips, pushing deeper into her mouth and she reached out, cupping his balls and stroking his cock with her hand as she sucked, moaning around his cock. Sucking hard, her cheeks sunk in. She went faster, rubbing her clit at the same speed she sucked, bobbing her head on his cock.

Gripping the back of the couch, he came. It was a long, drawn out orgasm that made his body shake. She came at the same time, sucking every bit of his cum and swallowing, cleaning him off with her tongue as he slowly pulled her mouth from him.

Bending down, he kissed her, hard. Her lips were still sticky. "You did good," he murmured against her mouth.

"Yeah," she breathed heavily, trying to catch her breath. "Can… Can I stay here tonight?" She pressed her head against his belly and wrapped her arms about his waist, hugging him.

He stroked her hair. He wanted to say no. But she had no parents waiting for her, and he no longer had a wife to warm his bed. Sighing, he said, "Sure. Why not."

"Carry me upstairs?"

He chuckled. "Sure."

"Do you have a big bed? I bet you have a big bed, to match your big cock."

He grinned. "Oh yeah."

"While I sleep, will you fuck me again?" She looked up at him expectantly.

18

He laughed.

"No, I mean it. I want you to fuck me until I wake up. Sleeping beauty was awakened with a kiss. I wanna be woken up with your cock deep inside me."

"But…"

She sighed, a soft moan escaping. It was a sleepy sound and she stroked his cock, almost absentmindedly.

He felt a familiar stirring as she touched him.

"Please, Michael. If I'm going to be in your bed, please, make love to me. Fuck me hard. I know I'll feel it. I'll even dream about your cock before I wake up."

"Tina, I can't."

She leaned back against the couch, her hands dropping beside her on the couch. Eyes closed, she sighed again. Her breathing became deep and slow. "It's what I want. I've always dreamed of your cock. And now I've had it, I want more of it. Please. Fuck me after I fall asleep."

With her lips slightly parted, she seemed to fall immediately into sleep. Her breathing steady and slow.

Michael put one hand over his mouth, and the other on his hardening cock.

She slipped down the couch until she lay on her side. With a huff, she rolled on to her back, but didn't wake up. Her breasts didn't move to the side at all, even though her nipples flatted a bit.

Hesitant, he reached out and gently touched her breasts, brushing the pad of his thumb over her nipple. She made a soft noise, but didn't stir.

She was so beautiful. Bending over, he kissed her lightly. First on her jaw, then her neck. She made another noise, but again didn't stir.

He watched her a moment, then finally picked her up, putting one arm under her knees and another under her neck. He scooped her up and held her close to him, her breasts pressed against his chest, her arm dangling limply. He carried her to the bedroom. She was surprisingly light, and he again marvelled at her beauty.

Chapter Four:

He placed her on the bed, on her back. She lay completely naked on the white comforter. The soft light from the moon illuminated her soft skin. She was so slender. He placed his hand lightly on her throat as if to choke her, then brushing his fingertips over her supple breasts, down her soft stomach, but stopping before reaching her pussy.

He sat on the edge of the bed and watched her sleep, his heart and breath quickening as his arousal grew.

At length, he stripped. His cock was only half hard, so he stroked it while he teased her soft skin with his hands, careful not to wake her.

Climbing on the bed, he straddled her, her trim waist between his knees. Careful not to wake his sleeping beauty, he rubbed the tip of his cock against her nipples. He watched, fascinated, as it wrinkled and stiffened until it her nipple was as hard as his cock. He did the same to the other nipple, and it came to attention fast than the first.

She made a noise and he froze. But she didn't stir. She was in the deep sleep of the drunk.

Stroking his cock faster, he kissed her chest between her tits, the scooted back, his mouth tracing a trail to her flat stomach.

She made louder noises, and shifted in her sleep, her legs spreading slightly.

He continued his trail of kisses, passed her belly button and down to her shaved pussy. He kissed the top of her thigh, and used his hands to slowly and very carefully spread her legs a little more. He checked to make sure she was still sleeping before kissing the inside of her thigh.

Her pussy smelled sweet, and he used his fingers to spread her pussy lips open. Like a flower in the spring, it opened for him. He ran his tongue softly over the outter lips, then flicked her clit with the tip of his tongue.

She shifted again, and her hips moved in slow, small circles. Her breathing quickened, but she did not wake.

He slid a finger inside her and sucked her clit. He pulled his wet finger from her, and touched her asshole with it. She let out a small moan, louder than the other noises she'd made, but she didn't wake.

Her asshole contracted. He couldn't wait any longer. He grabbed his cock and slid the swollen head between her hot, wet pussy lips, using it to rub her clit.

"God," he groaned, looking down at her perfect body. Her breath was speeding up and her lips had parted, but her eyes were still closed though they seemed to flutter behind the closed lids.

He stroked her clit once more with the tip of his cock before sliding the swollen head into her tight pussy. He froze, and flexed his cock, stretching her. After a moment, he slid the rest of the way into her. Her pussy was so hot it almost burned. He bit back and moan and pressed as deep into her as he could.

"Michael," she breathed. She hadn't opened her eyes, but her pussy was pulsating against his shaft, clenching and pulling him deeper as he slowly stroked, in and out.

"God," he moaned again. She felt so good. She was so wet and tight against his cock. He held himself over her, with his arms straight, and thrust a little faster, a little harder. It was better than anything he'd ever felt before.

Her sleeping body was responding to his motions.

She whispered his name again, and her eyes opened and she met him thrust for thrust.

He pounded into her, hard and fast. Her body trembled, and her leg shook as her pussy clenched around him, making it almost impossible to move, but she was so wet he could. She flushed red against the white comforter, and when he couldn't take it any longer, he pulled out and came. His hot white cum landed on her belly.

She reached down, swiped it with a finger, then rubbed it on her nipple before closing her eyes and falling back asleep quickly.

He stroked his cock, the last drop of cum dropping just above her pussy.

She was his perfect sex toy. He watched her sleep before falling into sleep himself.

The End

Moving Day

He moved her furniture and stole her heart

By Lonely Woman

Lonely Woman

Chapter One:

lizabeth unlocked her door, excited. She was a home-owner now! She tucked a strand of her blonde hair behind her ear, and pushed the door open. Home! The inside was exactly as it had been when she'd looked before buying, but now it was hers. A feeling a pride surged through her. Tomorrow, the movers would be here with her stuff. For now, she had a cheap air mattress to sleep on. She wanted to spend the night in her new home, and not at the motel she'd called home for the past three years.

She walked through her house, opening doors and cupboards, running the water, and pinching the carpet between her toes. According to her watch, it was almost midnight. She wasn't ready for bed yet. She was so excited about her new home, she wanted to spend her night exploring and touching everything. But the movers would be by first thing in the morning.

She made her way to the master bedroom and unrolled her air mattress. It had a built-in pump, but would need an outlet. She dragged the bed near a wall and plugged it in, closed the air valve, and turned the pump on. She watched in delight as the mattress began inflating with air.

A door slammed shut elsewhere in the house, and she jumped, quickly turning off the pump. The mattress was almost full, but what had made that noise? She decided to investigate.

All was as it should be, but the kitchen cupboards were all shut now. She wondered if she had shut them or not earlier. She'd opened and closed everything so many times it was hard to remember. But what had made that noise? It had to have been the wind.

She wrapped her arms around herself and shivered. There was a draft coming from somewhere. She made her way through the house, shutting all the doors and windows tight. If they were already closed, she'd opened them and reclosed them, making sure to lock all the locks.

She turned a slow circle in the living room. Satisfied she'd shut everything down, she turned off all the lights as she made her way back to her room. She didn't need a three-bedroom house, but it was nice to have the space.

She striped down, and climbed onto the mattress, pulling her soft blanket up to her chin. She fell asleep dreaming of what she was going to do with all the space. A library in one room, an office space in the other. Her bedroom would have a large bed, with a headboard. She could even buy mirrors to put on the closet doors.

She woke to the sound of scratching at her window. Her heart was racing, and it took her a moment to remember where she was. She was home. The thought calmed her, but the scratching continued. There was no way she was going to investigate. She'd seen enough horror movies to know better. She'd check it out in the morning while the movers were here.

The scratching wouldn't stop. She rolled over and found her phone where she'd left it when she'd gone to sleep; , next to the mattress, on top of her clothes.

She squinted at the bright screen in the dark room. Almost six. She groaned, and shoved her headphones into her ears. She tapped a music app, and turned the volume up. Once the scratching couldn't be heard, she fell back asleep.

Chapter Two

lizabeth directed the movers. She'd pulled on her clothes from the day before, and was tired. The leader of the movers was an older man, his balding head and wrinkled face putting him at about fifty. She wrinkled her nose in distaste. He gave her the creeps. When he announced after an hour he would be back to check their work, she'd breathed a sigh of relief. The two movers remaining were in their twenties. The taller of the two wore a tight white shirt, his muscles rippling through the material as he moved the heavy dresser to the master bedroom.

When her grandmother had passed away, she'd been left with a hefty life insurance payout, and all of grandma's furniture. Heavy, antique pieces that had been well loved.

"Wait," she said, stopping the shorter of the two movers. "That one goes in the library. Last door on the right," she clarified at his confused look.

He nodded, and took the heavy shelf.

Once all the furniture had been placed, the movers began hauling in brown boxes of various sizes. They'd been in storage since her divorce three years ago. Though dusty, they were all still clearly labeled. The men took almost an hour to put all the boxes in the appropriate rooms.

"Thank you, guys," she said, standing in the kitchen. "Can I get you anything to drink?"

The shorter one ignored her and went out to the truck, but the tall cute one stayed back. He shoved his hands into his pockets, his thick brown hair mussed from working so hard.

"No, ma'am," he said in an adorable Texan drawl.

Her stomach clenched. It'd been a long time since she'd found a man attractive. "Oh," she said, not knowing what to say.

He took a step toward her and her heart started racing in her chest.

She looked up at him. She was tall, but he was taller.

He looked down on her, a look in his dark brown eyes she didn't recognize. A small smile played about his full lips. He put his hand on her cheek, bent down, and brushed his lips against hers.

She stood motionless. It had been nothing more than the barest of kisses, but it had affected her in a way she'd never thought possible. Slowly, she opened her eyes to see the desire in his.

"Your number," he said, taking a step back.

"My number?"

His lips made a full smile this time. "Yeah. So I can call you. I want to take you to dinner."

"Dinner?" Her brain hadn't figured out how to function yet.

He stepped closer and put an arm around her waist, pulling her limp body close.

She closed her eyes, waiting for another kiss.

His face rubbed against her, his stubble rough against her soft skin. He breathed in her ear, and a tremor shot down her spine, and warmth rushed to her groin.

Her lips parted, and she pressed against his cock. He wasn't hard yet, but it was starting to get that way. When his mouth met hers, she opened up, matching his tongue's movements with her own.

He groaned against her lips, and her panties got wet. One hand roamed her back and the other gripped her braless tit, teasing her hard nipple through her shirt. She moaned.

He pulled away, and she gasped for air.

Had she just... She saw his rock-hard cock straining against his tight jeans, and knew he felt the same way. Looking out the front window, she saw his buddy was sitting in the driver's seat of the moving truck, eating something from a Tupperware.

She grabbed his hand, and pulled him back toward the bedroom. She hadn't felt this aroused, this awake, this horny, in years. And she wasn't going to let it pass without satisfying her body's desires.

He followed without protest, slapped her ass, and shut the door once they were in the bedroom.

The newly set up four-poster king bed was in the middle of the room. The mattress didn't even have sheets on it, and she didn't care.

She turned into his embrace, and met his passion with her own.

He pushed her backward onto the bed, climbing on top of her. He put a knee against her wet pussy, and she spread her legs for him. He pushed her shirt up, revealing her firm tits and taught nipples.

Her panties were getting wetter by the second, an orgasm building in her belly.

He groaned appreciatively before putting his mouth on first one tit, then the other. Reaching between them, he unbuttoned her pants, running his finger along the waistband of her panties.

He slid off her, and she threw her arms over her head, allowing him full access to her body. From the foot of her bed, he tugged her pants down, and she raised her hips to help. Once the pants where on the floor, he stood between her knees, undoing his own pants. He pushed them down over his hips. He stroked his hard cock, looking at her body.

She started to move, but he lay back on top of her, he cock pushing against her wet pussy, the thin material of her silk panties making it somehow more erotic. He kissed and licked his way from her mouth, to her ears, to her neck and down her body, leaving her wanting more.

He made his way to her panties, and nipped the material, pulling at them with his teeth. But he didn't take them off. He slid a finger in the side, stroking her wet lips with one finger while stroking his cock with his other hand. She started rocking her hips, wanting him inside her, and he groaned.

He pulled her panties down, and replaced his finger with his mouth, sliding his tongue inside her, then around her clit, then finally applied his tongue directly to her clit. He slid his fingers inside, spreading them apart and rubbing the sensitive ridge inside.

When he pulled his mouth away, he used his thumb to rub her clit. He put his other hand on her tit and started teasing her nipple the way he had her clit.

She was about to cum when he stopped. She opened her eyes, and he pulled her to a seated position. She grabbed his cock, gripping it firmly, marveling at the silky-smooth hardness of it.

He bent down and kissed her. When he pulled his face away, he nudged the back of her head toward his cock.

She licked it first, then opened wide. She couldn't fit all of him in her mouth, so she stroked the exposed shaft with her hand. She sucked, running her tongue along the underside of his cock. She used her other hand to cradle his balls, squeezing gently and rolling them around.

He moaned and the tip of his cock swelled.

He pulled out of her mouth and pushed her onto her back.

She watched as he climbed on top of her, sliding his cock into her wet pussy.

He went slowly, and she winced a little at his girth, but her pussy stretched, and he sucked her nipples, making her forget any discomfort. Once he was inside her, he began moving his hips.

She met him move for move. Tingles shot out from her pussy, and she wanted him completely.

He pulled all the way out and stood, pulling her ass forward and sliding the tip of his cock in, teasing her with his cock while he rubbed her clit.

She moaned until she couldn't take it anymore. "Fuck me," she begged. She needed him inside.

He slammed into her, and gripped her hips, pulling her against him. She exploded, her pussy clenching on his cock, as waves of ecstasy washed over her. She heard him moan, and felt a warmth that could only be his own climax. He ran his thumb over her clit and she shuddered.

He slowly pulled out, tweaking a nipple as he did, and pulled his pants up.

She couldn't sit up if she wanted to. Her muscles were liquid from the most intense orgasm she'd ever had.

He left the room, shutting the door softly behind him.

Moments later, she heard the engine of the moving truck start, and she knew she'd never see him again.

Chapter Three

lizabeth cleaned her kitchen, scrubbing the counters
and stove. It'd been almost a month since she'd moved
in.

She'd tried to regret her random encounter with the mover, but couldn't. It had been an encounter she frequently replayed in her mind when she lay in bed, lonely. She threw away the wrapper from a candy bar she'd eaten last week during her period.

With a sigh, she looked out the front window, and made a mental note to go to the thrift store and get some curtains. She saw the mailman across the street and put the sponge behind the faucet on the kitchen sink so she could check the mail.

She sorted through the stack of letters. Throwing away the junk mail and stuff for prior residents.

She pulled out the only letter. It was from the clinic. She tore it open and scanned the results. Clean. Thank goodness. The only thing she'd have changed about that day would be to use a condom. Since then, she'd bought two boxes and had stashed them in various locations around the house. It was better to be prepared.

She threw the letter in the trash with the rest, and finished cleaning the kitchen.

Hours later, she stood at her clean counter eating her cup of noodles with disposable chopsticks. The doorbell rang. Wondering who it could be she peeked out the front window. There was a motorcycle parked in the driveway.

Leaving the security chain latched, she opened the door.

She was greeted by the sight of a well-muscled chest under a tight shirt. Black this time. A chest she'd fantasized about many times. She shut the door enough to take the security chain off and opened the door the rest of the way.

"Hi." She held on to the door and spoke through the screen.

"Hi," he said. He brought around a hand that was holding a colorful bouquet of flowers.

She unlocked the screen door and pushed it open. "Come in."

He pulled the screen open the rest of the way and came it, letting the screen shut behind him. He stood in the living room and she shut the front door, locking the security chain and deadbolt.

"I didn't think I'd ever see you again. Hungry?" She made her way to the kitchen.

He followed. "Looks nice," he said looking around. "Did you get all the boxes unpacked?"

"Most, yeah." She took a bite and looked at him.

"Didn't mean to interrupt you." He ran a hand through his thick hair, still holding the flowers with the other.

"Your fine," she said around a mouthful of noodles.

He smirked and she flushed, remembering the last time he'd seen her mouth full.

Setting her noodles on the counter, she opened a cupboard and pulled out a vase for the flowers.

He stood behind her and took the vase from her hand. "Let me," he said, taking over the task of putting the flowers away. "Eat your noodles."

She shrugged, and sidled around him and back to her dinner.

Once the flowers had been situated in their vase, he turned to her with his hands shoved in his pockets. "Look," he began.

33

She interrupted. "I don't want to hear it. I was just as guilty as you."

He ran a hand through his hair again. "I know, but I need to say it, okay?"

She shrugged and shoved the last bite in her mouth and put the Styrofoam cup and chopsticks in the trash.

"I've never gone without a condom. And never within hours of meeting someone. You're sexy as hell, but I don't know why I didn't control myself. If you end up pregnant, I'll support you no matter what you want to do with the baby. If I didn't want to be a father, I should have used a condom, right? And even if you're not pregnant, I still want to see you. But If you aren't interested I understand." He took a deep breath and waited for her to respond.

She closed her mouth. That was the last thing she'd expected to hear. She shook her head, clearing it. "First, I'm not pregnant. Had my period last week. Second, you weren't the only one who lost control. Takes two, remember? And third, I'd love to see you more."

He closed the space between them, and she lifted her face. The expected kiss didn't come. Instead, he cupped her cheek with his hand. "Thank god," he whispered, then kissed her.

She felt the warmth pooling between her legs just as he pulled back.

"Not yet." He took a step back, and grabbed her hand. "I was hoping you would give me a tour of your house." He grinned.

She grinned back, and led him on a tour. He made appreciative noises, and asked questions here and there. Once they'd made their way back to the kitchen, she looked at him and he closed the distance between them again.

He pulled her into an embrace, running his lips along her jaw line. "Now we can," he said in her ear. "I just need to go buy some condoms."

She laughed, and he raised his face from her neck to look in her eyes. "I already did."

He chuckled, then put his hands under her ass and picked her up.

She wrapped her legs around his waist, and he carried her toward the bedroom.

"Library," she said, nibbling on his ear.

He turned into the library and walked to the far wall, pushing her against it. His mouth began exploring her body with a renewed fervor. She unbuttoned his pants and pushed them down, stroking his cock once it'd been freed. She set her feet on the floor and he pulled away to give her full access.

He moaned.

They tore their clothes off, hands and lips exploring each other as they did. He put her wrists in his hand and held them over her head and sucked on her neck, teasing her nipples with his other hand.

She squirmed, playing along and not pulling her hands free.

His mouth replaced the hand at her breast, and his fingers trailed down her side before resting on her hip.

He pulled his mouth back, breathing heavily, his eyes hooded. Seeing the desk, he steered her toward it, holding her hands behind her back.

Her butt pushed against the edge of the table, and she arched her back. He held her hands against the top of the desk, but kneeled in front of her, tasting her wet pussy with his tongue.

She squeezed the side of his head with her thighs, twitching with each flick of his tongue against her clit. She moaned, and came, holding his head with her legs as he licked and sucked.

Once she'd come down, he flipped her around, bending her over the table, holding her hands behind her back with one of his.

He slapped her ass and she cried out in pleasure. His cock push against her ass cheeks. "Condom," he panted.

He let her go, and she reached over the desk to pull one out of the drawer, thankful she'd left them all over the house. She tore it open and pulled the slippery thing out, rolling it on his cock while he sucked on her neck and ears. Once he was covered, he flipped her around again, and recaptured her hands in his.

He ran his cock along the inside of her pussy lips, putting pressure on her clit. She shuddered. He felt so good. He put the tip in, and worked the rest his large cock in. Once he'd made it in, he began a steady rhythm. He reached around and rubbed her clit while he fucked her.

She got close to climax, and he let go of her hands, grabbing her hips, and slamming her onto his cock. She grabbed the desk and held on. They came together, and her pussy exploded around his cock. She couldn't feel his cum, but she could feel his body clench and his cock swelled as he grunted.

Satisfied, they made their way to her bedroom. By the time they'd climbed under the covers, his cock was hard again.

Chapter Four

S he woke to his hands playing with her hair. He was leaning on his elbow, looking down at her.

"Mornin, beautiful."

"Hey, yourself." She pushed up onto her elbow and looked at him, pulling the sheet up to cover herself. "I think now would be a good time for you to tell me your name."

He looked at her blankly a moment, the barked out a laugh. "My names Sam."

"Elizabeth." She darted her head forward and lightly bit his shoulder, reaching down to stroke his cock.

"Not yet, darlin," he said, pushing her hand away. "I need the bathroom."

She watched his tight ass waddle from the room, a smile on her face.

She'd almost fallen back asleep when he climbed back into the large bed, pulling the blankets down. Her nipples hardened in the cold morning air.

"Mmm," he said, nuzzling her neck.

"Mm, yourself, cowboy." She reached down and began stroking him. He was already hard.

He lay back and she straddled him, letting his cock slip between her lips. She was already soaking wet from anticipation. He let her hold his hands over his head and she kissed him, then trailed kisses along his jaw, and down his neck, tugging on his ears with her lips.

She nipped his shoulder with her teeth and kissed it. He rotated his hips, the tip of his cock slipping inside her.

"You feel so good," he moaned.

She grinned, and teased the tip of his cock with her pussy. Letting go of his hands, she reached into the drawer and pulled out a condom, putting it in his hand. She slid down his body, tracing his skin with her hands.

She reached his cock, and looked up at him. She watched his eyes roll back before closing as she licked his shaft. She took his cock into her mouth, while playing with his balls. When she felt his cock flexing, she pulled her mouth off, sucking hard as she did so. He ran his hands through her hair and she wrapped her tits around his cock.

"Hang on," he said, sitting up.

He moved her off the bed. "Kneel."

She did as she was told.

He sat on the edge of the bed, with her kneeling in front of him. "Now you can," he said, leaning back onto the palms of his hands.

She took him back in her mouth, circling the tip of his cock with her tongue. He groaned, and held the back of her head, quickening her pace. When she sensed he was about to cum she pulled off, and he groaned.

Still kneeling, she wrapped her tits back around his cock.

"Oh yes," he said, pushing his cock between her tits.

She bent her neck, licking the tip when it came up. When he was about to cum, she looked up at him and sat back. He stroked his cock, tilting his hips toward her, and came, his hot cum landing on her tits and neck. He rubbed it into her nipple with the tip of his cock, and she moaned.

"My turn," she said, climbing back on the bed. She stopped him from climbing off, and pulled a latex dildo from the drawer next to the bed. "This," she said, handing it to him.

He sucked her nipple, avoiding his cum, and fucked her with the dildo while she rubbed her clit. She rocked her hips to his rhythm. "Don't stop," she begged. "Faster."

He slammed the latex cock into her, and stroked his own cock. It was coming back to life. Seeing it, she came, her body trembling and her toes curling

Once she was done, he rolled the condom onto his cock and slipped inside her. Going slowly, teasing them both back to climax. Close to cumming again, he got up on his knees, and put her legs on his shoulders. He rubbed her clit, and they both came, before collapsing onto the bed.

"Oh my god," she said, still trembling.

"Yeah," he agreed.

"do you work today?" She asked.

"Definitely not. When I can move again I'm going to call off. I don't think we're finished here yet."

"Oh good," she said, running a hand lazily along his stomach.

They lay together for a few more minutes before the alarm on his phone went off. "Time to wake up for work," he chuckled. "Let me call off. Then we can eat, and see how well the couch works." He winked and got out of bed.

She grinned, and got up to make breakfast.

She didn't even need to get dressed, and the smile never left her face. She'd finally found someone to trust.

The End

Lonely Woman

A Daddy for Naughty Emily

A DD/lg love story
By Lonely Woman

Chapter One: Emily

"Come on, Emily," Her best friend said, exasperated. "You're over thinking this."

Emily turned to Sasha, and gasped. "Are you serious? Over thinking? I have never been to a kink party. I don't want to stand out like a sore thumb."

Sasha rolled her eyes. "I've been to plenty. You'll fit right in."

Emily went back to her closet and dug around. She heard Sasha's exasperated sigh and grabbed a knee-length white dress with cherries on it, and pulled it from the closet. Holding it up to her, she turned to her friend. "What about this one?"

Sasha reached down and held out the skirt for a better look. "This is cute. And you look good in these retro dresses. I really like how the skirt has the weird under stuff to poof it out."

Emily smiled, and pulled the dress over her head. "Zip me up?"

Sasha pulled the zipper up, and the heart shaped bodice hugged Emily's curves in seductive innocent.

"Come on," Sasha said. "Let's do you make up." She led the way from the bedroom, stepping over the discarded pile of clothes in front of the door.

Emily scowled. She didn't like doing make up.

"Don't give me that look!" Sasha said from the hallway.

Emily quickly replaced her scowl. How could Sasha see her face? She rolled her eyes and tromped from the room after Sasha.

In the bathroom, Sasha had already pulled a bunch of makeup from her bag. "Sit on the toilet. I'll do it for you, and don't you dare roll your eyes at me."

Emily sat on the toilet seat obediently.

Sasha smiled. "Good girl. Now hold still."

Emily sat while Sasha did her makeup. She kept fidgeting with the hem of her dress, and earned several well-placed whacks with the makeup brush for it.

"Close your eyes," Sasha said, lifting her chin up.

Emily did as she was told, and tried not to flinch each time the brush landed on her lids.

"There. All done."

Emily opened her eyes and smiled at Sasha. "Can I see?"

Sasha handed her the mirror and Emily took it. She examined her face, turning it this way and that, as she admired Sasha's skill with a brush.

"Wow," Emily said. "I look good! You're the best." She smiled at Sasha.

Sasha returned her smile, and picked up the hair brush. "Turn." She made a circle in the air with the brush.

Emily sighed. She'd much rather just pretend hair wasn't a thing, but did as she was told.

She winced, and held her head as still as possible while Sasha pulled the brush through it.

"How do you want it?"

"I don't know."

Sasha sighed. "Fine. You're getting pigtails."

Emily giggled, but didn't object. If Sasha thought a weird hairdo would convince Emily to brush her own hair, Sasha was sadly mistaken!

With a tug on one of her pigtails, Sasha declared Emily was ready.

Emily stood in front of the full-length mirror on the back of the bathroom door and admired her appearance. She held out her skirt and spun in a circle. She loved the way her dress flared out from her hips, and accentuated her legs.

"Thanks." She hugged Sasha, and her shampoo reminded Emily of cupcakes.

Sasha hugged her back. "No problem. Come on, we don't want to be late!"

The rushed to leave Emily's third-floor apartment, and horridly grabbed purses and keys as they ran out the door.

In the hall, they giggled together as they made their way to the elevator. Emily was already having second thoughts about attending something called a kink party, but her best friend was doing a great job of easing her mind.

On the elevator, Emily clutched Sasha's elbow as they made the slow descent to the first floor. When the elevator dinged and the doors opened, Sasha stepped out into the lobby first, with a reluctant Emily following behind.

"You're going to love it! Stop worrying. I promise I won't leave you alone, okay?"

Emily nodded, and gave a brave smile. She trusted Sasha, and if she said it would be okay, then it would be.

"Good girl. Come on." Sasha took them out to her car, parked at the far end of the lot.

Once they were in the car, Sasha turned on the radio, and the two friends bobbed their heads as they sang along loudly with the music and made their way uptown.

Chapter Two: New Friends

The party was inside a local bank, on the fourth floor. The rooms were packed with people in varying degrees of undress. Some wore almost nothing, but for a few strips of well-placed leather, while others— like Emily —were looked like anyone you would see at a party. The air was thick with smoke and incense. Combined with the throng of bodies and the heavy pulsing music, Emily was not having much fun at all.

But Sasha had remained true to her word, and hadn't left Emily's side since they got there. Emily followed her friend around, even going so far as to keep a hand on her friends back to avoid losing her. A refreshment table had been set in one room, while the DJ and music was in another. There was even a room with people having sex in it. Not just a few people, but more than half a dozen.

Emily averted her eyes as she followed Sasha to the refreshment table. She was starting to get a headache, but didn't want to ruin her friends good time. They made their way through the crowd, and Emily grabbed the back of Sasha's top with a grip death would have been jealous of. She breathed a sigh of relief when they finally made it to the refreshment table.

46

Sasha leaned in close. "Hey, you okay?"

Emily forced a smile. "I'm good. You having fun?"

Sasha's grin went from ear to ear. "Yeah. Thanks for coming with me! I have to use the bathroom. You mind waiting here for me to come back?"

Emily's stomach tied itself in knots, but her forced smile never faltered. "Yeah! I'll stay right here!"

Sasha nodded, but didn't bother to yell back over the music, and disappeared into the crowd.

Emily needed something to do while she waited, and poured herself a glass of red punch.

A deep voice behind her startled her.

"Hey, are you here with anyone?"

Some punch spilled from her cup as she quickly turned to face him. He was the most beautiful man she'd ever lay eyes on. He wore a simple polo and khakis, but she wanted to lick his dark skin. The thought shocked her. She'd never had thoughts like that before about anyone!

"Oh, sorry. Didn't mean to scare you." He put a hand on her shoulder, and helped steady the cup in her hand.

She smiled up at him gratefully. "Sorry, I didn't get you, did I?"

He chuckled. "No, I'm fine. My name's Devin, by the way. And you?"

"Emily."

He stuck out a hand. "Nice to meet you Emily. So, are you a sub?"

"A what?" Her brows lowered in consternation. What he talking about sandwiches?

He leaned closer. "A sub?"

She forced another smile. "I'm sorry, but I don't know what you're talking about..." she trailed off, not knowing what to say. Where was Sasha to rescue her?

"A submissive. Are you new to the lifestyle?"

Oh, he was talking about the kink stuff the party was for! "Sorry, I just came with a friend."

She stood on her tiptoes, and surveyed the room, but didn't see Sasha.

"Did you lose your friend?" He was turning in a slow circle, as if he were trying to find Sasha.

"She went to the bathroom, but she said she wouldn't leave me." She stopped as she felt the tears threatening. She was not going to cry.

"I can stay here with you 'til your friend gets back."

Emily gave her first real smile of the night as she looked up at him. "Thank you, I'd really appreciate that. You said your name is Devin?"

He nodded. "Since we're waiting, do you want to dance?"

She shook her head. She just wanted her friend to come back.

He seemed to sense her discomfort, even though his presence helped a little. "Can you call her?"

Emily shook her head, and felt the tears welling up in her eyes.

"Okay, it's okay. Do you want me to stay with you or do you want me to see if I can find your friend?"

Emily squeezed her eyes shut, and willed the tears away. She wanted her friend, but she didn't want to be left alone. She cursed the small clutch purse that was big enough for her keys but not her phone.

A hand wrapped around her waist, and Devin's woody scent filled her nose. She felt safe, and turned her head into his shoulder.

He rubbed her back slowly, and swayed gently to the pulsing beat of the music. "There, it'll be okay. Do you want to tell me about your friend?"

She sniffled, but shook her head. She didn't want to talk. She just wanted to go home.

His deep voice rumbled in his chest as he said, "Hey, is this your friend?"

Emily looked up and yelled, "Sasha!" She pushed from Devin and hugged her bestie tight.

Devin shoved his hands into his pockets and chuckled. "Are you going to introduce me?"

Emily stepped away from Sasha as she smiled up at him. "This is Sasha. She's the one I came with. And this is Devin. He's been keeping me company while you were gone."

Sasha eyed Devin a moment, but then smiled and stuck her hand out. "Nice to meet you."

They shook, and Devin said, "Same."

Emily beamed at them. She had found a new friend.

Chapter Three: Make a Date

They stood at the refreshment table talking about this and that as they got to know one another. When the crowd of people started to leave the party, Devin checked his phone.

"It's almost three in the morning."

Emily gaped. "Already?"

Sasha checked her own phone. "We should get going."

Devin nodded. "Emily, what's your number. I want to go out with you some time soon."

Emily wrung her hands. "Oh, I didn't bring my phone."

He raised a brow, but turned to Sasha. "What's her number?"

Sasha chuckled, but programed Emily's number into Devin's phone and said, "One of these days you're going to learn your own number."

The blood rushed to Emily's face and she averted her eyes. "I know."

Devin pat her on the head, then pulled her close and hugged her. "You're adorable."

She grinned up at him. "I know."

50

He shook his head. "Baby girl, I'll see you tomorrow."

"Oh, but I have class tomorrow."

Devin stiffened. "How old are you?"

Emily cocked her head to the side. "Nineteen. Why?"

His arm fell from its place around her waist and Emily frowned. "What's wrong?"

He shook his head. "I didn't know you were in high school."

Emily gaped, then laughed.

Devin looked at her quizzically, but Sasha explained. "She means college courses. We attend the university."

Devin's face cleared. "Oh! Great. Then I'll see you tomorrow, Em. I'll text you and we'll figure out a time."

Emily's laughter subsided, but the smile remained. "Okay."

Sasha tugged her hand. "Come on. We have to be up early."

"Bye, Devin." Emily smiled and waved back at him as Sasha pulled her away.

He smiled and waved back, and Emily turned her attention to Sasha.

Once they made it outside and into Sasha's car, Emily sighed happily. "I like him"

"Who, Devin?"

"Yes."

Sasha nodded and reached over to pat her knee. "Good. Did you have fun?"

Emily gushed. "Oh, yes. It wasn't at first, because I only knew you. And then I was scared when you left me alone, but I met Devin and he's such a sweet guy. And? He wants to take me out tomorrow!"

Sasha chuckled. "Yes, I heard."

Emily figited in her seat. "You had fun, right?"

Sasha switched the hand on the wheel and sighed. "Yeah, it was fun."

"Okay."

They rode in silence the rest of the way back to Emily's place. "Are you staying here tonight?"

Sasha shook her head. "Nah, I need to get home, and water my plants."

Emily smiled as she stepped from the car. "Okay. Drive safe. And thanks again. I'm really glad I went."

The elevator's dinged and Emily watched as Sasha pulled away before she stepped into the box that would take her to the third floor.

Chapter Four: Mornings Suck

The next morning, Emily woke with a pounding headache and dry eyes. She'd been up way too late, and seven in the morning was too early to be up. She groaned, and stretched before she reached over and swiped off the phone's alarm. The shirt she'd slept it was wrinkled and wrapped around her body uncomfortably, and she wondered how much she'd tossed and turned last night.

She collapsed back onto her pillows, and wondered if she really needed to go in today. But the eight am class was econ, and she had a low 'D' in the class. If she didn't go, she'd plummet the rest of the way into 'F' territory. And she wouldn't be able to recover before the end of the term.

She groaned again, but sat up in time to hear someone pounding at the front door. Head pounding with the movement, she made her way to the front door. At only 5'2", she wasn't tall enough to see through the peephole. She left the security chain latched, and cracked open the door, keeping her body hidden behind the door and she peeked out.

It was Devin!

"Hey, darlin. Sasha gave me your address. Said I could take you to class. Looks like you just got up."

She shut the door enough to unlock the security chain, and opened the door the full way. He came in and glanced around the living room.

She ran a hand through her hair, still up but falling out from the night before. "Hey, I didn't expect you."

He grinned at her. "Yeah, wanted to surprise you. Here." He handed her a small brown paper bag.

She cocked her head to the side, and opened the bag. Doughnuts! Eagerly, she pulled out a chocolate frosted one. She took a giant bite, and with her mouth full said, "I love these!"

He laughed. "Mind showing me around?"

She shrugged, and swallowed. "Not much to show. Living room. Kitchen in there. Hall goes to the bathroom, and bedroom."

He raised an eyebrow. "That's now how you show someone around. If the house is clean, as it should be, you're supposed to walk your guest and show them each room."

She blushed and put the rest of the donut into the bag. "Oh. Sorry, Devin. May I show you around?"

He grinned and nodded. "Good girl. You can have both donuts."

She grinned, and escorted him through the small apartment. In her room, he toed the pile of discarded clothes from the night before. Bending down, she grabbed the clothes and put them on her twin bed.

He raised an eyebrow.

She grinned. "They're from last night. Clean. I just need to hang them all back up."

He nodded, and the ghost of a smile played about his lips. His eyes drifted to her chest, and she suddenly realized how exposed she was. Wearing nothing but a white graphic tee, and a pair of panties. Heat rushed into her belly and she stepped closer to him.

His smile grew, but he took a step back.

Rejected, she lowered her eyes.

He put a finger under her chin and lifted her eyes to his. "You're beautiful."

54

A smile covered her face and the sting of rejection faded.

He pulled his hand away. "But we need to get you to class and talk a bit before we go any further."

With a sigh, she nodded her agreement. She really didn't know him yet. The woodsy scent he wore wafted under her nose and she closed her eyes. When she opened them again, he stood at her bed as he dug though her clean clothes.

She caught a pair of shorts and the tank he tossed at her.

"Get dressed. You have class in ten minutes."

She nodded, and grabbed a bra from the top drawer before going into the bathroom to change. A glance in the mirror revealed her hair in disarray and eye liner streaked under her eyes. She stuck her tongue out at her reflection, and wiped her face with a baby wipe. How could he call her beautiful with her looking like this?

Dressed, she pulled her hair down, and tied it back into a bun without brushing it. She made her way to the living room where he sat on the couch. His arms were spread out on the back behind him, his legs spread slightly.

When she appeared, he stood, and stepped to her. He ran his hands up her arms, and kissed her forehead.

With a chuckle he said, "Next time you need to brush your hair."

She made a face, but didn't argue.

"Come on, let's get you to class. If you want to give me your schedule, I have today off. I can bring you home when you're done for the day and I'll take you out to eat."

"My last class today is at noon. But I was hoping to get a nap afterward."

He grinned, and she wondered what he found amusing.

"Okay," he said. "I'll pick you up at noon. Take your nap, and I'll make arrangements for dinner."

"Deal!" She stood on her tiptoes, and stretched up to kiss the bottom of his jaw. "Thank you."

He grabbed her hand and led her out the door. "Got your key?"

She held it up and he locked the door.

They held hands until they got to his car, a sleek black sports car. He was such a gentleman, he opened her door and helped her in before jogging around to his own seat.

The engine started silently, and he pulled carefully from the parking lot.

Once they were on the freeway, he turned the radio down. "I'm a dom."

"Okay?"

He sighed. "The kink party last night. We don't normally let anyone in who isn't part of the lifestyle. You looked like a little girl, lost and alone. It's probably why you weren't asked to leave."

"But I'm not a little girl. I'm in college." Her brow furrowed in confusion.

He drummed his fingers on the steering wheel. "I know. Let me explain what I mean by dom, sub, and little girl. It's not quite as literal as all that."

She nodded, but shifted in her seat so she could look at him. His strong jaw was shadowed by the hint of stubble, and his nose had a little bump in it at the bridge. The full lips of his mouth were curved down, and his eyebrows were pressed together, as though he were deep in thought.

He cleared his throat. "Tell me what you know about last night's party."

She thought about that a moment before she answered. "Well, Sasha said it was a kink party. There were a lot more people there than I'd expected. Goodness, did you see the room of people having sex? That was weird. But it was fun, and no one grabbed me or tried to kiss me like they do at the parties on campus."

He nodded. "Yeah. Kink. It's a polite way to encompass a lot of different things, but last nights party was specifically for the BDSM crowd."

"What's that."

"Oh man. Well, it's a lot of things. But you fit the D/s category."

"Like the game system?" She bounced in her seat. She loved her handheld DS.

56

"Um. No. Stands for dominant and submissive. Thought usually, we just call it dom and sub."

Suddenly she understood. "Oh! Like that book that recently came out. Sasha loved it, but I didn't read it. The internet said it wasn't a good representation at all. Is that it?"

"Yes. You should read it. Wasn't bad. Not good, but not bad either."

"Okay. I'll see if she'll will let me borrow her copies."

He nodded. "Okay. Do that. And we can go online later and look into it more, and see if you're interested. I am what's called a daddy dom. I like to take care of the women in my life."

"Women, like more than one?" She raised her brow at him. She was open to looking into the kink stuff. But she did not want to date a man who wanted lots of women.

"Yes, plural. No, not at the same time."

"Oh, okay." She smiled as relief washed over her.

He pulled into the campus parking lot. "I'll be here at noon to get you. Do you have your phone?"

She patted her pocket. "Yeah."

"I'll text. You should be able to find me though."

"Okay." She reached over to open her door, and turned back.

Devin had lifted her hand. He placed a kiss on the back of it and ran his thumb over her knuckles. "Have a good day, sweetie."

She smiled as butterflies filled her stomach. She wanted to kiss him, but he'd already dropped her hand.

"Okay. See ya."

She climbed from the car and made her way to class. Her headache was gone, but now she couldn't seem to stop thinking about Devin and what he'd said.

Chapter Five: Dinner

D evin picked her up from class at noon, and took her home. He even tucked her in, and kissed her forehead before leaving.

When her phone starting ringing, she woke up. It was Devin, and it was after five. She groaned, but answered the call. "Ugh."

He laughed. "Time to wake up sleepy head. I'm at the door. Let me in."

She got up, and rushed to open the front door. He must've locked it when he left earlier.

"Morning, sleepy head." His kissed the top of her head.

"Yup." She turned away and hurried to the bathroom. She needed to go!

When she'd finished, she found him in the living room.

He stood. "I want to take you somewhere nice. Let's find you something to wear."

She shrugged, led the way to her bedroom and opened the closet. Sasha had come by while she was in class and hung her clean clothes back up.

The hangers scratched against the wooden rail as he slid them aside. Spying a yellow dress, similar to the one she'd worn the night before, he pulled it out and held it to her. With a smile, he handed her the hanger.

"This one?"

"Yes. Get dressed." He left the bedroom, and shut the door behind.

She pulled off her shorts and tank, and pulled the dress on over her head, then went into the living room.

He smiled when he saw her.

She turned, showing him her bare back. "Zip me up?"

"Please."

"Please." She added.

His warm hands brushed her skin as he pulled the up the zipper. Resting his hands on her shoulders, he spun her around and inspected her appearance.

"Good?" She wanted his approval.

"Very. You want to put on makeup?"

She made a face. "No. I hate putting it on."

He raised an eyebrow. "Who did it last night?"

"Sasha. She did my makeup and my hair. She usually does." Emily shrugged.

"Okay. No makeup. But we need to get your hair done."

She nodded, and they made their way back to the bathroom. He pulled out her hair tie, and brushed her hair before braiding it. He tugged the braid and she smiled.

"Come on," he said. "Let's go."

"Where are we going?" She followed him from the apartment, and he locked the door behind them.

"A nice little Mexican place uptown."

"Oh, I love Taco Bell!"

He chuckled as he grabbed her hand. "This isn't like that."

"Oh."

He held her hand until they reached the car, then he opened the door and helped her get in.

She smiled up at him as he closed the door, then jogged around and climbed into his own seat.

Once they were on the freeway, he turned the radio down. It was just like this morning when he'd taken her to school.

"Have you had a chance to look up DD/lg?"

She shook her head. "No, I was tired."

"Okay. Basically, I want to be your daddy. But not like, literally. I want to take care of you. But, I want to have sex with you, too."

She raised an eyebrow. "Both of those sound good to me."

He smiled, but the look didn't meet his eyes. "There's more to it. If you decide you want to be in a relationship with me, there will be rules."

"Like, for sex?"

"No, for the house. You'll have a curfew, and will be expected to keep your room clean. Stuff like that. I want to tuck you in when you sleep, and be excited when you get good grades."

"Isn't that what boyfriends do, anyway?"

"Not quite. Because if you break the rules, I will punish you."

She shivered. The word sounded sexy when he said it. "I think I could like that."

"No. You will go to time out, or not be allowed to be near me. If necessary I will spank you. But that one will be both when you're in trouble, and when we're playing in the bedroom."

She nodded. "So far so good."

"I do not want a slave. But I do expect you to obey when given a command or request."

She hesitated. "What if I'm not comfortable with what you ask for?"

"There's a safe word for in the bedroom. And before we do anything you'll need to tell me any soft or hard limits you have."

"Okay. But what about out of the bedroom?"

He reached over and brought her hand to his lips. "Then you ask me nicely or tell me what the problem is. If I'm not listening, you can use the safe word if you need to."

He pulled into a parking space in front of a small restaurant. There was a line of people dressed in nice clothes that started at the door, and wrapped around the block. Emily craned her neck, but couldn't see where the line ended.

"Geeze. Maybe we should go somewhere else. I'm kind of hungry now."

He climbed from the car as she undid her seatbelt, and he came around and opened the door for her.

He held her hand as she climbed from the car. "Don't worry. I know a guy."

She smiled up at him, and held on to his hand as he led the way to the entrance.

A large man with dark skin and a shirt that read 'security' stood in front of a velvet rope. This was just like the club Sasha had taken her to after they'd graduated high school.

Devin smiled at the security guy, and pulled Emily closer.

Without any words spoken, the security guy unlatched the rope and stepped aside, allowing them entrance. The line of people booed, but there didn't seem to be any malice in it.

The inside was cozy. Wall sconces and hurricane lamps on each table lit the interior, but it was dim, and Emily couldn't see anyone's face clearly. Every table had someone seated at it.

Devin led her to a podium. A man in a suit stood there with his nose in the air. A handful of people were seated on the benches in the lobby, chit chatting quietly among themselves.

The man at the podium must've seen them somehow, because when Devin approached, he spoke with a nasal tone, reminiscent of the snotty butler in the old black and white movies.

"Name?" He sniffed as he spoke the word.

"Devereaux."

The man looked at Devin. Actually took his nose out of the air, and looked at him. He fumbled around at the podium a moment.

"Right this way, Mr. Devereaux." The guy turned away, and led them through the crowded restaurant to an empty booth in a back corner.

There steps were silent on the carpeted floor, and the other guests quieted as they walked passed. Nervous, Emily clutched Devin's hand, afraid he would let go.

He squeezed her hand reassuringly as she slid into the booth. Kissing the back of her hand, he let her hand go and took a seat in the booth opposite.

He waved away the menus the man tried to give him, and put his hands on the table, palms up.

Emily put her hands in his, and smiled shyly. The scent of fried corn tortillas permeated the restaurant and made her mouth water.

"When we're done eating, I want you to do some research. I do not want you entering into this relationship lightly."

She shrugged. "I guess. But you're a great guy, and you seem honest. I trust you."

He smiled back at her. "Good. I plan to have the enchilada plate. Do you have any food dislikes?"

"Peaches." She wrinkled her nose.

He laughed. "Really?"

"Yes. I hate them."

"Okay. Then I think, for your first time here, you should try the monster burrito platter."

"Geeze. Sounds… monstrous." She held her hands in front of her as she giggled.

"Trust me. You'll like it." He smiled, and she could feel her heart melting.

Moments later, a waiter appeared. He was wearing a suit similar to the one worn by the guy who'd been behind the podium.

He bowed, and spoke to Devin in Spanish while Emily looked between them, confused. The waiter walked away, and a woman approached the table and put their drinks down, and walked away without a word.

She looked at Devin, a question on her lips, but he answered before she was able to ask.

"It's horchata. It's good. Try it."

Hesitantly, she picked up her cup and took a sip. Her eyebrows shot up in surprise. It was smooth, but not creamy, though it was thick. It tasted of vanilla and cinnamon.

"This is really good!" She took another sip.

He smiled. "I'm glad you like it. So, tell me about yourself."

She shrugged, but kept sipping. He raised a brow and she caught herself before rolling her eyes.

"What do you want to know?"

"Everything." His voice dropped an octave, and warmth filled her belly.

"I don't know where to start." She shifted uncomfortably in her seat.

"You can start with your college. What's your major? What do you plan to do with your degree?"

She brightened at that. Those were questions she knew the answer to! "I'm a sophomore. I graduated from high school early. I'm working on my CPA. I want to be a tax accountant."

"Why taxes?"

She shrugged and took a sip before answering. "Because it's what my parents wanted me to do."

"Past tense?"

"Well, father passed on two years ago. Mother travels a lot. She's in Europe right now. She pays for my tuition and books."

"Do *you* want to be an accountant?"

She cocked her head to the side, and for the first time actually considered it. "I don't know. I've never really thought about it. I don't *not* want to be an accountant."

They were discussing music preferences when their waiter came buy, a large platter balanced on his crooked arm.

He said something to Devin in Spanish before setting their plants on the table in front of them.

Emily's mouth watered. Her burrito was as monstrous as it sounded and was covered in a pale greenish sauce with chunks. She leaned down and inhaled deeply, then sneezed. There was some spice to that dish!

A smaller plate was placed at her elbow. She grabbed some of the cool, crisp lettuce and sprinkled it over her burrito, then scooped on the chilled sour cream and guacamole. Devin passed her a small bowl with pico de gallo, and she spooned a small amount on as well.

Using his fork and knife, he cut into his enchiladas. She followed his lead, and cut into her burrito. When the bite hit her mouth, it was like a flavor explosion. She closed her eyes, and savored the different textures, temperatures, and flavors.

She swallowed. "Wow."

"I'm glad you approve."

She nodded and took another bite.

The spent the rest of the meal getting to know each other. Likes, dislikes, and amusing anecdotes from childhood. She'd eaten less than half her burrito before she was full to bursting. She leaned back and groaned, putting a hand on her belly.

Devin smiled. "You can take the rest home, but I hope you saved room for dessert."

He motioned with his hand, and the waiter appeared moments later with two plates of a weird looking dessert.

She eyed it warily. "What is it?"

"Fried ice cream."

She wrinkled her nose at it. "You can't fry ice cream."

He chuckled, but scooped some on to his spoon. "Try it."

She sighed, but took a bite. As with the horchata, she was pleasantly surprised. The inside was still cold but the crispy outside was warm. She pushed the soft ice cream against the roof of her mouth. It was just vanilla, but it'd never tasted so good.

"See?"

She nodded. "I think I'm going to like being your girl, if this is how I get fed!"

"Good. But I don't want to wait much longer before you agree to be mine."

She peeked up at him from under her lashes, and her eyes met his smoldering gaze.

"Come on. Let's get you to bed."

She giggled, but held out her hand.

He stood, took it, and helped her from her seat.

They made their way out of the dimly lit restaurant, and back to her place.

Chapter Six: Surprises

B ack at her apartment, she handed him the key and he unlocked the door. He held it open for her, and she went inside. She stopped short, and he bumped into her.

He grabbed her shoulders, and pushed her back into the hallway, and she backed all the way to the door on the opposite side of the hall, her hand over her mouth. Her apartment had been trashed.

A moment later, Devin came back outside, his phone to his ear. "Yes, a break-in. No, not that I found. Yes. Okay. Thank you." He hung up the phone and pulled the door shut behind him.

"You can stay with me tonight."

She nodded, and put her hand in his as he led the way back out to his car.

Once she was safe outside, the tears welled up in the back of her eyes. She sniffed, and tried to blink them away. Strong arms wrapped around her, and pulled her close. His woodsy scent filling her senses with him.

She couldn't be strong anymore. She closed her eyes, and silently cried into his chest. Her apartment didn't have much, but it was hers. She had an old nineteen-inch television that was decades old, and didn't have a remote. Even her sofa was cheap. A neighbor was moving and didn't want to haul it down the stairs, and had given it to her. The only thing of real value were the clothes in her closet.

Her shoulders shook but her tears remained silent as he rubbed her back and murmured soothing sounds into her ear.

After some time had passed, the tears subsided. Someone may have taken her stuff, but at least she was okay. And she had only seen how trashed the apartment was. For all she knew, someone had been searching for who-knows-what, and left after they made the mess.

"Okay?" He set her at arm's length and looked down at her.

She forced a watery smile and nodded.

"Good. Police said to take pictures and go to the station tomorrow and file a report. For now, let's get you home."

She nodded, but her lips trembled. What if she'd been inside?

He pulled her close again. "Shh. It's okay. Let's get in the car."

She nodded, and stepped back from him as she swiped angrily at the tears on her cheeks.

He helped her into the car, and he took her to his house.

***

Emily kept her eyes shut the whole way to his house. The car made effortless stops, merges, and turns. Her forehead pressed to the cool glass of the window, she fought the tears that threatened. She felt violated, and wanted only to curl up and sleep.

After what seemed like forever, the car slowed to a stop.

"We're here." Devin spoke softly.

Emily opened her eyes. They were in a well-lit, underground parking garage. She rubbed her eyes, and unbuckled. Devin had already come around to her side, and opened the door for her. She grabbed his proffered hand and let him help her up. She stood shakily, her legs not wanting to carry her. It was as if the weight of the last hour were heavy on her shoulders, making it hard to stand. She stepped close to him, her hands rested on his chest.

He held her a moment, then bent over, put his arm behind her knees, and lifted her up.

Emily wrapped her arms around his neck, and snuggled her head into his chest.

He carried her to an elevator that dinged as he approached without him pushing any buttons. He stepped inside. The doors closed, soundlessly, and took them rapidly up before slowing to a smooth stop.

She didn't bother to check the floor number. It didn't matter. She was safe. She sighed, and snuggled closer to him as he carried her.

"I have to set you down, little one."

She nodded, and he set her on her feet.

He kept one arm wrapped around her as he slid a key into the heavy wooden door. It opened as soundlessly as the elevator had. Once he'd put his keys back in his pocket, he scooped her back up and carried her inside, and used his foot to shut the door behind them.

He sat on the couch, and arranged her on his lap. She sniffled, but didn't want to cry again.

"Now. Enough of that. You're safe."

She sniffled again, and wiped her nose with the back of her hand.

He handed her a handkerchief in silent reproach.

Taking it, she cleaned the back of her hand and her nose.

He pulled his phone from his pocket, tapped the screen a few times.

She looked down to see he had google open.

"Here, we can read this article together."

She nodded, and moved her head so she could see the screen comfortably. It was an article for beginners, and what the lifestyle entailed. It was a short article, and once she'd finished reading, she tapped the back button.

"Well?"

"Are you into all that?"

He shifted underneath her. "All what?"

"Hurting people?"

He chuckled, the sound reverberating in his chest. "No. I'm into control. Bondage, mostly. Some light impact, but never pain."

"Oh." She wiggled on his lap as she looked around his living room. It was easily the same size as her entire apartment. Every decoration was white. The couch they sat on was white microfiber. White counters, white chairs, white paintings, even a white carpet. The walls were all different colors, one wall was a vivid green, one was violet, and the other was rose. The last was dominated by a large, plate glass window next to a set of French doors.

They opened onto a balcony, and she could see the skyline from where she sat. Gasping, she climbed up from his lap and made her way to the glass doors. The curtains were open, and she put a hand on the cool glass. She could see his reflection behind her as he joined her at the doors.

He reached around her and opened the door, the cool night air was refreshing. She stepped out, and leaned a little over the balcony as she closed her eyes and lifted her face to the breeze. She breathed deeply, the smell of car fumes, flowers, and Devin's woodsy scent filled her nose.

His strong arms wrapped around her waist as he whispered in her ear. "This is nothing compared to your own beauty."

She turned in his arm and looked up at him. He was so tall, but they fit so perfectly together. Resting her hands on his chest, she leaned against the banister behind her. The only thing keeping her from falling to her death.

He pulled her close.

She was expecting him to kiss the top of her head or her forehead, but instead, he brushed his lips against hers. Her eyes fluttered shut, and she was disappointed when he pulled away.

"You need to sleep." His voice had a husky, almost hoarse quality to it.

She smiled shyly. "But, I don't want to sleep now."

He pulled her against his chest, and buried his face in her hair. "You don't know what you're asking."

She grabbed his shirt with her hands, and turned her face up. She waited the barest of breaths then stood on her tiptoes and kissed him.

He growled, and held her tight as he deepened the kiss, parting her lips with his tongue.

She opened to him gladly as her hands slid up his chest to wrap around his neck. Her insides were quivering with desire, and she put a hand on the back of his head. She wanted him closer. Her tongue met his, tentatively at first, then matching his desire with her own.

Grabbing her bottom, he lifted her up, not taking his mouth from hers.

She wrapped her legs about his waist, and ran her hands along his back. She pulled her mouth from his to trail kisses along his square jaw to his ears as his arousal pressed into her.

He carried her back into the house, and down the hall to a bedroom, done in the same white décor as the living room but the walls were a mint color. He lay her gently onto the bed, and pulled away from her.

She moaned, and poked her lip out in a pout. Her heart was hammering in her chest.

He was panting, but kneeled in front of the bed. Grabbing her hips, he pulled her to the edge and lifted her dress. She wiggled her hips as he hooked his thumbs into her panties and pulled them off.

His hot breath on her wet pussy sent tingles up her spine. He kissed the inside of her leg as his fingertips trailed up her thigh.

Moaning in anticipation, she moved her hands to his head. But he grabbed her hands and held them on the mattress beside her. His mouth moved closer and closer to where she wanted it. She moved her hands, and he put them back, and moved his face farther away.

She moaned, this time in frustration.

He looked up at her, a stern look on his face. "If you think you can do this, now's you chance to try it. Nothing crazy. If you ever need me to stop or feel uncomfortable, you just say 'stop'. Now, keep your hands at your side. You may move your hips, but not your hands."

"Okay," she murmured as she rocked her hips experimentally.

His fingers began exploring her legs, teasing her with their closeness. "Okay, daddy," he said, not breaking eye contact.

She swallowed, but whispered. "Okay, daddy."

He smiled, and a fingertip traced her slit.

Her eyes closed, and her back arched, but she didn't take her hands from where he'd put them as his breath teased her. Her breasts grew heavy, her arousal tightened her nipples, she moaned, and gripped the blanket, but didn't move her hands.

He spread her lips with his fingers, and trailed the tip of his tongue up her pussy. He stopped at her clit, and flicked it as he slowly slid a finger inside.

Her hands opened and closed, wanting to hold his mouth to her pussy, but she knew he'd take his mouth away if she did.

He sucked her clit, then licked it, putting pressure on it in ways she'd never felt. He was driving her body over the edge, her legs trembling with need. She'd get to the edge, and he'd slow down, or move his mouth, teasing her with an orgasm so close.

"Please," she moaned.

"Please, what?" His hot breath on her pussy arousing her more.

"Please, let me cum."

He pulled his finger from inside her, but teased her opening. "Please, what."

It took her a moment then she said, "Please, daddy. Make me cum."

He pushed his fingers deep inside and rubbed her g-spot as he teased her clit with his mouth.

Waves of pleasure crashed into her. She bucked her hips, but his mouth didn't leave her pussy. Her legs trembled, and her hands opened and closed on the blanket as she came.

He took his mouth from her clit, and rubbed his thumb next to it, his motions slowing as he brought her down from her climax. His teeth nipped her inner thigh, and she moaned with pleasure.

She was panting, her heart pounding in her chest, and he climbed onto the bed next to her.

"You may move your hands now." He whispered, then pulled on her ear with his lips.

A jolt of pleasure shot through her body and she shuddered. Slowly, she lifted her hand, but let it fall back to the bed. The effort was too great.

"Thank you, daddy," she panted.

"Mmm, baby girl, you are more than welcome."

Turning her head, she looked over at him. His dark eyes bored into hers, with an intensity she couldn't fathom.

"Wow."

He chuckled. "Glad you liked it."

She cupped his cheek, and whispered, "Where's the bathroom?"

He laughed then, a full bellied sound, and stood then pulled her to her feet. "I'll show you."

It was strange, being dressed but missing her panties, but it was also sexy.

A door in the bedroom opened to the master bath. It was bigger than her kitchen. She turned in a slow circle, and tried to take it all in. It was white, like the rest of the house, but the walls were a soft blue color, and anything that wasn't white was nickel plated.

The bathtub was a jetted affair, large enough to hold two people easily. A shower was next to it. Clear glass and tile surrounded it, and multiple shower head were positioned inside. A wall separated the toilet from the double sink, making it feel even more private.

She opened the door, and revealed a linen closet stuffed with fluffy white towels and other toiletries. It closed soundlessly, and she opened the cabinets under the sink. There was nothing unusual, and she smiled. He was definitely someone she could trust.

She used the facilities, and washed her hands before rejoining him in the bedroom.

He was sitting on the foot of the large, king-sized bed. When he saw her, he stood, and made his way to her side. Brushing a stray bit of hair from her cheek, he kissed her forehead and grabbed her hand.

She smiled up at him.

He returned the smile. "Come on. Bed time."

He led her from the room, and into a bedroom across the hall. It was different than the rest of the house she'd seen so far. The walls were a dusky rose, but the white bedspread had a floral print. The carpet was a blueish green that matched the shade of the wall, and was the same color as some of the flowers on the bedspread.

"This is beautiful."

"I'm glad you like it. It's yours as long as you want it." He led her to the twin bed.

She sat on the edge and he kneeled in front of her, holding her hand. Her heart sped up, wondering if they were going to have a repeat performance.

He took her shoes off, and stood, reached behind her, and unzipped her dress. He slid it form her shoulders, his hands brushing her skin. His woodsy sent filled her nostrils, and she closed her eyes.

He pulled her to her feet, and her dress fell to the floor. His hands ran up her arms, and down her chest, brushing her breasts as he made his way to her stomach before going around behind and unhooking her bra. He slid the straps from her arms, and it fell to the floor as well.

He stepped back, and eyed her body appreciatively.

Uncomfortable, she put her hands over her breasts and neatly trimmed pussy.

But he moved her hands and held them aloft. "You're beautiful. You don't ever need to hide your body from me."

She smiled shyly, and he stepped close as he ran his hands from her wrists to her shoulders, then down her back. He kissed the top of her head so softly she thought she may have imagined it.

"Do you want a t-shirt to sleep in? Or are you comfortable sleeping naked."

She chewed the inside of her cheek. "I think a shirt."

He nodded, then left the room.

She shivered, somehow colder without his presence.

He returned a moment later with a plain tee, and a pair of cotton panties.

She raised an eyebrow. "I really hope you don't think I'm going to wear a pair of stranger's panties."

A look of confusion crossed his face, but amusement quickly replaced it. "No, these are new. See?" He held them so she could see a store tag hanging from them.

She giggled behind her hand. "Oh."

He pulled the shirt over her head, but handed her the panties to put on. While she did, he pulled the tie from her braided hair, and separated the thick strands.

"Sit, I'll get the brush."

She sat, and when he got back, she asked, "Why?"

"Because I would like to brush your hair every night before bed. Do you want it left loose or braided?"

She shrugged. "Either works. I usually just sleep in it however."

"Then let's leave it free tonight."

As he brushed her hair, wafts of his cologne kept drifting to her nose. Shutting her eyes halfway, she tried to capture as many smells as she could. It'd been a long time since she felt as safe as she did right now.

Once he'd finished, he pulled back the covers and she climbed under. He fluffed her pillow, and tucked her in before kissing her forehead and saying goodnight.

Her eyes closed and he turned out the light before leaving the room.

Chapter Seven: Daddy

The next morning, she woke and stretched before she snuggled back down into her warm bed. Her eyes popped open. This wasn't her bed. The events of the night before came crashing in, but she smiled. Devin was going to take care of her.

Emily rose from bed, and made her way to the bathroom in Devin's room. She didn't know where another one was, and didn't want to explore his apartment without him.

In the living room, the smell of bacon made her mouth water. She could hear someone cooking, and made her way through the living room into a small entryway she hadn't noticed the night before. She crept through the room, her steps were silent on the soft white. It was so plush, she wanted to lay down on it, or curl her toes into it.

Her mouth dropped open as she stepped through the arched doorway. A full dining room with kitchen lay beyond. The walls were a pale yellow, like sunshine after a rain. Devin was already dressed for the day in a dark blue polo shirt and khakis. He stood in front of a white stove and bacon sizzled in the pan in front of him.

He looked up and smiled. "Good morning, baby girl. How'd you sleep?"

"Good," she stepped hesitantly onto the cool tile floor.

"Breakfast will be done in a minute. Take a seat. Orange juice is in the fridge." He pointed with his chin to the large fridge dominating the outside wall. It was white, but had several magnets scattered on the front.

Opening the fridge, she saw it held more food then Devin could possibly eat in a month. But the orange juice sat, half empty, in the door. Putting it on the counter, she looked around. She had no idea where he kept cups, and she suspected he wasn't the type to leave clean dishes in the dishwasher.

As if reading her mind, he turned from the stove, and opened the cabinet next to the sink before turning back to the bacon as it popped angrily in the pan.

"Thanks," she murmured as she poured the juice. A square wooden table, surrounded by four chairs, was stationed in the dining room next to the kitchen. She took a seat, and quickly stood back up. The chair was cold. She pulled her shirt down as far as she could then retook her seat.

He turned off the stove, and set the table. His dishes were plain white, but they were glass and matched each other. He carried two platters to the table, and set them down before taking his own seat.

He added bacon, eggs and buttered toast to their plates. "When do you have class today?"

"I only go Monday, Wednesday, and Friday." She picked up a strip of bacon and took a bite.

"Good." He nodded and took his own bite. "We need to go to the police and file a report later. Then we'll go over my relationship expectations in greater detail. Have you asked Sasha if you could read her book?"

She shook her head. "No, I haven't seen her since the party."

"We'll pick you up a copy then."

She mentally calculated what was probably in her bank account. Mother deposited money on the first and fifteenth of every month, but if she wanted to focus on school rather than work, she needed to make it last.

"I'll just call Sasha after we get done at the police station."

"Okay. We can do that after breakfast. Get it over with."

She nodded, and they finished their breakfast in silence.

Once they'd finished eating, he leaned back in his chair and held out a hand.

She took it and smiled at him.

"Baby girl, I need to apologize to you."

"For what?"

"I would love to have you call me daddy. All the time. But, I shouldn't have taunted you with orgasm to do it. I want you to call me that because you want to. Not because I make you."

She smiled shyly. "I liked it."

He grinned, and the corners of his eyes crinkled with delight. "Good. But I don't want you to ever feel as if you are a slave or somehow lesser than me. If we do this, if we decide to start dating, I want you to be a partner."

She cocked her head to the side. "But, isn't a sub supposed to be like a slave?"

He chuckled. "If you serve me, I want it to be by choice. No matter what is bothering you, communication is the most important thing. If you feel demeaned by me, I need you to tell me. Need. If you can't do that, then this isn't going to work."

She nodded. "I'll do my best. But this is all new. What if I mess up."

He squeezed her hand. "We will both make mistakes. It's why we're human. The hope is? We can fix our mistakes and communicate our wants and needs with each other."

He stood, then pulled out her seat to help her stand as well.

"Do I have to do chores?"

He grinned again. "No. I have a service I pay to do that. Let's get you dressed."

He held her hand and led her back to her bedroom, where he opened the closet and pulled out a pair of black slacks, and a yellow flowy blouse. She pulled open the top drawer of the dresser, and saw it was filled with underthings, with tags still on. He was at the door, but she stopped him.

"Daddy," she turned to him, and wrung her hands.

"Hmm?" He turned to face her.

"Why do you have new clothes here."

"I was really hoping you would move in with me."

"But, I have my own clothes. And my own place."

He sighed. "Baby girl. Get dressed. Ask me when you're done."

Her lower lip pushed out in a pout. "But, I want to know now. I might forget later."

He closed his eyes a moment, as if he were mentally counting to ten, then took the three steps to stand in front of her. He rested his hands on her shoulders and they locked eyes. "Baby doll, I cannot think straight with you braless, wearing nothing but my shirt and a pair of panties. And I cannot stand arguing. I will not let you forget. Get dressed. I don't think you're ready to be spanked yet for being naughty." He chucked her chin with a finger and strode from the room, the door shutting behind him.

She swallowed. That was the single hottest thing that had probably ever happened to her. She quickly dressed, and marveled at the soft, luxuriant textures of the clothes. She had a floofy shirt like this in her apartment, but it was course and rough. This felt like a cloud.

She pulled on a pair of nylon socks, and found a pair of ballet shoes in the closet. They were her size, and matched the outfit better than her trainers. But these weren't like the ballet shoes she had at home. As with the rest of her outfit, these were higher quality. They had a padded sole, and if she stepped on pebble wearing these, her feet wouldn't get stabbed.

Satisfied with her outfit, she hurried from the room back to Devin. A large smile spread across her face at the look of approval in his eyes. She did a slow turn. "Am I pretty?"

He stood, and chuckled. "You're beautiful. But we need to do something with your hair."

She gasped, and a her hand shot up to her head.

He moved her hand down, and leaned in close. "The things I want to do with you right now, cannot be said in polite company. I like your hair the way it is, but I don't want anyone else to see you the way I do at this moment." His breath on her ear sent shivers down her spine.

Her eyes closed, and she turned her face to his.

His lips brushed hers, the kiss no more than the barest of whispers.

She whimpered when he stepped back, frustrated. She wanted him. And she wanted all of him this time.

His eyes were dark with desire. "We need to go to the police station." But he didn't step back.

She hesitantly placed her hands on his chest, then stood on her tip toes. "Can't it wait?" She whispered, then kissed his chin.

He groaned, and bent his head. His lips met hers and the familiar warmth of desire spread from her belly.

He parted her lips with his tongue, and her tongue met his with an equal passion. His hands wrapped around her, and his hardness pressed into her belly.

When his mouth moved from hers, to her neck and ears, she moaned as she panted, her heart racing.

Reaching down, he picked her up. Her legs wrapped around his waist and he took three steps to put her back against the wall. His fingers undid the buttons on her blouse, and his mouth moved to her chest.

Her breath came in rapid gasps as she gripped the back of his shirt and bunched it up before pulling it over his head.

His own breathing was ragged. He'd opened her shirt, and pulled the cups of her bra down, revealing her hard nipples and pert breasts. He sucked first one nipple, then the other.

She ran her hands over his bare back. She wanted him closer. She wanted him inside her.

He undid the clasp on her slacks, and rubbed her slit through her wet panties.

She moaned.

He moved her from the wall, and set her on the couch.

78

She looked up at him, her eyes hooded, and her pussy throbbing with need.

He unbuckled his belt and opened his pants before pushing them down over his hips. His hard cock sprang forth, and she gasped.

She reached up to stroke it, but he grabbed her wrist, and moved her hand to his hip.

He sat on the couch next to her and pulled her onto his lap.

She leaned forward, putting her breasts in his face, and he teased her taught nipples. His hand rubbed her pussy through her clothes. She wrapped her arms about his neck as she rocked her hips.

His hands made their way to her backside, pulling her slack down over her hips. He grabbed her ass, his fingertips digging into the soft flesh.

Panting, she whispered, "Daddy, I need you. Please." She wanted to beg.

He flipped her over, and stood between her legs. He pulled her slacks down, and she raised her hips to let them pass.

He kissed her deeply, then sucked her bottom lip as he pulled away. A finger teased her pussy over her wet panties, before sliding them to the side and entering her.

She gasped. "Yes," she moaned, her eyes closing. Her hands fisted beside her.

"Open your mouth." He voice was husky, and she peeked up at him from under her lashes, but did as she was told.

He put one foot on the couch beside her, and she leaned forward.

She licked the tip of his hard cock, tasting the clear bead that had formed.

He ran his fingers through her hair, then stopped at the back of her head as he guided her mouth onto his cock.

She sucked, her head moving with his guidance, her tongue teasing his shaft.

"Touch yourself."

She did as she was asked, her finger sliding inside her wetness before going to her clit.

He cupped her breast with his other hand, and pinched her nipple gently.

"I want you to swallow."

She sucked harder in agreement, and he groaned.

She rubbed her clit faster, sucking harder as she neared climax. Spit filled her mouth.

He grabbed either side of her face, and fucked her mouth, the head of his cock hitting the back of her throat. She moaned, and her hips bucked. Her legs twitched as she came, her body exploding with pleasure.

He grunted, and his seed filled the back of her throat.

She swallowed reflexively, but didn't taste it.

With a final thrust, he slowly pulled his cock from her mouth.

She sucked, not wanting it to be over, as she rubbed the sensitive areas next to her clit, coming down from her climax.

He stepped back, his breathing ragged. "Damn."

She looked up at him, and slid her hand from her pussy to her breast, trailing a finger around a nipple. "Did I do good, daddy?"

"Oh yeah."

They dressed, and she giggled as he stuffed his semi-hard cock back into his pants.

He tucked his shirt in, and held out a hand. "Come on. We need to get going."

She nodded, and they left for the police station.

Chapter Eight: Decisions

Emily handed her house keys to Devin in the elevator, headed up to her apartment. They'd filed a report at the police station, and she had zero faith they would make any apprehensions on her behalf.

As they walked down the hall to her door, her stomach tied itself into knots. She didn't want to deal with the aftermath. The closer they got, the more violated she felt. But no matter how stupid she told herself she was being, the discomfort grew.

At the door, Devin turned toward her and held up a hand. "I want you to wait out here, understood?"

She nodded and wrung her hands. "Alright."

He nodded, and unlocked the door. He went in, but shut the door behind himself. The longer he was in there, the more worried she grew. The seconds turned into minutes, but would the minutes turn to hours? What if someone was in there, waiting, and now he was lying on the floor, injured. Or worse. She blinked back the tears that were forming. Devin would be fine.

He was only minutes later when the door opened, but her heart jumped into her throat. The time it took for the door to open, and

Devin to appear, seemed interminable. She breathed a sigh of relief when she finally saw him. She jumped on him, wrapping her arms around his neck and her legs around his waist.

He stumbled back a step or two, but didn't fall. "Okay. Shh, baby girl. It's okay."

She nuzzled his necked, and just held him close, his woodsy scent comforting. Sighing, she loosened her hold, and he set her down.

"Better?"

She nodded.

"Good. Let's take care of your apartment." He wrapped a hand about her waist and they stepped inside.

She gasped, and was thankful for his support. She hadn't realized how badly it'd been trashed last night. The acrid scent of sour milk assaulted her nostrils, and her beige couch was flipped on its end and stood straight up in the center of the living room, with its cushions lying about haphazardly. Pictures had been knocked off the wall, the ones she'd done in art class and had been so proud of.

The tears that had threatened in the hall fell freely from her eyes. It wasn't just stuff that could be replaced. It was the smashed knick-knacks her Mother had sent back from Africa. Before Father died, they'd never sent her anything, and now they were crushed, ground into dust in the threadbare carpet. It was the painting she'd done of water lilies. She'd even gotten an 'A' on it. It was her shoes, cut up and slashed, laying like fallen soldiers among the upended trashcan in the center of the hall.

She took a steadying breath and nodded. The physical keepsakes may be broken, but she could still remember. And she was safe. She took a step, and Devin let go of her waist to grab her hand. She led the way through the small hallway to check the bathroom and her bedroom. Both were in similar condition to the living room.

She held onto the door frame, just staring at the disarray. Everything she owned had been tossed, or destroyed. Whoever had broken in must have been really angry at not finding anything worth stealing. Maybe they didn't realize she was an unemployed student.

The tears that had threatened earlier silently fell, unheeded, down her cheek. There was nothing for her to do now. She would need

82

to get large trash bags and throw out most of her stuff. There wasn't enough glue and patience in the world to put the pieces back together. She only wondered if she would ever feel safe here again, or if there wasn't enough glue still.

He tugged her hand. "Let's go."

She turned away from the destruction, and Devin lead her from the wreckage. There wasn't anything for her here anymore.

***

They drove in silence. He'd asked her if she needed to call Mother, or Sasha, but she'd just shaken her head. She didn't want to talk to anyone. Just wanted to wallow in self-pity. After a while, she was shaken from her revere by the odd scenery passing by the window. Rather than the skyscrapers and congested traffic of the city, they were driving through suburbs, with cookie cutter houses, and manicured lawns.

"Where are we?"

"I thought I'd take you somewhere special."

"Like, a treat?"

He smiled. "Are you sure you've never been in the lifestyle before?"

She chewed the inside of her cheek, trying to decide if that was a compliment or not.

He reached over and squeezed her knee. "It's a joke, baby. I'm very proud of how you handled yourself back there."

She reached over and cupped his cheek, his stubble rough on her skin.

He turned his face enough to kiss her palm, and she lowered her hand.

She turned back to looking out the window. "So, where are we going?"

"There a lake just out of town. I like to go there and camp in the summer."

"I've never been camping."

"I hope you like it. It's still too cool out for it, but…" he trailed off, and she remembered they needed to talk more.

She cleared her throat. "About that."

The muscle in his jaw ticked. "Have you thought about it?"

"I really want to try it. With you, not anyone else. And I want to be exclusive. I want to be your only girl."

He nodded.

Encouraged, she continued. "And I want you to teach me. I don't want to disappoint you. I feel safe with you. And I know I'm going to screw up, but I'm hoping you still want me."

He slowed as they approached a dirt turn off. Within moments they were driving on a gravel road, surrounded by tall pines. The road wound through the trees without regard for fasted route. Both his hands gripped the wheel, and he leaned forward in his seat. He cursed under his breath, and she winced.

"I should've brought the truck. Forgot how rough this road could be in the spring."

She gripped the door, but didn't speak.

He pulled into a clearing. There was a picnic table, and a metal drum with a trash bag in it. "This is as far as we can go this time."

He cut the engine, and they climbed from the car.

The cool breeze caught a stay bit of hair, and it tickled her cheek.

He came up behind her and wrapped his arms around her waist as he kissed her neck. "This isn't the lake. But this is good too."

She put her hands on his arms, and swayed with him. They were in a designated camping spot, according to the large sign off to the side. The air smelled of pine, dirt, and a hint of water. Just like Devin. She snuggled back against his chest, and he tightened his hold on her waist.

They stood together a moment longer before he let go. Grabbing her hand, he led her to a small footpath at the edge of the small clearing. She followed as he led them into the forest, until the clearing disappeared.

When they left the small foot path and wandered deeper into the forest, she tugged his hand. "Daddy, I'm scared."

84

He stopped and looked back at her, and stopped. "Baby, I'm sorry. This should be far enough."

She forced a small smile. She liked that he tried to be so considerate all the time.

He pulled her into his embrace, and he kissed the top of her head. "Thank you for telling me how you felt. I think you deserve a reward."

With her hands on his chest, she looked up at him and stretched to kiss his jaw. She could feel his heart speed up. She closed her eyes, and wrapped her arms around his neck. His lips met here upturned mouth, and she licked his lower lip.

He growled, and pulled her closer, his mouth ravishing hers, before trailing down to her neck.

With ragged breaths, she tossed her head back and arched her back, giving him full access to her body. Warmth spread from her belly, and she squeezed her thighs together as the excitement built.

He lifted her, and lowed them both to the ground. Pine needles dug into her bag, but they didn't hurt. His fingers flicked open her buttons one by one, and followed with his mouth.

Her hips were rocking and her need grew. She didn't just want him, she needed him. She needed his hands and mouth on her, and him inside her. She dug her fingers into his back, bunching his shirt.

He got to his knees and pulled his shirt off, his hard muscles flexing, and sweat glistening in the dappled sunlight. Reaching down, he flicked her slacks open with one hand, and undid his pants with the other.

Sitting up, she pulled her shoes and clothes off, and tugged his pants off his hips. His cock was hard, as if he needed her as much as she needed him. Looking up at him, she ran her hand up his hard thigh. "I want to taste you."

He thrust his hips slightly.

She opened her mouth, and stretched her tongue out.

He grabbed his cock and rubbed the tip on her tongue as she gazed up at him.

"May I touch it, daddy?"

"Yes."

She wrapped her hand around his girth, the silky texture at odds with the hardness of it.

He put his hand on hers, and adjusted her grip, teaching her how to do it through his guidance. "Touch yourself, not just me."

She rubbed her hand over her breasts, brushing her hard nipples, then moved her hand down her body while stroking his cock. When she reached her pussy, the ran a finger over the slit, the silky wetness covering her finger as rubbed her clit.

"Open up."

She did as she was told, a tremor running through her at the command. She sucked his cock into her mouth, stroking his shaft and balls with her hand while she rubbed her clit. Her pleasure was mounting, and she sucked harder, close to her climax.

When he grabbed her breast and teased the nipple, she was thrown over the edge. He pulled his cock from her mouth, and she moaned, her body shaking as each wave of ecstasy hit.

He sat next to her on the ground, and pulled her into his lap. She straddled him, his hard cock under her wet pussy.

She moaned, and wriggled her hips on his lap. She could feel the pleasure building again. Her breasts were heavy with desire as he put his mouth on them, sucking her nipple into his mouth.

He lifted her by her ass, and lowered her slowly onto his cock. "Ride me."

She rode him, her legs tingling as her breasts bounced.

He leaned back on his hands, his cock flexed inside her. She moaned again.

"Touch yourself. I want you to cum for me."

She reached between them to rub her clit, her back arched, she grabbed her breast with her other hand, her fingers digging into the soft flesh. He tilted his hips, his cock hitting the back of her pussy.

Climax claimed her, and she cried out. "Oh, daddy, yes!"

He sat up and grabbed her hips, and lifted her up then dropping her back down on his cock as the orgasm wracked through her body, every muscle clenching.

He grunted, and pushed his cock deep inside her.

They were both panting, and she could feel his cum dripping from her, mixed with her own. He held her close as their breathing came in ragged pants, his skin slick with sweat. He grabbed her ass.

"Again, daddy?" She giggled, and nuzzled his neck.

He chuckled. "Not yet. This was your reward. You handled today very well. But when we get home, we need to talk about limits. Because I don't want you to run away."

She nipped his neck. "I'll be yours as long as you'll have me."

He gave a sad laugh, and she pulled away.

There was a sad smile playing about his mouth. "What's wrong, daddy?"

"Baby, I am thirty-seven years old. I know you mean what you say. But you were probably raised vanilla. And I'm afraid you won't enjoy playing with me once it stops being vanilla. But even if you don't want to fuck me, I'll still take care of you as long as you want."

This. This right here was the moment she wanted to remember forever. He didn't want to just have sex, but he wanted to care for her no matter what. Her heart melted, and she kissed him. "You're the best daddy."

He grinned, the sadness in his eyes slowly disappearing. "Yeah. But I'm the only daddy you've had."

"And the only one I want."

"I think we should go home now."

He stood, and set her on the ground, and held her hand as they made their way back to the car.

Chapter Nine: Limits

They pulled into an underground parking garage under a towering building downtown. She tilted her head up, but couldn't see the imposing structure from the car.

"This is where you live." She'd be so distracted, she hadn't noticed where he lived.

He nodded, and turned the wheel, to make the necessary turns to park in a reserved spot.

She raised a brow. "Doctor?"

He chuckled. "Yep. Dr. Deveraux."

Her mouth dropped open. "But…"

"I'll fill you in once we get inside."

She waited for him to open her door, and he led the way to an elevator a short distance from his parking space.

They rode in silence to the top of the building. When the doors opened, they stepped into a small foyer with two doors. He unlocked and opened the door to the left, and held the door while she stepped into his apartment. He closed the door softly behind them as she made her way to the white sofa.

She plopped into the seat, and grinned.

"Now stand up and sit back down five times. We don't plop on the furniture."

She could tell he was serious by the tick in the muscle in his jaw. With a sigh, she stood and sat five times in a row.

"Good girl." He joined her on the couch. "Limits."

"You keep saying that."

"Watch the tone. And yes. Here's the deal. Typical dom sub relationships stay in the bedroom. And most DD/lg is all the time. I like it all the time. I don't want to ever put you in a position you do not feel safe, or are afraid to tell me to stop."

She nodded. "You said there are safe words if necessary."

"Yes. I want you to say 'pineapple' if you tell me no and I think you're arguing or I'm just not listening."

"Okay."

"Anal sex."

She clenched her butt cheeks. "That sounds painful."

"Is it something you are not interested in at all? Or something you would like to explore and test."

"Not ever. At least, not anytime soon."

"That makes it a hard limit. You do not want to do it, no matter what. Do you think you might enjoy anal play? Fingers or small toys, but nothing large and no anal sex?"

"Oh! Then a soft limit is something I don't really want, but am interesting in testing and trying out?"

"Pretty much, yes." He beamed at her.

She smiled back. "Okay. Well, anal sex sounds horrid, but play would be optional. Soft limit. What else is there?"

He took a deep breath. "Bondage."

"Okay?"

"That's my preferred scene to create and play in."

"What do you mean?"

"Sex. Vanilla sex is the default. If I want to play, it's sometimes called a scene."

"Oh. Why?"

He chuckled. "I don't know. It just is. But I would like nothing better than having you tied up, or bound, and doing what I want to you."

She shuddered. "Me, too."

"Good. And I enjoy light impact play."

She cocked her head to the side.

"Spanking. Slapping. Impact."

She wrinkled her nose. "That's a soft limit. I think spanking is fine, but never my face."

"Toys?"

She shrugged. "I had some. But I never used them much."

He raised a brow, a look of shock on his face, but then it was replaced by amusement. "I don't mean dildos or vibrators. I mean paddles. Whips. Feathers."

"Oh!" she chuckled. "I think that's still a soft limit. I'm willing to try it out, but I don't know if I'll enjoy it."

"Okay." He pulled his shirt off over his head.

She gasped. He was gorgeous.

He pulled her into his lap, and her hands rested on his chest. "I want to play with you, baby girl."

She giggled. "That means sex."

He gave have a smile. "Yes."

She chewed the inside of her cheek. "But, you're a doctor."

"So? I like to care for others."

"But, what type of doctor are you?"

"General surgeon."

She wiggled on his lap, and smiled when his cock started to grow. "And you want to spank me now?"

He growled, and pulled her close. He ran his tongue along her jaw, then nibbled her ear. "I want to do more than that."

"Teach me, daddy," she moaned.

He lifted her from his lap and carried her back to the bedroom.

She wrapped herself around him, and kissed his neck, then tugged his ears with her lips.

He set her on her feet, and stepped away from her.

Her hands dropped to her side, hurt. She hoped he was teaching her and wasn't rejecting her. She stood motionless, and watched as he slowly undid his pants, but didn't take them off. It was almost as if he were taunting her.

He sat on the edge of the bed. "Go to the chair, and slowly take your shirt off."

She spied a wooden chair behind the bedroom door. She shuddered, knowing how much she was about to arouse her man. Facing him, she undid one button at a time on her blouse.

"Touch yourself, pretend your hands are mine."

She nodded, but thought for a moment. Closing her eyes, she ran her hands over her body. She didn't stop in one place, but explored her chest, her neck, her belly. When she would hit a button, she would undo it. Her hands rubbed her skin, as she pushed her blouse to the floor. She reached behind her to undo her bra, but he stopped her.

"No. Take of your pants."

She left her eyes closed, and slid her slacks off, running her hands over her wet panties. She was teasing him as much as she was teasing herself. Once she was standing, wearing nothing but her lacy satin bar and panty set, she waited, her hands still exploring her body.

"Come here."

Dropping her hands to her side, to made her way to him, stopping when she was still a step away.

"You are very good, but you tried to take off your bra without permission."

She chewed the inside of her cheek. "Sorry, daddy."

"I want you to bed over my knee. I am going to spank you three times."

She draped herself over his knee, butterflies in her stomach.

His hand smacked her backside, leaving a sharp sting. He rubbed the spot before doing it a second time. She gasped when the third strike hit.

"Remember, you are to tell me if you are uncomfortable with anything."

She nodded, but quickly forgot the sting as his hand rubbed he rear, soothing the hurt. When a finger pulled her panties aside and brushed outside her slit, she moaned.

"Do you like this?"

"Yes, daddy," she moaned.

Desire built in her belly, and she rocked her hips, wanting him touch more of her.

"You need to tell me what you want."

"I want you to touch me, daddy."

"Here?" His fingertips traced her spine, and she shivered.

"Yes, daddy."

He pulled her from his lap, standing her in front of him.

He grabbed her wrists when she started to touch her body. "I don't want you to move. Understood?"

"Yes, daddy. Will you please touch me?"

He reached behind her and unclasped her bra, his hot breath on her skin somehow more tantalizing than his hands would have been. He pulled it off, and flicked a taught nipple with the tip of his tongue.

She gasped, and her hand flicked at her side.

He pulled his head back. "Did you move baby?"

"Only my hand," she whispered. "Please, don't stop daddy."

His hands trailed to her panties, and pulled them down, but stopped part way. "Are you going to move?"

"No, daddy," she breathed, fighting every urge to pull his head to her, to run her hands along his bare back, to feel him under her and inside her. She closed her eyes, and took a shuddering breath. "Please, daddy."

She didn't even know what she wanted him to do.

He pulled her panties the rest of the way to the floor, and she stepped out of them. His hand met her ass with a sharp smack from his fingertips. "Don't move." He soothed the hurt, and kissed the hollow of her hip.

Moaning, she stood still, but wanted to do so much more.

He ran a finger along her wet slit, then slid a finger inside her.

She wanted to grab his shoulders, to bite down. Her toes curled in the carpet as she swayed, her passions moving her despite her best efforts.

Standing, he cupped a heavy breast, and teased her nipple with his thumb before leaning forward and putting his mouth on her neck. Licking, kissing, sucking.

She moaned, the desire building to a demanding height. "Please, daddy. I don't know how much longer I can be still."

In her ear he whispered, "lay on the bed, and show me how you pleasure yourself."

She practically jumped, laying on her back, she cupped her breast, and slid her fingers to her wet pussy. She spread her legs apart.

He stood, and watched her, his hand stroking his cock as she stroked her clit.

Her hips rocked as she teased herself to climax. Her legs twitched, and her body shuddered with orgasm. She brought herself down, and locked her gaze with his. "Did I do good, daddy?"

"Yes, baby." He grabbed her hips then pulled her forward so her legs dangled over the edge of the bed, and ran his tongue up her wet pussy before flicking her clit. She moaned.

"Grab the headboard. Make sure to cross your arms when you do."

Curious, she crawled to the bars on the headboard, crossed her arms at the elbows and grabbed hold. "Like this, daddy?"

He moved her hand over one bar, bringing them closer together, then reached between the mattress and headboard, and pulled up a pair of silicone restraints. There was no lock or clasp.

She looked at him quizzically, wondering how they worked. He moved her hand and slid it into the restraint, the silicone stretching to fit. He did the same with her other hand.

"Baby, if you ever need, you can pull from the restraint. But I'd hope you would tell me."

"Okay, daddy."

"Good girl. If you enjoy this, we can try leg restraints later." He moved to her feet, his hands rubbing her legs and ass as he explored her body.

She shuddered when his tongue joined the exploration. "I want you inside me, daddy."

He smacked her ass, then rubbed it as he kissed it better with his mouth. "Patience, baby girl."

She moaned again, and gripped the bars of the head board as he slid his fingers inside her wet pussy.

"Do you like this?"

"Yes, daddy," she moaned.

His tongue trailed her ass crack, and she shivered. He moved the fingers from her pussy to her ass, rubbing her butthole as he had her clit. It felt strange, but in a good way. She wiggled her ass as his finger pushed inside.

His hard cock pressed into her bum as he fingered her ass hole. He rubbed the tip of his cock along her slit. Her pussy lips spread, and he rubbed her clit with the tip before slipping it inside.

She bucked her hips, wanting him deeper. Her body quaked with the sensations he was causing. She couldn't think straight.

He pulled the tip out, and she moaned with disappointment. "Please, daddy," she begged. "I want it."

He slammed his cock into her, and her head bumped into the head board and she cried out, "Yes!"

Her body clenched as she came, her hands gripped the bars as if they were the only thing keeping her upright. Her legs trembled, and her heart beat a rapid staccato in her chest. He thrust again, and pulled out.

She gasped when he flipped her onto her back, uncrossing her arms.

From his knees, he moved her leg over his, so he was between them. Falling forward, he landed with his hands on either side of her, his face inches from her own.

He leaned in close, but stopped without kissing her.

Panting, she wondered what he would do to her next. She didn't have long to wait.

He straddled her chest, and scooted closer until his hard cock was in her face. She opened her mouth, but he pulled back. "Not this time, baby."

"But, I want to taste you."

"Don't argue or I'll have to spank you."

She closed her mouth.

He stroked his cock, as she watched with anticipation.

"You want my cum?"

"Yes, daddy, please."

"Where do you want it."

"In my mouth?" She looked up hopefully.

He shook his head. "Where else?"

"On my chest, daddy."

He scooted backward, his cock over her tits. He smiled, then pushed her tits together before lowering himself, and sliding his cock in her cleavage. With a frown, he moved his cock, and spit on her chest then spread it around with the tip then put his cock between her tits.

He teased her nipples with his thumbs as he thrust into her chest.

She watched as his cock appeared and disappeared. She moaned, she wanted to taste him. "I want to taste it, daddy."

"If your tongue can reach, you may."

She stuck out her tongue, able to lick the tip as he thrust. She moaned, wanting more, her need growing with each thrust.

"Daddy,"

He stopped and put a hand on the headboard as he lifted his hips, pointing the tip of his cock at her. "Tell me you want my cum, baby girl."

"Give it to me, daddy. I want it."

He panted, "Where?"

She squirmed against the restraints, wanting to feel his cock. "On my tits. Please, daddy."

He came, covering her tits in white cum. He stroked a final time, careful not to get any on his hand. "Want to clean it off, baby?"

"Yes, please, daddy. May I?"

He put his softening cock on her lips, and she opened wide. She sucked every drop she could, wanting his cock clean and ready for next time.

"Good girl." He pulled his cock from her mouth.

She squirmed, wanting to touch him, to be touched by him.

He chuckled. "Do you want to cum, baby?"

She nodded, "Yes, please."

He crouched between her legs, and ran his tongue along her slit before opening her and slipping his fingers inside her as he licked her clit.

Her hips were rocking with his rhythm when he began playing with her asshole. Instead of rocking, now she was bucking. She was so close, her body twitching and shuddering. "Daddy," she begged, now know what to ask for.

He put a hand on her breast, and pinched her nipple, harder than before, and she came, her body spasming and rocking with the orgasm that finally came.

"Yes, oh god, yes!"

He took his mouth off her pussy and slowly stopped his magical fingers, bringing her down form her climax.

Panting, she said, "Oh, daddy, that was amazing."

He grabbed a towel from the night stand and dried his fingers and her pussy. "You need a shower, baby girl."

"Mhm."

He pulled her wrists from the restraints, then tucked them back behind the bed, and helped her sit up. "Go shower. When you're done, we need to get your apartment cleaned."

"Can I sleep first?" Now that her heart had finally slowed, all she wanted was to take a nap. And *not* deal with a giant mess.

"Not today." He lifted her in his arms, and kissed the top of her head.

"Okay, daddy."

Chapter Ten: Clean Up

E mily stood in her living room and held the big black garbage bag as she turned in a slow circle. She had no idea where to start.

Devin kissed the top of her head. "Don't think about it baby girl. Start with the trash. And if it's broken, you throw it away."

"But... the memories. What they mean."

"If you don't think about it, it won't hurt as much while you work."

She nodded, and made her way to the upended trash can in the hall way. She'd never realized how much all her things had meant to her. She'd always thought of her apartment as minimalist and frugal, but now she understood. It wasn't about expensive things or fancy furnishings. It was about the memories her belongings held.

She moved slowly from the hall to the living room. A ceramic shepherd figurine lay in two pieces on the floor. It had been a gift from mother the week Father died. Mother had recited several scriptures as she told Emily there was no need to be sad.

But Emily had still been sad, and Mother went away to Europe. Then Asia. Now Africa.

A tear trickled from her eye. It made a tail down her cheek before it dripped off her chin.

"Baby girl, don't cry. Just put it in the trash and move on."

"But, you don't understand." She put down the bag and picked up the two pieces of the figure. "I don't have much, and mother was never much for affection. But, this is all I have right now. She's in Africa, remember? But I didn't tell you why."

He stopped what he was doing to look over at her. "Why?"

"Because I'm a terrible daughter. I was never thankful or appreciative of what they gave me before father died, but now he'd gone, and she gave me this. And I turned my nose up at it. It wasn't what I thought I'd wanted. And I hurt her so she left."

"Emily. It isn't your fault you mom left."

"Yes, it is. And now all the weird tokens she sent over the last two years are gone. All that are left are the memories." She threw the pieces on the ground and stomped on one to pick up a slashed painting. The water lilies. "I can't show her my art. I can't recreate it and I never took a picture. Everything has been ruined or destroyed somehow."

"Calm down. It's not that big a deal."

"To you maybe! You *have* parents that love you, you already graduated and you're doing a job you love! I don't even know what I want to do with my life!" Tear fell down her cheeks, and she angrily swiped them away.

He stepped toward her and she held up a hand to stop him.

"No. I don't want platitudes or sympathy. I want the person who did this to pay! They need to be arrested. But the police won't do it. They don't even care. Just like you don't!"

He nodded. "You need to grieve now. I get that. Do you want me to come back later, or do you want me to keep helping you."

"I don't need help! You and Sasha both think I'm incapable of doing the simplest of tasks. And maybe you're right. Maybe I rely on other people too much."

"What are you saying."

She took a deep breath, and looked over at him, her eyes full of the sorrow and defeat she felt. "Maybe you should just go. I need to grow up and handle my problems."

"Okay." He tied the trash bag he'd filled, and hefted it over his shoulder. "I'll be back in an hour."

She threw her hands to the side. "Haven't you been listening? I don't want help."

"Then text when you're done and I'll come pick you up and take you home."

"This *is* home! I'm not moving in with you! And you never told me why you had a closet and dresser full of clothes. Not the cheap ones, either. I don't want you to take care of me!"

"I see. Goodbye, baby girl."

She snarled. "Don't bother calling me that. I'm no one's baby girl. I'm just Emily. Broken, damaged, and completely useless Emily."

He hung his head, and walked out the door, taking the bag of trash with him.

Once the door latched behind him, she fell to the floor in a heap, as if she were nothing more than a discarded pair of pants. Useless, and unwanted. Even mother didn't want to be around her. And it was better Devin figured that out now, rather than down the road when it would hurt too much to let him go.

She curled in a ball on the floor, and the sharp edges of broken ceramic dug into her side. Tears fell freely, and she didn't bother wiping them away. This was it. There was nothing left for her. Even in school she was barely passing. Sasha hadn't called or texted in days. And she was alone.

Chapter Eleven: New Beginnings

Emily had no idea how long she'd lay on the floor and cried. It didn't matter. She'd gotten rid of Devin, and regretted it already. Mother couldn't be bothered to be in the same country, and unless it was the third, wouldn't be available for a phone call.

She sighed, and sat up, brushing off the small ceramic dust that had embedded itself into her clothes and hair. A piece in her hair jabbed her finger, and she pulled it back quickly. Ouch. She sniffled, but swallowed the tears that threatened to overcome again. She needed to be strong and take care of herself.

And that meant a shower. The bits of ceramic were painful. She spied her phone on the floor. It must have fallen from her pocket. The green notification light was flashing, so she swiped the screen to check it.

More than a dozen texts. Most were from Sasha! She had never been so thankful to see a text from her best friend before.

Sasha: Devin said ur upset. Whats goin on??

Sasha: Em? U ok?

Sasha: TF em! U need to txt or call me

Sasha: Getting worried here

Sasha: I called Devin. He said to talk to u. What happened??

Sasha: If he did something to you, I will chop off his fucking balls.

Sasha: Im comin over there

Devin: Baby girl Im worried about you. Lemme know youre ok.

Devin: babygirl, sasha's blowin up my phone. She thinks I did something to you.

Sasha: On my way now. Im gonna kill that jerk

Devin: Emily, I'm worried. I need you to talk to someone! Me or Sasha, doesn't matter. But you have to let us know youre ok.

Devin: Im coming back. God, pls be okay.

She checked the time stamps, and groaned. Devin and Sasha would both be here soon. Crap. She panicked, and started shoving everything she could into the trash bag. It needed to look like she'd at least done *something* after Devin left.

A pounding on the door prevented any further work. She stood motionless, like a deer caught in headlights, and the front door opened. Sasha and Devin were arguing.

Devin growled, while Sasha spoke. "…because she's fragile you jack hat!"

"Doesn't make her an idiot." Devin shot back.

The door opened the rest of the way, and Sasha came through first, her mouth opened in horror as she spotted the mess everywhere. Devin came through next, and a look of pure relief crossed his face when he saw Emily standing in the middle of the room. The relief was immediately hidden by a mask of indifference.

Sasha turned and grabbed Devin's shirt as he turned to leave. "Oh, no you don't. Get in here, you fucking coward. How dare you!?!?"

Devin's spine stiffened at the insult, and he slowly turned to face her. In a low voice he said, "What are you talking about."

Emily cowered back. Devin towered over Sasha's average five-foot-four-inches. But Sasha wasn't going to back down, and toed up with Devin.

"Don't you act innocent. I have eyes. I know you said you fought, you didn't say you tore up here damn apartment! Emily is tiny. There's no way in hell she's the one who did this."

"That's what you think?"

Sasha threw her hands up. "What I think? As if there is some other explanation for her apartment to look like a crime scene? The only thing missing is the body! Should I be thanking you for not providing one? Jesus, Devin! You knew from the beginning she was knew to all this!"

Devin shut the open front door with his foot. "Are you done?"

That angered Sasha more. Her back stiffed and she got on her toes, as much in his face as possible. "No, I'm not done. I'm not a sub you can boss around. I'm not a little that think you deserve respect. I'm fucking Sasha Jackson, and you *will* answer to me for this."

Devin raised a brow, and crossed his arms over his chest as he shifted his weight to his heels. But Sasha wasn't done.

Her chest was heaving with emotion. "You knew. KNEW she was new. I got special clearance from Sir to bring her. And I was right, she fit right in. But you have to come and ruin her for anyone else. After this? She's never going to want to be with another daddy, let alone a dom. And? And?? I *will* be texting Sir and telling him what's happened here."

"Do it." Devin spoke so softly, Emily almost didn't hear the words.

"Oh, I will. Don't you dare fucking leave." Sasha poked him in the chest and stepped carefully over the carpet to get to Emily.

Emily cowered back from the arm Sasha went to wrap around her.

The look of hurt on Sasha's face had Emily instantly regretting the reaction. Her best friend would never hurt her, and only wanted to help. Lowering her eyes, Emily held out her hand, and Sasha took it, and held it in both of hers.

"Emily, sweetie. Talk to me. Are you okay? Did he hurt you at all?"

Emily shook her head, not trusting her voice.

"It's okay. I won't let him touch you ever again. Just, tell me what you need me to do."

Emily sniffled, and waved an arm helplessly. She looked over to Devin who was still standing in front of the door, the mask of indifference firmly in place. Tears formed again, and Emily quickly looked away. But Sasha misinterpreted the gesture.

She strode back to Devin, not caring about the debris she stepped on. She pulled her hand back, and slapped Devin. The sound was sharp in the quiet room, and landed hard enough to make Devin's head snap to the side.

Devin raise his hand to his cheek, and pulled it away, as if he were looking for blood. He looked over at Emily, who was watching in horror. His face softened. "Emily," he murmured.

"Daddy," she sniffled.

That was all it took. He made it to her side in two long steps, and pulled her into his arms.

Emily buried her face in his shirt as he lifted her up, one arm under her knees and one behind her back. She couldn't hold the tears back any longer. Her shoulder's shook and she grabbed his shirt in her fists as she tried, unsuccessfully, to swallow back the tears.

Emily couldn't see Devin's face, but could hear the hardness in his tone. "Any more assumptions you wish to make before you call Sir? Or would you like to find out what actually happened."

Sasha joined Devin and Emily. She rubbed Emily's back, and pressed her face into Emily's belly. "Em."

The single syllable held more anguish, more hurt, and more emotion than her best friend had ever before shown. Emily's heart broke anew. Not only had she kicked Devin from her life, she'd hurt her best friend. She really was the worst person in the world. Emily broke, no longer able to hold back the sobs that shook her shoulders. The tears soaked Devin's shirt, as she cried, her heart was broken with the realization every problem in her life was her own fault.

She didn't know when Devin began walking, but she could feel the jostles as he stepped over the bigger bits of her broken belongings. He was whispering, but Emily couldn't understand what he was saying, and Sasha was no longer with her.

She hiccupped and pulled her face from Devin's chest. He was carrying down the hall.

He kicked her bedroom door the rest of the way open, and she saw Sasha standing next to her bed.

Devin sat on the bed, and arranged her in his lap so she could keep her face in his chest if she needed to, but could still look out. Sasha sat across from him.

The mess on the floor had been shoved aside, and a full-looking black bag sat near the closet. Sasha must've cleaned up in here. She looked between Devin and Sasha, the pushed against his chest. She shouldn't let Devin hold her like a baby.

He helped her sit up straight, but kept a protective arm around a her. She leaned back, her head rested on his collar bone. Sasha looked concerned, but didn't seem angry anymore. And the two of them must be getting along well enough.

"I'm sorry." Emily whispered, not meeting Sasha's gaze.

Sasha grabbed her hand. "Emily. Talk to me!"

Emily squeezed her eyes shut, and hiccupped. There were no more tears to cry, and she just wanted to sleep.

Devin's voice rumbled in his chest. "There was a break in. Emily's been sleeping at my place since then. We came back to clean up today, and I... I upset her."

Emily opened her eyes and nodded at Sasha.

Sasha took a deep breath, as if it pained her, and clasped her hands in her lap. As if she were trying her hardest not to be angry or upset. "Okay. And why was she upset."

Devin cleared his throat. "She said I wasn't listening to her."

Sasha's hand clenched in a fist, but she quickly released it. "And then?"

"She told me she didn't need me and never wanted to see me again."

"I see. Em?"

Emily nodded, and finally met Sasha's gaze. "I was horrid."

"What didn't he listen about."

"It's my fault," she whispered.

"What is. Em, I can't read your mind. You have to talk to us!"

Emily squeezed her eyes shut. Maybe the tears weren't all gone after all.

"Baby girl. Remember what I told you? No matter what, you have to tell me what you do or don't like. Anytime something upsets you."

She nodded, and took a steadying breath. He was right and she was being dumb. "It's just, he wanted to throw everything away, and he's right, but..." she shrugged.

Sasha sat back, a look of understanding on her face. "But even though you saw it as crap, it was all crap from your mom, or something you'd picked up to give her."

Emily nodded.

"And you didn't want to throw it away?"

"I need to. I know that. It's all ruined, but I still have my memories. I just. I don't know! I feel like everything is my fault, and I don't deserve Devin, and mother left because of me, and I guess I just got so angry at myself that I took it out on him."

Devin chuckled. "I heard you. I was pushing you too hard. I wanted you to clean first, grieve and be sad later. I was wrong."

Sasha shook her head. "Damn, Emily. You had me ready to call Sir on this guy."

Emily sat up, bumped Devin's chin with her head and leaned back down. "Sorry, daddy. Who's sir?"

Sasha looked to Devin, and Emily could feel him shaking his head. "Sir is the guy, or gal, who organized the party I took you to. They are held once a month, and the location rotates around. Sir is the one who organizes it, and makes sure they are safe. If you screw up, Sir is the one to spread the word, and they get blacklisted from all the local events."

Emily pushed her head back, looking up at Devin as best she could. "That's why you said guests were usually screened out."

He kissed her mouth, at the weird angel she'd put her head in. "Yep. And when you introduced me to Sasha, I understood."

"You never met Sasha before? But, don't you both go to parties?"

Devin chuckled. "I go a few times a year. I work, remember?"

"Oh." Blood rushed to her face in embarrassment, and she put her head back to rights. "But, you don't know who this Sir is?"

Sasha shook her head. "Nope. We just go to whichever location is designated, and enjoy ourselves."

"But, if you text him, then…"

Sasha sighed. "Then Sir is the one who would make sure Devin was blacklisted from any events in the futures. If it had been too terrible, Sir would have set you up with counseling."

Emily chuckled, the sound feeling oddly refreshing after all the tears. "I couldn't afford that and we both know it."

Devin kissed the top of her head. "No, Sir pays for it."

"Why?"

Sasha shrugged as Devin said, "Some people just like to make sure the rest are safe."

Emily gasped, and squirmed around to face Devin. "Nooo."

He raised an eyebrow, and said, "Nope."

She squinted at him. "Hmmm."

He winked, and her mouth dropped open. She turned back to Sasha, who was looking between them both, confusion on her face.

"Call Sir!" Emily was bouncing on Devin's lap.

Devin growled. "You are going to get spanked later for this."

Emily tossed a cheeky grin over her shoulder. "Nuh uh."

Sasha just sat there, confused. "What the hell, Emily. You were heart broken twenty minutes ago, and now your flirting with Devin?"

Emily grinned. "He's my daddy."

"Sit still baby girl. Sasha, think about it. It's just the emotional rubber band. When we got here, I was ready to leave since I knew she was okay. An hour ago, I had hopes, but I bet she was kicking herself, not knowing what to do, and thinking she'd ruined everything. From what I understand of her parents, she just thought I was going to disappear, too."

Emily nodded solemnly.

He turned her on his lap to face him. "And now you know. I will only walk away if you ask me to. But I meant it when I said I wanted to take care of you, even if you didn't want a sexual relationship."

Emily tossed her arms around his neck, and kissed him hard. "I know."

"Baby girl, you freaked out. I didn't know how to help you, and I was scared."

"I'm sorry, daddy."

"I know. But I was afraid I had lost you almost as soon as I'd found you. I love you, Emily. You're my baby girl, and I don't want to lose you."

Emily smiled so big she thought her cheeks might fall off her face. "I love you, too, daddy!"

He pulled her close, and hugged her as he kissed the top of her head.

"This is cute." Sasha sounded annoyed.

"What?"

"You two. Whatever. I'll see you later, Em. Maybe you could call me so I don't threaten your boyfriend next time he says you two argued."

Emily nodded from the safety of Devin's arms. "Sure thing. I love you, too, you know."

Sasha's face softened and a smile played about her lips. "I know. I'll come back tonight and clean up for you." She tucked a stray hair behind Emily's ear. "If I know you, you're going to want a nap."

Emily yawned in response as she nodded.

"Devin, call me later."

"Okay."

Sasha left, shutting the doors behind her as she made her way from the small apartment.

Chapter Twelve: Sink or Swim

*H*ome, Emily thought as she stepped into Devin's spacious apartment. The thought startled her, since she'd never thought of anywhere as 'home' before. But it was nice. Safe. And she wanted to be here with Devin.

He pulled her close. One arm around her waist, the other grabbed her hair, pulling her head back.

She gasped, but she wasn't afraid. He would never hurt her.

"You scared me," he growled, then lowered his mouth to hers in a demanding kiss.

She met his passion with her own as a fire ignited in her belly and between her legs.

His mouth trailed to her neck, kissing and biting, sending thrills of pleasure shooting through her. Grabbing her wrists, he moved them from around his neck, and put them behind her back.

She gasped. His power over her, knowing he could take whatever he wanted, but would never take what she wasn't willing to give, send thrills down her spine. She clenched her thighs together as her wetness grew.

"No more taking it easy. If you can't handle what I want from you, I need to know now." He bit her neck then sucked as a moan escaped her. "I can't go through that again. I thought I'd lost you."

"I don't want you to leave," she panted, her breaths coming in short gasps. His mouth was doing amazing things to her body.

Letting her hands go, he picked her up and carried her to the bedroom. Once there, he set her unceremoniously on her feet. "Kneel."

She hesitated. She was still dressed.

He snapped his fingers, and pointed to the floor. "Kneel," he growled.

She dropped to her knees, and winced as she hit the floor. By the time her eyes opened, he'd already undone his pants, and stood in front of her face with his hard cock out. Instinctively, she opened her mouth, tingles of anticipation spreading through her body.

He rubbed the tip of his cock on her lower lip, and her tongue darted out to lick it. He turned away, going to his nightstand.

She wanted to follow after, to put her mouth on his skin, and taste every inch of him. But he told her to kneel.

When he turned back around, he was holding a strange looking rope with knots in it.

"What's that?"

"This is to keep you where I put you." He moved to stand behind her.

Her eyes lowered, and she licked her lower lip. She could still taste him on her. She sat still as she felt the nylon rope being hooked over her ankles before he tightened it. It was snug, but didn't hurt as long as she wasn't fighting.

He put her hands together, and clasped her hands together behind her back before tightening them in a knot as well. The ropes scratched at her wrists and ankles as he got them how he wanted them. Once he was finished, she gently tugged on one to see if there was any give. There wasn't and it scratched her skin uncomfortably.

He stood in front of her, and stroked his cock. Reaching down with the other hand, he rubbed her wet pussy between her legs.

Her hips moved in pleasure as she joined his rhythm, but the ropes scratched, and reminded her she wasn't supposed to be moving.

When he stood, she moaned in frustration.

He tweaked a nipple, then put his hand on the back of her head, grabbing her hair with a fist.

Opening wide, her eyes closed as he put his dick in her mouth. She couldn't move without the ropes scratching, so she sat perfectly still. Using her tongue, she rubbed his cock while he fucked her face. She moaned, almost gagging on his cock.

When he pulled it out, she gasped for air, her chest heaving as she panted. He took a step back, and she almost leaned forward to be closer to him, but for the biting reminder from the ropes taught on her wrists and ankles.

Moving behind her, he held her shoulders, and she could feel him moving. His hands reached under her arms and lifted her up. It was necessary to tighten every muscle in her body to keep from pulling unnecessarily at the rope.

When he put her on the bed, her knees screamed in appreciation. She hadn't noticed how hard the floor was. When he ran his fingers over her shoulders and down her back, she shivered, her back arching reflexively. The ropes dug into her ankles, and she moaned.

There were so many sensations, none could keep her attention. The feel of his hands on her skin as he teased her. The coarse ropes on the sensitive flesh inside her wrists and on her ankles. His breath on her neck as his mouth, his mouth placed butterfly kisses across her shoulders and neck, sending goosebumps down her arms.

Her breasts were heavy with desire and she closed her eyes as she reveled in the sensations he caused. His hands moved to her front, teasing her nipples but a moment before moving elsewhere. By the time he reached between her legs, her body was ready to explode.

"Please, daddy, I need you," she begged.

He climbed up behind her on the bed, his legs straddled hers. His hard cock pressed into her ass.

Her mouth opened, and she licked her lower lip to moisten it from her panting. She no longer only wanted him. She needed him. To feel him inside her.

His fingers separated her slit before he pushed his cock inside her.

She gasped. It was what she wanted, and he felt so good, his girth stretching her tight pussy with his size.

He started moving, slowly. "Tell me what you feel."

"Oh, god, daddy," she panted. She was so close to climax, she couldn't think straight.

He grabbed her hair in his fist, and tugged.

She moaned, her eyes closed. "Daddy, please, fuck me harder!"

"Tell me." He squeezed, and her hair pulled enough to stave off her climax, allowing her to think.

"Your cock feels so good," she moaned. "The ropes are tight, and I can't move or they scratch me, but I want to move so they do."

He thrust, and his cock pushed deep inside.

She cried out, "Daddy, yes, harder!"

But he pulled out to just the tip again.

"I feel your hands on me, teasing me, and, daddy, I just want to cum. Please!"

He rammed into her, but didn't let go of her hair. He fucked her hard, pushing deep until she came.

With every twitch and tremor, the ropes reminded her he was her daddy, he would care for her always, and no matter how angry he might be, he would never hurt her. His hand in his hair reminding her she was his little girl.

As she came down from her climax, he pulled his cock out, his hot cum hitting her ass as he reached around to rub the area around her clit, slowing her descent from her orgasm.

Both were satisfied when he kissed her neck, and slapped her ass playfully before wiping her off. He loosened the ropes, his breath as heavy as her own.

"Baby, did you like that."

"Yes, daddy."

Once the ropes were off, he rubbed her skin where they'd been, and slowly moved her limbs. Her joints hurt from being in the same position for so long, and she loved the care he showed her.

He turned her around; he was already standing at the side of the bed. Putting her arms on either side of her, he locked his eyes with hers. "Did you like that. Do not tell me what you want to hear."

A smile played about her lips and, before he could react, she darted her head forward and picked a kiss on his lips. His mouth dropped open and she grinned. "I said, yes. I really did. Does this mean no more... um... Vanilla sex?"

He chuckled, sat next to her on the bed and pulled her into his lap.

She buried her face in his neck. He smelled of the woods, and she smiled as she remembered his surprise.

He stroked her hair. "Baby, I'm so glad to hear that. There are other toys, and other things to do. But I love when you give me power over you."

She smiled into his neck and licked him, his skin salty with sweat. "I want that. Maybe not all the time. But I liked it a lot. But, daddy?" She pulled her head away and looked up at him.

He was looking down at her, and she could see the love in his eyes.

"Aren't you Sir?"

He shifted around and looked away. "I'd rather you call me daddy, but if you'd rather call me sir, that's fine."

She sat up. "Daddy. You're *my* daddy. But you're also Sir, that Sasha was talking about."

She watched in fascination as the blood rushed to his face. "Yes."

She nodded and relaxed back into his arms on his lap. "Okay, good. Making sure."

He started rocking with her on his laps, and her eyes drifted shut.

Moments before falling asleep, she thought she heard him whisper, "I love you, baby girl."

The End

The Adventures of Mia Lovejoy

By Lonely Woman

Lonely Woman

Chapter One:

Professor Mia Lovejoy finished writing the theorem on her white board. She'd been teaching high school geometry for two years, and loved every second of it. Her all-male class seemed to love her back, and she never had the attendance issues other teachers seemed to have.

She turned to the class, her white button up blouse tight against her large, perky breasts. The size of her chest strained the buttons between her tits, allowing her white satin bra to peek through. She didn't mind. Her therapist had paid good money for these breasts, and she wanted everyone to appreciate them. Her black skirt was just over dress code guidelines, covering her pert ass and not much else. To avoid panty lines she didn't wear any, and kept her dark hair in a tight bun on the top of her head.

She sat on the corner of her desk, watching her students' eyes on her upper thighs as her skirt inched its way up beyond what was strictly appropriate. She was twenty-one and craved the attention her body received.

On her eighteenth birthday, she'd seduced her therapist. He'd tried to diagnose her with "nymphomania", but there was nothing wrong with liking sex. Her therapist had felt so guilty about it, he'd bought her breasts. When her mom had passed away a month later, he'd opened his home to her, taking care of her the way he took care of his girlfriends. He was the reason she'd gotten hired at this upstate private school. She would have to thank him and his newest girlfriend when she went by for dinner this weekend

She inhaled, stretching the limits of the buttons on her blouse. She suppressed a smile when she saw the young men in the front row widen their eyes. She knew they had a bet going around, wondering when her buttons would finally pop.

"Class, for homework you will write a proof for the theorem on page 362 of your books. Dismissed." The bell rang as soon as the words were out of her mouth.

The students stood, and gathered their belongings to leave. They all wore the same uniform. A navy-blue blazer with a white dress shirt and navy slacks with black loafers. Most of the boys were seniors, finally coming into their bodies. She enjoyed the eye candy some of the better built boys provided. The least she could do was be eye candy back.

Her classroom emptied, and she set about closing the blinds. She could see the parking lot from her windows, and watched as the other teaches got in their expensive cars to leave for the day. She liked being the last to leave.

Her breasts pushed against the wall as she reached up to latch the rod into the hook to turn the blinds closed. She wasn't very tall, even in her six-inch heels, and couldn't quite get the rod into the hook. A voice right behind her startled her.

"Can I help?"

She stumbled, dropping the rod.

Strong hands caught her, saving her from hitting the tile floor. She looked into the deep blue eyes of her savior, and lost the words she'd been about to say, her mouth hanging open. His jaw was strong and square, with a hint of a mustache on his upper lip. His brown hair was long, brushing the collar of his navy blazer. He lifted her to her feet. He wasn't one of her students.

"Thanks." She looked down and brushed herself off, adjusting her clothes.

He chuckled. "Sorry. Didn't mean to startle you. I can help with that." He bent and picked up the rod, reaching up effortlessly to close the blinds.

She made her way to her desk, and sat on the corner, crossing her arms over her belly. "I don't recognize you." She cocked her head to the side, considering him and what he could want, trying to ignore her increasing wetness.

"I'm new," he said, looking at her over his shoulder.

"Transfer student?" she spoke more to herself, but he answered.

"Yeah. Got held back too many times. So dad put me here." He shot her a grin from over his shoulder, and she took a deep, steadying breath. He was gorgeous.

"So you're eighteen?" She couldn't believe it. He was a student, she reminded herself. She had to keep her hands off. But she could look. She admired the way his ass looked in his navy slacks. When he turned, she caught an eyeful of his large package in the front. She slowly lifted her eyes to his face.

"Yeah." He took two steps toward her. "And I was supposed to be in this class for my last hour, but I had some trouble finding it." He took another step, his eyes focused on her lips.

She sighed. "Oh good." She shook her head. "I mean, glad to have you. Thanks for the help."

She stood from her desk, but didn't tug her skirt back into place.

He took another step, standing so close she had to look up into his eyes. He brushed his fingers along her cheek and jaw.

She closed her eyes and leaned slightly into his hand.

He bent down and cupped her neck with the back of his hand. Her mouth opened, and she inhaled, pressing her chest to his. He put his mouth a hairs breadth from her own, his mesmerizing blue eyes holding her captive.

He whispered against her mouth, "I'm nineteen." He brushed a kiss against her lips, flicking open her blouse with his free hand.

She kissed him back, her lips opening when his did, her tongue brushing against his in a dance as old as time. She clenched her thighs together, and pressed her hips against his, feeling his arousal push into her belly.

His hand moved from the back of her neck to the bun on top of her head. He tugged her hair free, the hair pins and tie went flying, clattering on the floor as her hair cascaded down her back. His hand fisted in her hair, pulling her head back. His mouth moved from hers to her neck.

She moaned, liquid fire in her belly as her desire built.

She nudged him, and he took a step back. She took an unsteady breath.

He tried to step in closer, but she held him at arm's length.

"I can't," she panted, shaking her head. "I could lose my job."

His mouth dropped open, and he looked angry.

The clang of the janitor's mop against its bucket in the hall interrupted whatever he'd been about to say.

He shot her a smoldering look full of promise, but didn't argue. He picked his back up from the floor where he'd dropped it, and walked away.

She shivered, and wrapped her arms around herself. She was alone once more, and the room felt somehow colder without his presence. Her therapist would be proud of her when she told him about her encounter today. The thought provided little solace to her groin, aching with need and desire.

Chapter Two:

Mia checked the time once more. Five minutes until she could release her class. She shot a look from the side of her eye to where her new student, Milo, sat in the back row. He had been staring at her chest or lips since class started, and it made her wet when she remembered what they'd almost done the afternoon before.

Even though he was not a minor, it was against school policy to engage in any sort of relationship with a student. She sat on the edge of her desk, letting her legs spread slightly, and flashing her trimmed pussy to the boys in the front row. She needed to figure out what to do about her attraction to her new student.

"Class, go ahead and leave early. It's Friday. I'm sure you all have things you'd rather be… doing." She glanced over at Milo as she said it, but his face was an unreadable mask.

The rest of her students grabbed their bags and left as quickly as possible, talking amongst themselves about their weekend plans. Milo was the last one to leave, dropping a folded piece of paper on her desk. His hands brushed her knee as he passed, then walked out the door.

She took a deep, steadying breath, and watched in amusement as the button on her shirt popped off. She chuckled. Shame her class missed it. A knock on her open classroom door startled her.

"Got a minute?" Dan Plough stood in the doorway. He was her fellow math teacher, and older than her therapist. Easily in his fifties or sixties. His eyes bulged from his balding head when she turned and he saw the missing button.

She laughed. "Come on in."

"Your, um, your button, there." He waved in the direction of her chest, averting his eyes.

She looked down. "Oh, right. It popped off a moment ago. I'll fix it when I get home. Did you need something?"

He walked the rest of the way into the room, and she covered Milo's note with her hand. She didn't know what it said, and was worried Dan would see it. She slid off her desk, and pushed the note under a stack of papers she needed to grade.

"You keep a nice classroom," he said, surveying the room.

"I don't want it to smell like teenaged boy," she said with a giggle.

He chuckled. "Right." He turned to look at her, keeping his eyes locked on hers, trying not to look at her pretty lace bra or cleavage, exposed by the missing button.

"And?" she prompted. He seemed to have forgotten why he'd come.

He blinked slowly. "Right! I was wondering if you wanted to go out tonight. Your father mentioned you were single..." he trailed off and cleared his throat uncomfortably.

"My father?" Her brow furrowed a moment. "Oh! You mean my therapist." She laughed.

He nodded, and looked away.

"I didn't have any plans." She wanted to tell him to go away, that he was old enough to be her grandfather, but she knew better. If her therapist had told Dan she was single, he must have approved. And if he approved, it meant Dan had serious cash.

He perked up, and glanced at her chest before quickly looking away. "How does dinner sound?"

"Sounds lovely. Come to my classroom at six. I should be finished with my grading by then."

"Yes, okay." He started backing away. "I'll see you at six."

"Dan," she said, stepping toward him.

He stopped, and looked at her.

She closed the distance between them, reaching up to cup his cheek in her palm. She knew how to handle older men. "Thank you," she whispered.

She dropped her hand and turned away, walking slowly back to her desk. She exaggerated the sway of her hips and heard his sharp intake of breath. She smiled. Yes, she knew how to handle men like him.

***

It was quarter to six, and time to wrap up her work. Milo's note had only held his cell number with a request to "text me". She'd added the number to her own phone before tearing the paper and throwing it away. She sighed. She needed to focus on entertaining Dan Plough tonight.

The class door closed softly and she spun around. It was Milo! "You can't be here!" She'd already closed the blinds, but what if Dan showed up early.

He didn't speak. He dropped his bag in front of the door and strode over, pulling her roughly against him. He lowered his mouth to hers and she tried to push him away, but me was stronger.

"Milo, we can't. Mr. Plough will be here any minute!"

He growled, and she felt a familiar warmth spread in her groin.

He spun her around, pushing her toward the desk. If she didn't obey, she would fall in her six-inch work heels. Her hands splayed on the desk in front of her as he pushed her head down. He reached around, and ripped her shirt open. Her buttons flew off, pinging off the whiteboard, and bouncing on the floor.

"Milo! You have to stop. I said no."

He yanked her shirt halfway down her arms, preventing her from moving them, and pushed her skirt up, her pert ass hanging out. Fighting would be useless.

"Hurry up, before Mr. Plough comes," she surrendered. Fighting now would be pointless, and she didn't want to risk losing her job.

She heard his zipper drop, and felt his cock slide between her pussy lips. He slammed his cock into her.

"Faster," she urged.

He pushed her head down, so she was half laying on the desk, her face turned to the side, the metal cool against her cheek.

Moments later, she felt his hot cum fill her pussy. He finally released her, and zipped himself back up. Without saying a word, he left, before she'd even pulled her skirt back into place.

She gaped at the closed door, wondering what had just happened. Five-til-six. Shit. She pulled her skirt down, and looked down at her torn shirt. There was no way she could hide it. She rushed to the staff bathroom next to her classroom. Mr. Plough was at the end of the hallway, coming closer, his footsteps echoing in the empty corridor.

She shut the bathroom door, and squatted over the toilet, trying desperately to push the cum out. She dried off, hoping she'd gotten all of it. The musky scent of Milo's sex filled the air.

She flushed the evidence and looked in the mirror. Her hair was a mess. She took the hair tie and pins out, then ran her fingers through it to smooth it out. Her shirt still hung open.

"Mia?" She could hear Dan in the hallway, looking for her.

There was only one thing she could do. She opened the bathroom door. "Dan," she whispered.

He lowered his voice. "Mia? That you?" He came around to the open door and gaped at her.

She cocked a hip, and peeked up at him through her lashes, then beckoned him with a finger.

He came closer. "What happened to your shirt." His voice was full of concern.

She shut the bathroom door behind him, and shrugged her shirt off. "I was waiting for you." She stepped closer to him, and pulled his shirt from his waistband.

"Mia, we're in a bathroom."

"So?" She unbuttoned his shirt, and leaned in close to suck his hear.

He groaned, and closed his eyes.

She backed him up to the wall, and undid his pants, her mouth trailing down his undershirt. She pushed his boxer shorts below his half-mast cock. She kneeled, lifting his undershirt to run her hand along his stomach, stroking his cock with her other had. She looked up at him, hoping he couldn't smell Milo's sex.

She licked his cock, starting at his balls, and slowly making her way to the tip. He shuddered, and a bead of precum appeared. She licked the tip, then took him into her mouth. As she sucked, he got harder.

"Mia," he groaned. He ran his hands through her hair, making a fist but not pushing her head the way Milo had.

She pulled off, sucked his balls, and teased his cock with her tongue. She moaned.

"Not like this," he said, using her hair to pull her mouth off his cock.

She looked up at him, leaving her mouth open. Her nipples hardened, seeing him standing there with his fully erect dick.

"Please?" She said the word as almost a whisper, looking up at him with sultry eyes.

He groaned, but wouldn't let her suck his cock. She stood, and reached behind her, locked her eyes with his, and slipped her lacy bra off, shaking it to the floor. She was completely topless, her large breasts heavy with arousal.

His gazed dropped to her tits, desire in his eyes.

She stepped closer, and pushed his shirt off his shoulders, letting it fall to the floor. She leaned in, pressing her body against his. She kissed his neck, then took his mouth with hers.

His mouth welcomed hers, and she pressed her hips into his. He was willing to kiss her after his cock had been in her mouth, and it

125

was such a turn on, she didn't need to act anymore. She wanted to please this man.

She grabbed his undershirt, and lifted it, running her hands against his sides. They broke their kiss as she stretched to pull it off him, letting her breasts brush against him. She whispered in his ear, "I'm not wearing any panties."

He groaned, and wrapped an arm about her waist, pulling her close. He kissed her neck, and reached down to fondle her breast, teasing her nipple with his thumb.

She moaned, slid his pants down and pulled her skirt up.

His hands roamed downward, squeezing her ass and she nipped his shoulder.

She pulled back, and reached between them to stroke his cock. He cupped her breast, and brought his head down to suck her hard nipple. She guided his hand to her pussy, and he slid his finger inside her, getting it wet, before pulling it out to rub her clit. She twitched. He might be old, but he knew how to please her. She turned, pressing her ass against his cock. They were perfectly lined up, thanks to the heels.

He grabbed her hips, and walked her forward to the sink. She looked at him in the mirror, and squeezed her ass cheeks together.

He looked down, then rubbed his cock between her ass cheeks before slowly pushing into her pussy. He pumped a few times, then licked his finger, his eyes watching her in the mirror.

She reached between her legs to stroke his cock and her clit.

He rubbed the outside of her asshole, then fingered her ass.

She closed her eyes, as her muscles started to twitch. She was so close. "Don't stop," she begged.

He pumped faster, and she came, her pussy squeezing his cock. Her legs twitched and tried to give out on her, and he gripped her hips, pushing into her as deep as he could. He slapped her ass as she came down from her climax and she moaned.

He pulled out, and rubbed her wetness on her asshole. "I don't have a condom," he said.

The tip of his cock pushed on her asshole, and she relaxed. He slowly pushed into her.

She cried out when he tried to go too fast.

126

He pumped hand soap into his hand, and smeared it on his cock and her asshole, then slipped the rest of the way in. He moved slowly, letting her get used to his girth in her ass.

She moaned, and started rubbing her clit again. His cock felt so good inside her.

He started going faster, holding her hips, and guiding her.

When she came again, she collapsed on to the sink, her entire body spasming as wave after wave of pleasure washed over her.

He grunted, and pushed deep inside, and she felt his hot cum fill her ass as they rode the climax together.

When she finally started breathing again, she panted, her chest heaving and her heart pounding.

He slowly pulled out of her, and immediately placed paper towels between her legs.

"Thank you," she murmured, then waddled to the toilet.

He stuck his cock, back to being half hard, over the side of the sink and turned on the water. She looked away, not wanting to watch him clean himself off.

Chapter Three:

She pulled up to her therapist's mansion on Saturday morning. She'd enjoyed a nice dinner with Dan. The only thing about him she found appealing was his amazing ability to make her cum. She shivered, remembering their "dessert".

She turned off the engine of the expensive car her therapist had bought her, and stepped out. She looked up at the palatial home, craning her neck to see the top. It had been painted since the last time she was here.

The valet approached, and she handed him her keys with a muttered "Thanks."

She climbed the flight of steps in front of the house, and pushed the front door open, closing it softly behind her. The sound echoed in the large, spacious entry way. "Daddy?"

She peeked in the public rooms. He wasn't here. She sighed. She'd told him she was going to come by today. The door to his first-floor study was closed. Maybe he was in there. She made her way down the hall, and tapped lightly on the door before pushing it open.

He was laying on the couch, his pants open with is cock in his hand. The sound of porn came from the speakers of the phone in his other hand. She remembered the first time she'd seen his cock. It was her birthday, and she'd gotten him drunk. He hadn't been able to tell her no. She'd seduced him, and his then-girlfriend. She smiled, remembering the car he'd bought her afterward because he'd felt bad. Then the tits he bought her the second time she did it.

She shut the door behind her, and he looked up.

"Get on or get out." He turned back to his phone.

She rolled her eyes and sat at his desk.

He ignored her, and continued stroking his cock.

She stood, hiked her skirt up, and sat back down at the desk. She stroked her clit as she watched him pleasure himself.

He stopped before he came, and she let out a frustrated moan. He stood, came to where she was seated behind his desk, and spun the chair to face him. Without needing to be told, she opened her mouth and relaxed her throat. She knew what to do.

He fucked her face while she rubbed her clit, wetting the leather chair she sat on. Her body tensed, she was on the edge. When he reached down and pinched her nipple, it threw her over, and she came.

He grabbed the back of her head, holding her face on his cock, and came, filling her throat with his cum. She swallowed like a good girl, and stroked around her clit, bringing herself down from her climax. She sighed, and leaned back in his chair.

"Good girl." He shoved his cock into his pants and zipped up. "Now. What did you want."

She wiped her mouth, and sighed again, trying to get her racing heart to slow.

He plopped down on the couch, waiting for her to compose herself. She shuddered one last time, and used a tissue to dry her finger. She wiggled her ass, making sure to get his leather chair as wet as possible.

"Dan Plough."

"Oh him." He rolled his eyes. "Good family. Lots of money. Doesn't need Viagra."

"Okay, so why did you set me up with him?"

He shrugged and threw his hands up. "How do you expect to find a husband to take care of you if you come here, questioning me, when I send good ones your way."

"Good?" She gaped. "He's older than you are!"

"And?"

She shook her head. "Whatever." She stood, and tugged her skirt down. "If you think he's a good match, I'll give him another chance. As of right now? I have zero interest."

"Spoiled brat."

She winked at him. "Maybe later you can spank me. For now, I have an appointment. Let me know if you need me." She sauntered out of the room, knowing he watched her ass as she left.

***

She pulled up to the school, and unlocked the door. She'd texted Milo to meet her here. She pushed open the door, and waited just inside. She wanted to let him in when he got there. She didn't have to wait long.

He drove an expensive car, like all the kids in this school. His dark brown hair still needed to be cut, and he was gorgeous. But she had a lesson to teach him.

She cracked the door open as he approached, and bit back a smile at his startled look. He hadn't expected her to be waiting for him. He came inside, and pulled the door shut behind him.

He reached out and squeezed her tit, hard, making her wince.

"Come with me." She smiled and stepped back, then turned and led the way down the hall to an open classroom. It wasn't hers, but that didn't matter. She looked over her shoulder at him, and went in the room.

He came in after her, unzipping his pants.

"Strip." She ordered.

He paused, as if considering, then shrugged. He kicked his shoes off and pulled down his jeans. He wasn't wearing any underwear, and pulled his shirt off. He put his hands on his hips, and thrust his raging hard-on toward her.

She smiled. She wasn't wearing a bra, and her nipples could be seen through the thin material. Her heart was pounding in her chest, knowing what she was about to do.

Milo stroked his cock.

"Come here," she said, getting on her knees. The boy needed to be taught how to take no for an answer. She grit her teeth.

He came toward her, and she quickly stood. He growled.

She reached out and grabbed his cock in her hands, giving a gentle squeeze. "I own you, Milo Jenson."

He tried to remove her from his cock, but she squeezed tighter, and used her other hand to grab his balls. She cocked her head to the side, and saw fear in his eyes. She squeezed his balls, and smiled in satisfaction as his pained yelp.

"I told you no yesterday."

He stood there silent. That wasn't good enough. She tugged. "I said, I told you no yesterday."

He nodded. "Yep."

"What does no mean, Milo Jenson."

He swallowed. "Don't do it."

"Exactly. And what is it called when you're told no, and do it anyway?"

He hesitated a moment and she squeezed.

"Rape! It's called rape!"

"Good boy. Do you like raping women? Does it turn you on?"

He shook his head.

"Then why did you ignore me."

"I thought you were playing hard to get."

"Milo." She squeezed again. "Is that really what you thought?"

"Yes!"

"Monday, you are going to go to the office and drop out. You will tell your father you are no longer welcome at this school." She smiled confidently, but her mind was racing with everything that could go wrong.

"I can't! He'll kill me!" The panicked look on his face gave truth to the words he spoke.

She leaned in close. "And if I ever catch you at this school again, I will chop your dick off and feed it to you. After I tell your father what you did, and how worried I am I could be pregnant."

He swallowed hard and the color drained from his face.

She was on birth control, but he didn't need to know that. "Do you understand me?"

"Yes."

"Good." She gave a final squeeze, and he cried out. She let go suddenly, knowing the rush of blood would hurt as much as the squeezing had.

He doubled over, holding his cock in his hand.

"Get out of my school." She pointed to the door.

He curled up and groaned.

"Three." She held up three fingers.

He got to his hands and knees, grabbing his shirt and pants in one hand, his shoes with the other.

"Two." She held up two fingers.

He started crawling to the door.

"One." She said the word slowly, and watched with amusement as he got to his feet, holding his clothes, and ran naked from the room.

"Smart boy." She mentally counted to five, and breathed a sigh of relief when she heard the front door to the school slam open.

She sat down, and closed her eyes. Her heart was racing, and she was shaking. Had Milo been any older, or any stronger, and that wouldn't have worked. She held out a hand and tried to steady it, but failed. She put her head between her knees, forcing herself to breath slowly. She was safe. Milo would never hurt her again.

After a while, her heart slowed, and her breath evened out. She need an orgasm. And dinner. She needed her therapist.

Chapter Four:

She lay on the couch in her therapist's study. He wasn't home, and was between girlfriends currently. She had the house to herself. She gave the staff the rest of the night off when she'd arrived, and was alone in the big house. She'd cried, and hated herself for letting Milo rape her, and for feeling so guilty she'd fucked Dan to cover it up. But what was done was done.

She sat up from the couch and wiped her eyes with the corner of a throw pillow. What she needed now was a bath. And pizza.

She ordered a pizza as she made her way up the stairs to the master bath with the large, two-person, jetted tub. She ran the water, adding bubbles and oils. The pizza would be here by the time the tub finished filling. She lit several candles, and placed them around the bathroom before turning out the overhead light.

When the tub was half full, the front bell rang. She rushed down the stairs to answer it, since she'd sent the staff home. She was out of breath when she opened the door. The delivery driver gaped, and she looked down; she was only wearing a fluffy white terrycloth bathrobe. She looked up and smiled, holding out cash to pay for the pizza. "Keep the change." She winked and took the pizza.

"Th..th...thanks," he stammered, slowly backing from the door.

She shut the door and shook her head. Hadn't the kid seen a porn before? Didn't he know when a woman answers wearing a bathrobe he's supposed to proposition her? She probably would have said no, but at least he could have tried.

She took the pizza to the bathroom and set it on the sink. The tub was almost full. She turned off the water, and poured herself a glass of wine.

She dropped the robe on the floor, and opened the pizza box. It was hot. She took a piece and put it on the paper plate the delivery boy had included.

Drink in one hand, pizza in the other, she climbed into the fragrant bath water. She slid along the bottom of the tub until the water came up to her neck, and set her drink and plate on the side of the tub. She slid the pizza to the edge of the plate, and took a bite. She exhaled quickly, trying to cool the hot pizza, and quickly sipped her chilled wine.

She'd burned her mouth. She laughed, and blew on the pizza before taking another bite. This was heaven, she thought, closing her eyes and leaning her head back as she chewed.

She must have fallen asleep, or at least dozed off. She sat up quickly and looked around. Her bubbles were gone, and her pizza was room temperature. She took a deep breath to slow her heart, wondering what had startled her.

She didn't hear anything, and stepped slowly from the tub. Pulling her bathrobe on, she checked the lock on the bathroom door before breathing a little easier. She sat in the almost silence, listening. Something had startled her, and she didn't want to drain the tub or make noise until she knew what it was.

Then she heard it. Someone was in the hallway. She must've heard them on the stairs. She held her breath, her heart pounding

"Damn it, Mia."

She laughed, realizing it was just her therapist. She pulled the drain on the tub, and wrapped the robe tighter around her. She took a bite of the cold pizza, and opened the bathroom door.

134

He'd been drinking. She could see it in his eyes.

"You sent the staff home." His words were slurred, and she took a step back.

She stiffened her spine. She'd wanted an orgasm. Now was as good a time as any to get one.

"Yes, daddy." She forced a meekness in her voice. He liked to be in control.

"You've been a… a bad girl!"

"Yes, daddy." She dropped her robe, letting it pool around her ankles.

He stepped toward her and wobbled. He glared at her, as if it were her fault he'd drank too much.

She walked slowly toward the bed, so he could keep up. "You're going to need to teach me a lesson, daddy." She grabbed hold of the wooden beam on his four-poster bed, and looked over her shoulder at him.

He pulled his belt from his pants, folded it on itself, then snapped it. "Bend over."

She did as she was told. She cried out when the leather of his belt met the soft skin of her ass. It hurt, but it felt good. "Again, daddy."

The leather belt hit her ass again, and she knew there would be a red mark there.

She shivered in anticipation. She knew what came next. "That hurt me, daddy." She forced a tremor into her voice. "Will you kiss it better?"

She looked over her shoulder at him, and he was unbuttoning his pants. She smiled, and jiggled her ass, eager for what would happen next. "Please, daddy," she begged. "Kiss it better."

He bent down, using the beam to keep from falling, and kissed her sloppily on her ass where he'd spanked her. He stood back up and she rolled over, sitting on the edge of the bed.

"Let me make it better, daddy." She looked up at him, and tugged his pants down to his knees. Standing, she rubbed her chest on him as she pulled his shirt off. He groaned, and his cock moved. But he'd drank too much and wasn't very hard. He closed his eyes.

She bit his neck and pulled on his ear with her lips.

He opened his eyes and pushed her back onto the bed.

She giggled, and spread her legs. She ran her hands along her body, teasing her nipples, and feeling her soft skin, still warm from the bath. She arched her back, teasing herself, wanting to rub her clit. But not yet.

"You want to be a good girl?" He was stroking his cock.

She moaned. "Yes. Please daddy, yes."

"Show daddy how you like to touch yourself."

She sighed with pleasure, and slid a finger between her pussy lips and into herself, getting her finger wet. She pulled the wetness to her clit and began rubbing, tantalizingly slow. She cupped a large breast in her other hand, pinching her nipple with her thumb and forefinger. She moaned, and arched her back, rocking her hips. Tingles of pleasure began radiating from her groin. She was getting close.

He climbed on the bed next to her, his cock a little harder, but still soft.

"Am I doing a good job, daddy?" She was panting, holding back, not ready to cum yet.

"Be a good girl, and show daddy how you like to touch him."

She let go of her tit, and grabbed his cock. It was soft, and she squeezed it gently as she tugged it, stroking it and trying to bring it to life.

Once it was halfway hard, she put her mouth on it, sucking and licking, teasing it with her tongue. He groaned, and flexed his cock. Soon, he was completely hard, and she took her mouth off, licking her lips.

"Am I a good girl, daddy?"

He sat on the edge of the bed. "Come here."

She did as she was told, climbing from the bed, and standing in front of him.

He grabbed her tit and squeezed, then pinched the nipple. He tugged her tits and she stepped closer, shoving her tit into his mouth. He sucked, then let go and kissed her chest, then took the other nipple in his mouth. He wrapped his hand around her and grabbed her ass, pulling her on to his lap.

136

She wrapped her legs around his waist, grinding her wet pussy on his cock. She tossed her head back, reveling in the sensations he was causing with his mouth. "Daddy, I want to cum," she moaned.

He lifted her by her ass, and slid his cock inside her, not taking his mouth off her tits. She arched her back, and rode his hard cock. She pushed away, and he lay on the bed. She slid her hand between them, rubbing her clit. She tensed, and her toes curled as she came. He grabbed her hips and flexed his cock in her, increasing the intensity of her orgasm.

She collapsed onto his chest, and kissed him.

"I want to taste you," he grunted. She sat up and climbed off his cock. On her knees, she crawled to his head, and straddled his face. He wrapped his arms around her thighs, and pulled her pussy to his mouth, licking and slurping.

She wanted to suck his cock, but his mouth felt so good. She grabbed her tits, and teased her nipples. When her toes started to curl and her thighs clenched, she rode the wave of pleasure, her therapist licking her dry.

She climbed from his face, and lay back, slowly rubbing around her clit.

He looked at her, and she smiled up at him. "Did I do good, daddy?"

He grunted, and pushed her back onto the bed, and straddled her chest. "I bought these tits." He pushed them together, and slid his cock between them. She looked at the tip of his cock between her tits, and she stuck her tongue out to lick it.

He stopped, and shoved his dick in her face. She opened wide and he fucked her mouth. She moaned. She loved the way her cum tasted on his cock.

He pulled his dick from her mouth and started fucking her tits. She held them together for him, and he pinched her nipples. Pleasure shot from her nipples straight to her pussy and she moaned, writhing under him in agonized ecstasy. She was going to cum again.

He grunted, and released his load, spilling his cum on her neck and chest. When he was done, he climbed off. He ran his finger through his cum, and stuck it in her mouth.

137

She sucked.

"You're daddy's good girl." He slid a finger over her clit, and inside her, rubbing the sensitive g-spot. She grinded her hips against his hand, sucking the finger in her mouth.

She came, her pussy tightening, soaking his hand with her juices. Her stomach tensed and her legs twitched. As she came down, her entire body was trembling. She shuddered a final time, and he pulled his fingers out of her, wiping them on the bed.

He turned away from her. "Get out of my sight."

She stepped up behind him, and wrapped her arms around his waist. "You're the best daddy ever." She kissed his back, and stroked his limp dick.

He barked a laugh. "I don't know why I let you do this to me. Go. Unless you need another spanking."

She released him and hurried from the room. She did not want to feel his belt on her ass again tonight.

Chapter Five:

She stretched and moan, her skin sliding against her satin sheets. She didn't live with her therapist anymore, but he kept a room for her and that's where she'd slept last night.

Rolling over, she checked the clock on the night stand. It was almost ten. The best part of the weekend was sleeping in. She closed her eyes, relaxing her muscles, then sighed. It was time to get up.

She took a coral silk blouse, with one of her favorite black pencil skirts, from the closet. She didn't want to wear a bra, but her tits hurt her back when she didn't. She grabbed a lacy coral bra to match her shirt.

She dressed quickly and made her way down the stairs to the breakfast nook. Her therapist was already there. The aroma from his morning coffee filled the air, and she inhaled deeply. He looked up from the news he'd been reading on his phone, showing no ill effects from his drinking last night.

"Good morning, daddy." She walked to him and leaned down, kissing his forehead.

He grunted in response.

She poured herself a cup of coffee, and sat next to him. She took a sip then said, "Jenson family. Tell me what you know."

He set his cup down on the table and looked at her a moment. "What happened."

She shrugged, and looked away, bringing her cup to her face and closing her eyes.

He locked his phone and set it on the table. "Mia. You can't lie to me."

She felt tears well in her eyes, and she set her cup down, trying to blink the tears away. It didn't work and they fell to her cheek.

"Oh, Mia." He pushed his chair back and stood, standing beside her, and wrapping his arms around her.

She turned her face to his belly, and let out the pent-up emotions from the last two days.

He said nothing, just stroking her hair, and making soothing sounds as she sobbed.

When her cried subsided, she wrapped her arms around his waist, sniffling as she cried out the last dregs of tears.

He held her tight.

After a few moments, she loosened her grip and he let go, sitting back down.

"Tell me." He picked up his cup, took a sip, and wrinkled his nose. His coffee had grown cold.

Mia sighed, picking up her own cup. It no longer warmed her hands. She stared morosely into the cup, as if her cold coffee held the answers she needed.

He stood, and grabbed the carafe from the side board. He poured two new cups, and set one at her elbow.

She gave him a watery smile. "Thanks, daddy."

He shook his head and sat back down. "The longer you hold it in, the hard it will be to tell me."

She sighed, and grabbed her new cup, the heat radiating into her hands and giving her courage. "Milo Jensen was transferred to my school. To my class. Thursday, he kissed me. But you would have been so proud!" She set the cup down, and reached over to grab his hand. "I didn't have sex with him!"

140

His eyebrows shot up. "You were able to say no?"

"Yes!" She brought her hand back to her cup. "I turned him down."

"But?"

She sighed again. "Friday. Dan Plough asked me to dinner. He was going to meet me in my classroom at six and take me out." She paused.

"Okay," he prompted.

She swallowed the lump that had formed in her throat. "Milo came to my class a bit before six."

"You didn't."

"No! Well, yes, but no!" She shook her head.

"I told him no, that Mr. Plough would be there any minute."

He sat silently, but she could see the rage radiating from him.

"He didn't take no for an answer. He ripped the buttons from my shirt. I wasn't wearing any panties or those would have been ripped, too."

He drummed his fingers on the table.

"So, I cleaned up in the bathroom, and convinced Dan to fuck me. He never asked about my shirt, but we both got off." She shrugged. "I handled Milo, though."

"How." The muscle in his jaw was ticking. He was pissed.

"I called Milo and invited him to the school yesterday." She rushed to finish when he pushed his chair back. "I had him strip, and I did what you taught me. I grabbed his dick and his balls, and told him he is never allowed to return, or I would tell his father what he'd done, and say how worried I am that I might be pregnant." She reached out and grabbed his hand. "But I told him no. At least twice!"

He shook his head, and took a deep breath. "Mia."

She hung her head, and stared back into her mug. "I know."

"No. You don't know! He will be back on Monday. I know the family. Jenson's kid has been kicked from three other schools for being a trouble maker. I'd never heard what he did. But if he did it to you, he's probably done it before, and his family is paying to keep the others quiet."

She looked up at him, her mouth open. She'd never thought of that!

He sighed. "I'll ring up his father and invite him over. I will make sure he won't be there Monday, and make sure you get appropriate compensation. You still have the implant in your arm?"

"Yes." He'd gotten her the implant birth control the day after she'd seduced him the first time.

"Good. When you get off work tomorrow, go down and get tested for STD's." He sighed heavily.

"I'm sorry, daddy."

He squeezed her thigh, just above her knee. "You did exactly as you ought, telling him no. I'll take care of this." His hand slid further up her thigh. "Was Dan a good lover?"

She put her hand on his, sliding further still, pulling her skirt up. "Not as good as you." She winked at him.

He laughed. "Well, I have some calls to make." He pulled his hand away, and took out his wallet, handing her a card. "Go to the spa, and relax. You did nothing wrong. By the time you get back, I should have it all handled. But I want you to stay here tonight. I don't know if the Jenson kid is crazy or not."

"Yes, daddy." She took his card. "Can I sleep in your bed tonight?"

He chuckled. "No. I have a fiancé now."

She gaped. "I didn't know you were seeing anyone!"

He shrugged. "About a month now. We've been talking about flying to Vegas to get married. She's widowed, and has a step-kid about your age."

She pushed her chair back and stood, adjusting her skirt. "Well, let me know when you get tired of her, and I'll... soothe your broken heart." She grinned saucily at him, and sauntered from the room, making sure to exaggerate the shake of her ass.

Chapter Six:

She pulled up to her therapist's mansion, and handed the keys to the valet. She'd spent the afternoon at the spa, and every muscle felt relaxed and refreshed. She unlocked the front door and shoved it open with her hip. Voices came from the sitting room, and she remembered her therapist had said he had a fiancé now. She patted herself down, making sure her clothes were in order, and pasted a smile to her face. Time to meet the newest trophy piece.

She stood in the doorway, surveying the room's occupants. They hadn't noticed her yet. The woman was plainer than Mia had expected, with mouse brown hair, and a chest that didn't exceed a 'C' cup. She had laugh lines around her eyes and nose, and Mia guessed her to be in her forties. She wore a seafoam green cocktail dress, and her calves looked like she enjoyed walking, or at least wearing heels.

A young man sat next to her, about Mia's own age, with blonde hair and a square jaw free of any stubble. He was handsome, wearing a matching seafoam green polo shirt over a pair of light khaki's and loafers the same color as his pants. His muscles bulged through his one-size-too-small shirt, and Mia licked her lips.

Her therapist— seated in a chair across from the sofa seating the other two —spotted her first. "Mia!" He stood, holding his arms open.

She walked toward him, and he grabbed her shoulders, kissing the top of her head before wrapping a fatherly arm around her. She smiled at the others.

"Laura, Carlton, I want to introduce you to my charge, Mia." He held out an arm, and led her to the arm chair on the other side of the couch.

She took her seat, and smiled at their guests. "Pleasure to meet you both."

"Same." Carlton seemed disinterested, looking at the well-manicured fingernails on his hand rather than at her.

"You are a very lovely young woman, Mia." Laura's voice held approval.

"Thank you, Miss Laura." Mia lowered her eyes diminutively.

Laura laughed, a sound like tinkling bells. "Please, call me Laura." She lowered her voice dramatically. "If I have my way, I'll be marrying your guardian."

Carlton laughed, a bitter sound, and Mia wondered what his deal was.

Her therapist stood. "I'm going to check on dinner. The three of you can get to know one another." He smiled, and left the room.

That was the first real smile he'd directed at anyone other than her in years, and Mia pushed back a pang of jealousy. If this woman made him happy, she needed to be happy for him. Mia turned back to Laura, speaking softly as she'd been taught. "Laura." She smiled. "What do you like to do?"

Laura turned her attention from the empty doorway to Mia. "I like to read, and paint. You?"

"I don't have much time for hobbies. Most of my time is spent working."

"Oh? What do you do?"

"I'm a teacher at a private school upstate. You?"

"Oh, I don't work." She shook her head to add emphasis, as if the thought of working disgusted her. "My late husband worked, and when he passed away, he left his fortune to me."

Mia raised a brow. "I'm so sorry for your loss."

Laura waved a hand dismissively. "It was years ago. And I still have my Carlton. He's attending school, learning how to run his father's business."

"Oh, Carlton is your son?" Mia raised a hand to her mouth in mock astonishment. "I thought he was your personal assistant. Surely you aren't old enough to be a mother to a grown man!"

Carlton scowled, and Laura placed a hand possessively on his knee. "Oh no, he's technically my step son. I married his father a little over a year before he died, when Carlton was 21. He's 25 now." She turned a smile to Carlton, who's jaw clenched.

"Oh, I see." Mia wondered if her therapist knew this woman's story. He must, or she wouldn't be so open to sharing with Mia.

Carlton stood, looked at Mia, and sat right back down, his mouth hanging open.

Mia smiled shyly, and took a deep breath, peeking up at him from under her lashes. "Carlton," Mia breathed. "Do you have any—" "she paused for half a beat, "—hobbies?"

He swallowed, and she knew he hadn't missed her innuendo. "I ride and hunt."

Mia feigned shock, gasping softly. "What a coincidence. I, too, enjoy a good ride."

Laura's brow furrowed for a moment before clearing. She placed her hand back on Carlton's knee and squeezed. "So do I, my dear." She smiled at Mia.

"We should all arrange a ride soon. I'm sure my guardian can arrange it."

"Speaking of." Laura tapped her chin thoughtfully with a long nail. "How long is he to remain your guardian? You must be at least twenty-seven by now, surely."

Mia smiled sweetly, ignoring the dig at her age. She was younger than Carlton! "He will remain my guardian until he passes to the next life." Mia shook her head sadly. "I try not to think such unhappy thoughts." She looked to the open door. "Here he comes now."

Her therapist came stepped inside the room, a forced smile on his face. "Dinner shall be ready shortly. Mia, may I have a moment?"

Mia stood gracefully, and inclined her head toward Laura and Carlton. "If you will excuse me?" She turned and followed her therapist from the sitting room to his study.

He shut the door quietly behind her. "Mia," he began.

She held up a hand, stopping him. "Daddy, do you love her?"

He stepped closer to her, cupping her cheek in his hand. "Yes, baby girl, I think I do."

Mia hugged him, resting her head on his chest, and his arms wrapped around her. "Then, for your sake, I will learn to love her, too. But daddy?"

"Yes?" He whispered into her hair.

"Can I keep Carlton?"

He laughed. "If he will let you."

She frowned into his shirt. "But Laura wants to keep him, too."

He held her away from him, studying her face. "What do you mean?"

She shrugged and tried to hug him, but he held her at arm length. "Mia." The word held a warning.

She sighed. "She kept putting her hand on his knee. The way you do with mine. And if you plan to marry Laura, are you going to stop playing with me? And will she stop playing with him? I'm worried. If I don't have a guaranteed release, I'm afraid I'll go back to some of the unsafe things I used to do."

"Oh, baby girl." He pulled her close. "I'll make sure you always have the release you need. Don't worry. We'll figure it out." He squeezed her tight a final time before letting her go. "Hungry?"

She cocked her head and lowered her lids, smiling up at him. "Daddy." The word came out as a husky breath. "We don't have time for that."

He grunted and turned away.

She closed her eyes and took a deep breath, trying to will away the arousal between her thighs, thankful hers would never be as obvious as his.

"You can take Carlton out after dinner. I'll distract Laura. I'll join you in the dining room in a few."

She sauntered passed, then turned to face him. His eyes were closed. She took half a step forward, and rubbed his semi-hard cock through his pants, then breathed into his ears. "I'll be thinking of you." She left before he could chastise her.

***

Dinner had been a boring affair, with small talk and words that meant nothing. But she did her best to stay nice to Laura. If her therapist was happy, then she would be happy for him. She might have been reading too much into Laura's actions and words. She had seemed fine after they'd all been seated together at the large table. But her therapist had kept his word, and pulled Laura away once dinner had been cleared, allowing her a chance to get to know Carlton.

They were walking across the back lawn under the full moon, the scent of the blooming rose bushes near the house filling the air. Once they were out of earshot of the house, she turned to Carlton.

"Do you always talk this much?"

He seemed taken aback. "Excuse me?"

"You haven't said much since I arrived. I wonder. Is it me? Or are you always this quiet."

He shook his head. "It's Laura. She gets pissed and freaks out sometimes when I say the wrong things at the wrong time."

Mia took a step closer to him. "Oh, I'm sorry," she whispered.

Their gazes locked, and she was entranced by the intensity in his pale blue eyes. "Are they real?"

His words snapped her from her thoughts. "What?"

"Your tits. Are they real?"

She laughed. "Blunt. No. My guardian gave them to me for my eighteenth birthday. Are you fucking Laura?"

His jaw dropped open. "How did you…" he trailed off and shook his head.

She winked at him. "She's clingy and obvious. Does she at least let you have girlfriends?"

He shoved his hands into his pockets and shrugged, then turned away and resumed strolling across the lawn.

She rushed to catch up, placing a hand on his shoulder. She was glad she'd changed into a pair of ballet flats. "Hey," she said, sounding breathless.

He looked down at her, and his eyes strayed to her cleavage.

"If Laura marries him, maybe you and I could… get to know each other." She smiled up at him, and the tips of his ears turned red.

"Maybe."

The resumed their stroll, heading back to the house. Mia tried to ignore the growing tension in her belly, and the demands of her body. She shuddered, and took a deep breath. Her therapist would help her tonight.

Back at the house, Laura was at the door, pulling on a pair of thin gloves even though it was summer.

"Are you leaving?" Mia asked, disappointed. She'd wanted to test the waters with Laura. Maybe Laura would be willing to help with her growing physical needs, too.

"Yes." She gave Carlton a pointed look. "We'll be back next weekend. Henry, your guardian, has invited us to come live with him."

Mia clasped her hands together in front of her chest. "Oh, how wonderful!" She was surprised to realize she meant it.

Laura smiled at her and hooked her arm through Carlton's. "We look forward to seeing you soon," she said, and they left.

The butler shut the door behind them, and Mia turned to her therapist and raised a brow. "I need therapy." She didn't want to be obvious in front of the staff, but the ache in her belly wasn't going to wait much longer.

He nodded at her, and led the way to his study.

Chapter Seven:

Mia followed him to his study, shutting the door behind her.

"Mia," he warned when she stepped toward him.

She stopped, and looked up at him. "Yes, daddy?"

"One hour. You need to wait one hour, then we can go upstairs."

"But, daddy…"

"No." He shook his head. "You know the rule. You asked for therapy."

She sighed. She did know better. "Did you get ahold of Mr. Jenson?" She wanted to change the subject. She draped herself on the couch, and squeezed her thighs together, trying to assuage the burning desire building there.

"Yes." He took a seat behind his desk. If anyone knocked, they would be in the appropriate positions. "Jenson says his boy will be enlisting in the army on Monday. You will also receive a lump sum deposit into your retirement account."

"The one you opened for me overseas?" She ran her hand along the exposed portion of her thigh. Her skin was so soft and smooth. She half-closed her eyes.

"Mia," he snapped at her.

She groaned in frustration and opened her eyes. "Yes daddy."

"Yes. The overseas account. I'll make sure the deposit is made." He looked down at a stack of papers in front of him on his desk.

She leaned her head onto the back of the couch, and slid down in her seat, her skirt riding up. She ran her hands further up her thighs, her fingers brushing her pussy but not exploring it. Her massive triple-D breasts grew heavy. She inhaled deeply, stretching the limits of her blouse.

Her therapist was either ignoring her or not paying attention. He pulled a pen from the holder, and scribbled some notes on the top sheet of paper on the stack he'd been looking at.

She brushed her nipples with her other hand, and her nipples perked to attention. She slid a hand to her pussy, slipping her thumb between the lips, and squeezed her thigh. She moaned softly, the sound escaping before she could stop it.

He sighed, and her eyes popped open. "Come here."

She jumped up, not bothering to pull her skirt down, and came around to where he was seated. She straddled his leg, and he ran a hand up her inner thigh. She closed her eyes, and ran her hands up her belly to her tits, the top buttons on her blouse popped open from the strain, but didn't fly off. Her body hummed to life.

She slipped a hand inside her bra, and pinched her excited nipple.

He slid a finger inside her waiting pussy. He rubbed her clit with his thumb, and she stumbled back, her ass hitting the edge of the desk. Her legs were growing weak.

He opened the rest of the buttons on her blouse, and leaned forward, running his hands up her thighs to her backside, and burying his face in her belly. She rocked her hips, and spread her legs, leaning back on her hands, her back arching in anticipation.

Lonely Woman

Chapter Eight:

Mia arrived at work Monday morning feeling completely refreshed. The last few days had been interesting, to say the least, and she was ready for the monotony of work. The parking lot was almost empty, and she took the spot closest to the doors.

She climbed from her car, and walked to the steps of the school, her heels clicking on the cement.

"Mia!"

She turned around and smiled. It was Dan Plough. "Hey, Dan." She waited until he'd joined her to make her way to her classroom.

"Glad I caught you." He walked next to her, and held the door open for her.

"Thanks. How come?"

"I wanted to tell you what a wonderful time I had on Friday." He cleared his throat. "And not just, um, before our date, or just our after dinner, um, dessert." He blushed slightly.

"Thanks, Dan. I had a good time, too."

"I was wondering, if you wanted to go out again this week? Not just, you know, for that. But to dinner or a movie."

She stopped in front of the door to her classroom. "Oh, that's so sweet." She smiled up at him. "I'll check my calendar and get back to you."

"Alright. Your shirt looks nice today, by the way."

She glanced down. She was wearing the usual white blouse she always wore at school. She just smiled again. "Thanks."

She pushed the door open to her class and stepped inside, shutting the door firmly behind her. She closed her eyes, leaning against the door a moment, clearing her head. She check and make sure she'd gotten all the papers graded. Not that it mattered. The parents of her students would have her head if any of their precious babies came home with anything less than a 'C' on a paper.

She opened the blinds on her windows before taking a seat behind her desk. "That's odd."

The papers that had been in her drawer Friday weren't there. She opened all her drawers, and her heart started racing. There were no student papers in her desk. Instead, there were sticky notes on the insides, with rude sayings and crude drawings. She pulled one off. It read, Fuck you. Another called her a whore. Another had a picture of a woman with her throat slashed, and another was a depiction of a cock with cum.

She shook her head, and pulled her phone from her hand bag. She needed to call her therapist. He would know what to do.

He picked up right away. "What."

"Daddy?" She heard the tremor in her voice, and swallowed.

"You okay?" He sounded concerned.

"Yeah." She took a deep breath. "It's probably nothing."

"But?"

"But, all the papers from my desk are gone, and there are… rude sticky notes."

"Okay. I'll call Jenson. Make sure he got his kid off to boot camp. For now, go find someone to keep you company."

She nodded, the remembered he couldn't see her. "Okay daddy. Thanks."

She ended the call, and pushed back from her desk wondering where all the papers had gone. Her desk had been packed with memo's, work books, master worksheets, and the like.

She jumped when a pencil fell to the floor. Stay calm, she reminded herself. But it didn't work. She rushed from her classroom to find Dan.

He was seated behind his desk in his classroom across the hall. He looked up when she came in, and stood, worry in his eyes. "Mia? What's wrong? You're pale."

She forced a smile. "Oh, it's probably nothing." She wrung her hands in front of her. "But, would you mind, coming with me?" She pointed with her thumb over her shoulder.

He came around his desk. "Sure." He put a hand under her elbow and escorted her to her classroom. It seemed so innocent, and nothing was out of place that she could see. But her desk, her personal space, had been violated.

She stopped.

He shot her a questioning look.

"My desk. The drawers. I had all my stuff in there. Would you mind looking. Maybe I've lost my mind and just missed it."

He raised a brow, but went to her desk. He pulled open the center drawer, ran a hand over his balding head, and whistled. He looked up at her. "You don't know who did this?"

She shook her head, blinking back the tears that were threatening to fall.

He shut the drawer, and pulled open the rest, shaking his head as he saw the stickies. He came around the desk, and put an arm around her waist. "Come on." He escorted her from the room.

She stopped in the hall. She was being silly. It was just her desk. It's not like someone had come to her home, or her therapists home. She took a wavering breath. "I need to find my workbooks, and the students' papers."

He nodded slowly. "Okay, but let's see Principal Spears first."

She leaned on him, and let him lead her to the principal's office.

Dan told Principal Spears what they'd found in her classroom. He ran a thick hand through his ginger hair that was liberally sprinkled with grey and white. He sighed, his jowls wobbling with the motion.

Mia wrinkled her nose, and quickly unwrinkled it. Principal Spears had the worst breath ever. She held tighter to Dan's arm.

"Miss Lovejoy, please take a seat. Mr. Plough, please go to her classroom and look around. Check the supply closet. See if you can find the stuff from her desk." There was an unspoken, *and check for any other signs of sticky notes or other vandalism.*

Dan walked Mia the few steps to the leather upholstered pair of arm chairs in front of Spears' desk. She took a seat, and looked up at him gratefully. "Thank you," she whispered.

Dan nodded, and left the classroom.

She turned to Principal Spears. "Sorry to bother you, sir." She averted her eyes. He was in a position of power, and even after almost nine months of working together, she still wasn't sure if he preferred submissive women or not.

"Miss Lovejoy." He sighed. "Who would want to do this."

She peeked up at him from under her lashes. "I'm not sure, sir."

He raised a brow. "I see the way you dress. And I know who got you this job. Anything said in this room will remain confidential."

She gave him a tremulous smile, but knew better than to trust his good-guy act. Getting fired or losing her job was not an option. "I don't know, sir. I'm very sorry to have bothered you."

He leaned forward, one arm over his desk, and one in his lap. "Miss Lovejoy. Mia." He shook his head. "I know you see me as your boss. But I would like you to see me as a friend. I want to help you fix this. Will you help me, help you?"

They locked gazed a moment, but she looked away first. His blue eyes were boring into her, and she felt her breasts swell with desire. For the first time in her life, she cursed the biology that made her want sex. "I wish I knew," she murmured.

Dan came back into the room. "Principal Spears? You're going to want to see this."

Principal Spears stood. "Stay here," he told Mia.

156

She did as she was told. She didn't want to see whatever it was.

Then men left, she breathed a sigh of relief. She should have a few minutes to take care of herself. She closed her eyes, and slid her hand under her skirt. She was already wet, but didn't waste time teasing herself. She put her finger on her clit, and quickly rubbed herself to orgasm.

Chapter Nine:

The school bell rang, and she dismissed her class. Milo Jenson hadn't show up, and she made a mental not to thank her therapist for his intervention. When the last student had left, she closed her eyes. It had been the longest day ever. Dan and Principal Spears had told her they couldn't find her papers. She could tell they were lying, but didn't want to know the truth.

Her class door opened a moment later and her eyes snapped open. It was just Dan.

He closed the door softly behind her. "How are you doing?" He spoke softly, making his way to her desk.

"Alright. Would you mind closing my blinds?"

He nodded, and did as he was asked.

He was a rather boring person, but he had a good heart. And his cock worked well. She eyed his delicious looking ass. She stood, and locked her classroom door as he closed the last blind. She stood in front of the door, leaning against it with her hands behind her back. Her shirt stretching across her large tits. She took a deep breath, and smiled with satisfaction when his eyes traveled down to her breasts.

"Dan," she breathed.

He came to where she was leaning, and tucked a stray strand of hair behind her ear. His eyes moved up to her lips, pausing before gazing into her eyes. "May I?"

She nodded. He could do whatever he wanted to her.

He cupped her cheek, and she leaned into his hand. It felt warm. It felt... right. His hands trailed to her hair, and he was painstakingly careful to remove the pins before shaking it loose from its tight bun. He ran his fingers through her hair. "So beautiful."

She closed her eyes, enjoying his touch. His hands moved down her back, pulling her against him. Her hands splayed on his chest. She turned her face up, and he breathed deeply, then nuzzled her neck.

"I want you," she whispered. That wasn't quite true. She needed him. But she didn't want to scare him away by telling him.

He groaned, fisted a hand in her hair, pulling her head back, and kissed her. Their tongues battled in their mouths, and the familiar warmth of desire spread from her belly to her pussy. She clenched. She needed to feel him inside her.

His hands roamed her back, untucking her shirt, then trailed down to her ass. He squeezed, lifting her.

"Take me," she moaned.

He pulled away, and turned them, backing her toward her desk. Her hands roamed his body, unbuttoning his pants and feeling his skin under his shirts. Her ass hit the edge of her desk, and he fisted his hand in her hair, tugging her head back. He put his mouth on her neck and ears, his hot breath sending goosebumps along her arms. She trembled.

He pulled away, still holding her head back, and popped open the buttons on her blouse, one by one.

She gasped, and bit her lower lip. She should tell him no, but it felt so good. She inhaled deeply, and he freed her breasts from their satin prison, pushing the cups of her bra down. He lowered his mouth to her pert nipples, teasing them with his lips and tongue.

She ran her fingers through his hair and down his back, then slid her hands under his shirt, feeling his skin, hot to the touch.

She lifted her ass, and perched on the edge of her desk. She shivered in anticipation when he pushed her blouse off her shoulders to her bent elbows. She held his head as he sucked her nipple into his mouth, nipping it with his teeth.

His hand trailed along her skin, down her waist, to her hip, and his mouth journeyed back up to her neck. She was panting. "I want you inside me."

He pushed her skirt up to her waist and stood between her spread legs.

He pushed her back, and she put her hands flat on the desk to support herself, thrusting her groin to meet his. He slid a finger between her pussy lips, and groaned into her neck. She smiled, and thrust her hips again. His his finger slid inside her.

She sat up, sliding forward to keep his roaming fingers inside, and pushed his pants down. His cock popped out, hard and ready. She stroked the silky shaft, gripping it firmly. He was so hard. She needed him inside her.

He pulled her to her feet and turned her around, slapping her tight ass before rubbing the tip of his cock between her ass cheeks.

She felt tremors in her thighs. She was close to climax. The tip of his cock push against her pussy, begging for entrance, and she spread her legs a little more, rocking her hips to put him further inside.

He put his hands on her shoulders, pulling her down on his cock.

She gasped, and reached a hand between her legs. She stroked his cock as it slid in and out, and rubbed her clit. Her pussy clenched on his cock, squeezing, and contracting with her orgasm. The edge of the desk dug into her belly as she came, her muscles twitching and shaking. Her heart pounded in her chest. He pulled out, and slapped her ass with his cock.

She moaned, and he turned her back around, her ass pushed against the desk his slid back in from the front, teasing her nipples with his mouth. She tossed her head back, moaning with pleasure, and wrapped her legs around him.

She reached between them, rubbing her clit, and felt the orgasm climb, electric tingles shooting from her groin into her toes. Climaxing, she trembled, and he pulled his cock out, stroking it. His hot cum shot onto the hand she rubbed her clit with. He covered her mouth with his own, muffling her moans with his tongue. He held her close, moving her hand from her clit, replacing it with the tip of his spent cock, smearing his cum around.

She shuddered a final time, her fingers digging into his shoulders, and buried her face in his necks, trying to catch her breath.

He stroked her hair, and held her close. They were both breathing heavy, and she could hear his heart hammering in his chest as rapidly as her own.

A gentle tap on the classroom door broke them from their post coital bliss.

"Shit," Dan said, quickly pulling away and buttoning his pants. He pulled his shirt down rather than tucking it in, and smoothed out the hairs that remained on his head.

She stood, tugging her skirt down and pulling her shirt back over her shoulders. She turned away from the door and adjusted her bra, and buttoning back up. There wasn't time to gather the hair pins from the floor. She was finger brushing her hair when she heard the click of the door unlocking.

She stayed turned away, trying to compose herself.

"Why was the door locked?" It was Principal Spears.

"I was comforting Mia. It's been a rough day."

"I see." From the tone of his voice, he clearly did.

"I'll see you later, Mia," Dan said, and she could hear his steps take him out of her room and across the hall. A door closed, and she was alone with her boss.

She took an unsteady breath, and turned to face him. She was as presentable as she could be under the circumstance.

Principal Spears shut the door behind him, and locked it.

Mia raised a brow.

"You were fucking him." His voice held desire, and accusation.

She nodded. It would do no good to lie.

He walked toward her. "Is that why your room was attacked? You fuck other teachers too?"

She took a step back, wincing as her hip made contact with the desk. "N..no, sir."

"Was it the students? I know you don't wear panties." His eyes roamed her body, and she felt exposed.

She threw her hair back. She wasn't going to be afraid. "I fucked Dan," she whispered. Despite her bravado, she *was* afraid. Her racing heart had nothing to do with her orgasm anymore.

"Who else," he said quietly, coming closer.

"I haven't willingly fucked anyone else here." She held her ground. The desk behind her helped.

"Fine. You're on thin ice. This is a school, not your private bedroom. Do not let it happen again."

She dropped her eyes, and saw his cock was bulging under his belly more than usual. "Yes, sir."

"Now. I've notified the parents there was a technical malfunction. There's only a week left before school lets out for the summer. You will need to give every student an 'A' for any assignments that are missing. Is that clear?"

"Yes, sir." She kept her eyes down.

"Are you dating Mr. Plough?"

She looked up, then quickly looked away. "Not exactly."

"What's that supposed to mean."

She started to shrug, but answered. "We've gone on a date and we've fucked. I don't know if he is looking for anything more, sir."

She peeked up and saw he was nodding, looking thoughtful. "Careful," he said, stroking his chin. "While it isn't against policy, dating a coworker is frowned upon."

"Yes, sir."

He stepped back. "Good. Don't lock your door again. I'll repeat. This is not your own personal room." He turned heel to leave, stopping only to unlock the door.

Once he was gone and the door was shut behind him, she breathed easier. That had been close. She opened the door and stepped into the hall. Dan wasn't in his classroom. She could only assume he'd already left for the night. She went back to her desk and grabbed her handbag from the bottom drawer and pulled out her phone.

Dad had already texted, saying he would see her tomorrow. She sighed. Did she really want to see him anymore? Or was she using him

162

for the sexual release he could provide. Her therapist had warned her about that. It didn't matter. She wasn't looking for someone to take care of her. When she settled down, she wanted it to be with someone who could entertain her mind, and not just her body.

When she got to her car, all four tires were flat. A pocket knife hung from the side wall of a back tire. They weren't just flat; they'd been slashed. Her heart raced, and she looked around. She wasn't the last one to leave today, and there were still plenty of cars in the parking lot. But she didn't see anyone out here.

With a shaking hand, she pulled her phone back out from her hand bag, and called her therapist. Her hands were shaking, and she'd had to retype the number several times before finally getting it right.

"Mia?"

She cupped her hand over her mouth and the phone, not wanting anyone to overhear. "Daddy, come get me." A noise from behind made her jump, but it was only dog, wandering between the cars. Normally she would have gone over to pet the dog and see if he had a home. But not this time. The dog could be a nasty trick.

"Where are you?"

"I'm in the parking lot at school. Please hurry."

"I'll be right there." He ended the call, but she didn't put her phone away. Her classroom wasn't safe. Her car wasn't safe. There was no where she could go that she would be safe. She felt tears fill her eyes, and she blinked quickly, trying to get rid of them. Now wasn't the time for tears. Right now, she needed to go to be around people. She was alone in the parking lot, and she wasn't safe here either.

When her therapist pulled up, she climbed into the sleek black two-door car.

She closed her eyes, leaning her head against the seat. He put a comforting hand on her knee and squeezed. "What's going on."

She told him about her desk, and her encounter with Principal Spears after fucking Dan in her classroom, then going out to find her tires had been slashed.

He didn't interrupt, making noncommittal noises in all the right places.

He stopped at the gate leading to the house and punched in the security code. "I need to get back to work. Laura's here with Carlton. I know you need release, and I can't do it for you. I'm sure you can figure it out. I'll be home later this evening. I have a meeting with Jenson after work. I can take care of you when I get back, if you still need it."

She shuddered in anticipation. "Thanks, daddy. I owe you one."

Chapter Ten:

She stepped into the house, and closed the door. She could hear moans and groans coming from the sitting room. Someone was having loud sex, and she squeezed her thighs together with a shudder. She closed her eyes, enjoying the sensations coursing through her.

She made her way to the sitting room door and peeked in. Laura was straddling Carlton on the couch. They were both naked. Carlton had his mouth on Laura's nipples, his hands squeezing her ass, guiding her on his cock. Laura was squeezing her other breast, her head back, riding Carlton and moaning.

Mia lifted her skirt, rubbing her pussy, and unbuttoned her blouse. Watching them fuck was sexy, and she didn't want to be left out. But she didn't want to interrupt and have them stop.

She reached into her bra, and teased her nipple, a sigh escaping her lips. Her eyes closed halfway, and she teased her clit, getting wetter. She moaned softly as Laura came.

Carlton must've heard her. He looked over, and his eyes widened. He turned back to Laura, and pulled her head to his shoulder and whispered something in her ear.

Mia couldn't hear over the sound of her pounding heart.

Laura looked over and smiled, then climbed off Carlton, revealing his rock hard cock. It was enormous, and Mia shuddered, imagining what it would feel like inside her.

Laura came to her and reached out, pushing Mia's blouse from her shoulders. It fell to the floor. Laura squeezed Mia's tit, and smiled.

Mia returned the smile, and tugged her skirt back into place, then unzipped it, letting it fall to the floor with her shirt.

Laura stepped closer, their tits separated only by Mia's bra. She reached behind Mia, undid the clasp, and pulled her bra off.

Mia stood naked in the doorway, her nipples hard as they brushed against Laura's nipples.

Laura stepped back, grabbed Mia's hand, and pulled her into the room. Laura stopped, and Mia reached around, pressing her hips into Laura's ass and grabbing her tit, teasing her nipples. She let go of Laura's hand.

She bit Laura's neck, then kissed it, running her hands over Laura's belly and down to her pussy.

Carton spread his legs, stroking his cock slowly as he watched.

Mia pressed her finger into Laura's clit, making her moan. Mia began rubbing, making small circles over the sensitive spot, her eyes locked with Carlton's.

Carlton got up, then stood behind Mia, his cock pushing into her ass. She rocked her hips, and started rubbing Laura faster.

Laura began twitching, and put her hands over Mia's, guiding her.

Carlton slid his hand between Mia's legs, then pinched her clit. A moment later, his cock was sliding into her wet, tight pussy, stretching it.

Mia moaned, and held onto Laura as she began trembling, her pussy clenching in climax.

Laura stepped away, and Mia moaned. Carlton's hands were on her hips, shoving his cock deep inside, his girth stretching her. The smell of sex filled the room. Mia ran her hands along her belly to her heavy breasts, teasing her nipples.

Laura pushed Mia's hand out of the way, and put her mouth on Mia's nipple. She pulled her nipple with her teeth, then opened her mouth and sucked. She reached down, rubbing Mia's clit, while Carlton slammed into her from behind.

Mia started twitching, close to orgasm, and Carlton wrapped his arms around the front of her thighs, lifting her, then sat with his cock still inside, and her on his lap.

Laura got on her hands and knees, licking the exposed shaft of Carlton's cock then licking Mia's clit, while rubbing her own. Mia cupped her breasts, rocking her hips, her head tossed back.

She came, shuddering and twitching.

Carlton's cock flexed inside her and she felt his hot cum fill her up, mixing with her own juices and soaking his cock.

Laura sucked her clit, and Mia's pussy clenched on Carlton's cock as waves of pleasure and ecstasy wracked through her body.

Laura pulled her mouth away, stroking the area around Mia's clit as Mia came down from her orgasm, still trembling, her breath coming in short bursts.

Carlton's cock slid out of her, and Mia scooted off, collapsing onto the sofa next to him.

She slowly slid a finger inside, feeling her wetness mixed with Carlton's cum. She slipped her finger up to her clit, circling it, then sliding back inside.

Carlton replaced her hands with his, and Laura stood.

Mia wiggled on the couch, laying her head on one cushion, with her ass over Carlton on the next cushion. "Sit on my face," she whispered to Laura.

Laura straddled her face, and Mia pulled her pussy closer to her mouth. She licked and slurped, tasting Laura, and moaned against her pussy when she grabbed Mia's tits, teasing her nipples.

Carlton was rubbing her g-spot, teasing her. He slid a second finger inside, stretching her tight pussy, and rubbing her clit with his thumb. He slid his other thumb over her asshole, teasing it, sending waves of pleasure shooting from her groin to her toes.

Laura's thighs squeezed her face, and Laura came, her pussy clenching and unclenching, over and over. Mia gripped tighter, holding her pussy to her face, licking every drop of Laura's cum.

Once Laura had finished, she climbed off Mia's face, and sat on the arm chair across from the couch, her body completely relaxed.

Carlton increased his pace, pressing harder on Mia's clit, and stroking the sensitive area inside her.

Mia grabbed her tits, closing her eyes.

Carlton slid a finger into her ass, throwing her body over the edge of her climax.

She shuddered, every muscle in her body contracting, curling her toes and her fingernails dug into the soft skin of her breasts.

Once she'd come down, she opened her eyes. Laura was no longer in the room.

Mia looked askance at Carlton, but his eyes were closed. Mia sat up, and cupped his cheek with her hand, turning his face toward her. She kissed him, tenderly at first, then deeper. Their tongues brushed against each other, and she moaned into his mouth. Pulling away, she whispered, "Thanks."

Then retrieved her clothes from the doorway and made her way to the master bedroom. She wanted a nap.

Chapter Eleven:

ia woke to the feeling she was being watched. Her heart was racing, and her skin was damp with sweat. She sat up, looking around the room, disoriented. Then she remembered. She was in her therapist's room. She'd fucked Carlton and Laura, and had wanted a nap. But she wasn't supposed to be in his room. He was seeing someone. She rubbed the sleep from her eyes, trying to figure out what had woken her.

Something caught her eye near the French doors that opened onto the balcony. The curtains were swaying in the breeze. She climbed naked from the bed.

That was odd. She hadn't opened the balcony door.

She slid back the curtain and gasped. Milo Jenson was on the balcony, holding a long, knife, the setting sun glinting off the thin blade. She took a step back, and inhaled deeply. She went to scream, but Milo was faster.

He rushed forward, slapping her face hard enough to knock her head sideways. Her screams died in her throat as she grabbed her cheek, the tears welling up in her eyes.

Milo grabbed her waist and threw her onto the bed. "Fucking bitch. My dad enlisted me in the army because of you."

She tried to scoot further away from him, but he grabbed her ankle, pulling her closer. She kicked out, and he squeezed tighter, his fingers cutting off the circulation in her foot.

"Stop kicking or I'll cut you." He brandished his knife, slicing it in the air.

She froze. The young man might be beautiful to look at, but he was an ugly person.

He pressed the knife to her calf, and a small drop of blood surfaced around the knife's tip. He glared at her. "Fucking cunt. You think you own me? I'll show you."

He lifted the knife and pulled her again, leaving her legs dangling off the bed, and pressing the knife to her belly. "Threaten to tell my dad you might be pregnant? I'll make sure you never get pregnant. Ever." He added pressure to the knife, and she cried out. He turned the knife, and it felt like her skin was being ripped open.

She cried out again. "Please!"

She watched as dark red blood pooled in the gaping hole he'd made in her skin. He turned the knife sideways, and pushed a hand on the wound, the pressure hurting as much as the knife had. She closed her eyes, tears streaming from her face.

"Beg, you slut."

She squeezed her eyes shut, trying to control the tears. Milo was going to kill her.

"Look at me!"

She forced her eyes open. The knife was in the hand pushing on her belly, but his cock was in his other hand. She felt her pussy get wet, her body wanting what her mind knew she didn't.

"Milo," she said, her voice a whisper. "Please. I'll do whatever you want. But put the knife down."

"Fucking whore. You think I'm stupid?" He let go of his cock, and backhanded her.

She tasted blood, the acrid metallic scent filling her nose.

The bedroom door flew open. Her therapist was standing there, gun drawn, and pointed at Milo. A man she didn't recognize stood behind him.

"Daddy!" She was so happy to see him, she called him daddy in front of strangers.

"Sit tight, baby girl." He stepped into the room, his aim never wavering, and stepped to the side. The stranger stepped and stood next to him.

"Father!" Milo stepped back from her, shock covering his face.

"You have disappointed me for the last time." The stranger, Milo's dad, stepped forward. He glanced down at Mia. "Young lady, you have my apologizes."

He turned back to Milo— who'd dropped his knife —and punched him in the gut.

Milo doubled over from pain.

Mr. Jenson grabbed his son's shoulders, and kneed him in the crotch. Milo grabbed his groin, and his knees hit the floor as he collapsed.

"The police are on their way."

Her therapist didn't put the gun down, keeping it trained on Milo.

Mr. Jenson stepped back, giving her therapist a clear shot in case it was needed. He pulled out his phone, and Mia heard sirens in the distance as the room went black.

Epilogue:

Mia lay in her therapist's bed, curled up against his side. Milo had been arrested and slapped with a slew of charges. Mr. Jenson had disowned him, and refused to pay legal expenses. Laura and Carlton had moved in while she was in the hospital getting stitched up.

The doctors had said the cut was deep, and the twisting blade meant they couldn't just stitch her up. Her therapist had insisted they keep her overnight. She'd tried to get her doctor to fuck her, but he'd given her a shot of some sort, and her need had gone away. Maybe her therapist was right, and she really was a nympho.

But she was home now, and safe in her therapist's arms. Milo was in jail and, thanks to Mr. Jenson's connections, he would likely be going to prison for a very long time. She sighed, and Laura stroked her hair, laying on the other side of her therapist. "Don't worry sweetie. You're safe."

Mia smiled, and pushed her as into Carlton's hip. He was laying behind her.

The four of them lay on the giant bed, each happy and safe. The effects of the drug they'd given her hadn't worn off. Her therapist said it was a good thing, since she shouldn't be having sex until she healed. But she still enjoyed the feel of Carlton's hip against her ass, daddy's chest under her fingertips, and Laura on the other side of daddy, stroking her hair.

She felt safe. And loved. And for the first time, she felt like she was finally where she belonged. She was home.

The End

President Rump and Vice President Penis Pound a Country's Ass Without Lube: Anal Tearing is Inevitable

By Lonely Woman

Contributing Author: Richard Longfellow

Chapter One:

Ronald Rump was the President of the greatest nation on earth. The States of United Americans. He looked in the mirror and fixed his tie with his tiny hands. He was almost eighty years old, and had lost his hair trying to build a corporate empire as good as his dads.

It hadn't worked, and the stress led to hair loss. He'd bought hair implants, so people wouldn't know the truth. It's also why he liked spray tan. It hid his pasty skin. His daddy had taught him all about image and how important it was.

A knock on the door to the oval office startled him, and he jumped. The door opened, and his second in command, his Vice President Penis, entered the room.

"Looking good, Rump!" Penis smiled. He walked to wear Rump stood in front of the mirror and slapped his ass. "I want to hit that."

"No, I can't right now, we have a meeting with the heads of state soon!"

Penis growled, a sound that rumbled in his chest, as he spun Ronald Rump around to face him. "Boy, I didn't ask." He shook a finger in Ronald's face.

Ronald gave a resigned sighed, and unbuttoned his pants. "I didn't take my erectile dysfunction pill today."

"I did." Penis undid his belt and unzipped his pants. His hard cock was proof he'd taken that pill.

Rump shuddered with anticipation, and splayed his hands on the wall in front of him.

Penis pushed his trousers down to his knees, and pressed his cock into Ronald's rump.

"I want you inside me," Rump said.

Penis reached around and stroked Ronald's soft cock, sliding his own cock between Ronald's ass cheeks. "Beg me," Penis whispered.

Rump whimpered. "Please, Penis. You should be the President, not me! Put your massive cock in my ass! I need you! Please!"

Penis smiled at him in the mirror, and guided his cock into Rump's ass. He put his hands on Ronald's shoulders, and slammed his cock into Ronald, hitting as deep as he could.

Ronald groaned, and pushed his hips out, turned his toes inward, and gave Penis better access access.

Penis pumped into him several times, and slapped Ronald's ass. "Call me daddy," he whispered into Ronald's ear.

Ronald groaned again, and practically yelled, "Fuck me harder, daddy!"

"Damn right." Penis flexed his cock, and came, filling Ronald's ass with his cum. Penis pulled out, and grabbed a tissue from Ronald's desk to wipe off with. "Pull your pants up, son. We have a meeting."

Ronald did as he was told. He knew better than to argue with Penis. He wanted to clean up, but he was going to be late if he didn't hurry. He was glad he'd skipped his little blue pill, or he'd have to walk the halls of the white house with a raging hard on.

Once his clothes were in order, and Penis's cum dripped into his boxers, he rushed from the room to his meeting.

Chapter Two:

"B" ut, Ivana, I don't understand!" Rump whined to his daughter over dinner. His wife, Mel, was living in New York still, and Ivana Put-In-Rump had been nice enough to come live with him and help him with all his duties.

Who knew being President would be so hard? It was more complicated than that stupid health care bill he'd been trying to push through the senate. And the supreme court? What a joke! Why did they pay judges to make rules about the rules that'd already been made? It was a waste of money. And Ronald Rump knew all about wasting money. Hell, his weekly golf trips were a perfect example.

But it sure was nice to enjoy life without being the one to foot the bill. Mel had talked about wanting to visit her home country of Sweden. Maybe he would take them on Air Force Five to the Bahamas. Sun, waves, and lots of fun.

Ivana sighed. She was starting to lose patience with him. "Give me the healthcare bills. I will look them over and tell you if they're good or not. Or tell me what you want to pass, and I'll compose the executive order for you. You'll just need to sign it."

"Okay." He hung his head. "But I'm the President. That means the people must love me! So why are they so mean to me on social media?"

She shook her head. "I don't know."

"Fine." He pushed back in his chair, and changed the subject. "Penis made me do bad things again today."

She rolled her eyes. "You told me they weren't bad things when I was younger and you didn't want me to tell mom. So you can deal with it."

"But, you wanted it! I don't!"

She laughed, a cold, hard sound. "I am not having this conversation with you."

He slammed his hand on the table and sat up straight. "You are here because I brought you here, and I can send you out just as fast. You want the easy meal ticket so you can run for office after I retire? You better not ever forget what I teach you. You can start by speaking softly. You know what the mainstream media wolves would do to you if they ever heard you speak like that? They'd tear you to peices."

Ivana raised a brow, and spoke softer than she had. "You're right. I'm sorry."

"Don't you forget it. Or I will bend you over my knee like I did when you were fifteen."

Ivana paled. "No, daddy. Please no."

Satisfied he was back in control, he leaned back. "Good. Now figure out the new health care bill. They are putting my name on it, it needs to be good. Amazing. The best. The best bill ever. The greatest bill of all time!"

She nodded.

He pushed away from the table and rebuttoned his jacket. "Mel will be here later. Make yourself scarce." Without waiting for a response, he left the room.

He made his way through the winding corridors to his room. Mel was his current wife. He'd had seven other wives, and at least two kids with each of them. But he only claimed some of his kids. He just sent money to the rest.

In his room, he called Penis. "I'll finish reading the bill this evening and get back to you."

Penis laughed from the other end of the line. "You can't read. Don't lie to me. Who are you having look it over? That sexy daughter of yours? Or your current wife. Her English might be terrible, but she sure is a fine piece of ass."

Rump glared, even though Penis couldn't see him. "How was dinner with the female prime mister of Germany. What's her name? Oh, that's right. You couldn't go unless you brought your wife with you. How does it feel, fucking the same pussy for forty years, knowing all those kids tore it up and it will never be the same."

"I wouldn't know. Haven't fucked that bitch in fifteen years. I fuck your ass instead, and don't you forget it."

Rump wanted to argue, but knew better. He'd had to get stitches in his ass last time, and Mel had tried to give him the cold shoulder. But he was the boss. And if she wanted to be a citizen, she knew better than to tell him no. He was a star, and when you're a star, women let you do whatever you want.

He stripped naked, and let his gut hang down. Clothes were so confining. He admired himself in the mirror. He'd need a little more spray tan soon, or his pasty skin would show, and that would damage his image.

He sucked in his gut, and put his hands close to the mirror. "You have the biggest hands," he told his reflection.

He lay on his massive bed— the biggest, most comfortable bed in the world, —and spread his legs. He had an hour before Mel would show up to service him, and he wanted to scroll his social media accounts.

The top stories were of the liars, the wolves, the mainstream media. They were talking about his bill, and how bad it was. He was mad, so super angry. It was the best bill ever! How dare they talk like that about it!

His fingers moved furiously across the screen and he penned several responses. That would show them! He smiled with satisfaction when he saw his numbers had gone up. He had five more followers than he'd had that morning! His official presidential account was losing followers. Whatever. He typed out a final message and Mel came in his room.

She was looking good in her pale green, fitted, floor length dress. He squinted at her and rose from the bed. "Your arms are flabby! You haven't been working out! How are you going to keep me happy if you let your body go! I have an image to uphold, and if you can't do what little I ask of you, why should I bother keeping you around? Millions of women would love to be my wife, especially now I'm the President. Billions! And they all want me."

He pulled a blue pill from his pocket and took it, forgoing any water. He looked down his nose at her and puckered his lips.

She cowed down, looking scared. "But, my husband," she said, in her heavy Swedish accent. "I have been traveling and taking care of our son! I will visit the gym first thing in morning, yes?" She ran her hands up his chest. "For now, I will take care of you." She smiled at him.

He sat on the edge of the bed, and spread his legs. His dick looked so small right now. He grimaced. He beckoned her to come forward, and she did as she was told. She got on her knees in front of him without him telling her to do so. She was well trained. Why else would he keep her around?

She lowered her mouth to his limp dick, and he leaned back on the bed. He rested on one hand, and held her head with the other. Her brown hair covered her face and he couldn't see what she was doing. He used his free hand to brush her hair back to one side. She knew better than to do her job without pulling her hair back, but he would yell at her late. For now, he could feel blood flowing to his cock. That little blue pill could work wonders.

His cock filled her mouth, and he shoved her head down, making sure she took it all in.

She reached up and fondled his balls while she sucked, and he groaned. His cock was almost hard. He tilted his hips, and pushed on her head, as he fucked her mouth, her spit soaking his cock and balls, as she deep throated him. A moment later, he came. He shuddered as he rammed his cock into the back of her throat. He wanted her to choke on his cum.

As soon as he was finished, he took his hand off the back of her head and she pulled off his cock. Her face was red, and she sputtered, trying to catch her breath. Damn, his dick must be good if she was breathless!

She stood, and put her hands behind her to take off her dress.

He stopped her. "Don't bother. I'm done. I want to sleep for a few hours before I post my three am update on social media." He stood, grabbed a towel from the side of the bed, and cleaned himself off before laying down to sleep.

She still stood at the foot of the bed.

He rolled his eyes. "Go visit Ivana or something. Hell, go visit Killary Clit for all I care. But go away. I'm tired."

"Yes, sir." She turned from him and left the room as he drifted peacefully into sleep, with thoughts of being loved and adored by all.

Chapter Three:

Rump stood on a balcony overlooking the white house lawn. A crowd was gathered. The crowd was so large, they spilled out into the streets and covered the entire area within a mile of his house. They were chanting his name, and he waved. He felt benevolent.

"Rump! Rump! Rump!" They chanted, over and over.

Someone handed him a large, heavy book and disappeared. The cover was blue, and it was bound with thin metal bolts. It had *How To Win At Love And Life* written in fancy gold letters on the front. This book would have all the answers.

He opened it to the first page, but the words swam in front of his face, making them hard to decipher. The crowd below grew impatient, and clouds rolled in overhead.

He frantically thumbed through the pages, desperate to find one that was legible. He looked up as he reached the final page. It was blank. The crowd had stopped chanting, and all looked like his father, with scowls of disappointed on their faces.

The crowd rushed his balcony and climbed up, making a human ladder to reach him. He backed away from the edge, and threw the book into the crowd. He needed more time! He backed into something, stopped, and turned slowly around, afraid of what he would see.

It was his hero, Vlak Put-in! His hero wrapped Ronald in his arms. Put-in had pulled him to safety when he woke up, alone in his bed. Sweat had beaded on his neck and chest, and his sheets were damp.

Cursing, he climbed from bed. "Fucking bullshit."

The red numbers on his clock radio illuminated the dark room. Three am. He sighed. Every damn night.

He pulled his sheets back so they could air dry, and sat in the chair by his closet while he scrolled his social media. He laughed at a post by his education secretary, Betty DeVoid. He was a genius putting her in charge. Stupid libtards were so focused on her idiocy they weren't paying attention to everything he did.

It'd been an hour and his sheets were mostly dry. He climbed into his bed, and fell back into sleep, confident he would have even more followers tomorrow.

Chapter Four:

Ronald Rump made his way to his daughter's room, and entered without knocking. His mouth fell open. Betty DeVoid wore a strap-on. Both DeVoid and Penis were pounding into her pussy the way he pounded into prostitutes! And at the same time!

He quickly backed away and shut the door, shaking his head. But maybe now he could get one up on Penis.

He wandered off, contemplating the possible ways he could use what he'd seen to his advantage. He pulled out his phone and dialed up his hero, and now good friend, Vlak Put-in.

"Hallo," the voice answered, his accent heavy.

"Hi, Vlak!"

"You do not to call me dat. You call me only Put-in."

"Sorry, Put-in."

"Good boy. Now, vut do ju want. I am a very busy man."

"Can I have those tapes back now?"

Put-in laughed. "Not any way possible no. You have not given me everything I want. But I may to allow you to come to my country and have my best girls do it again."

Ronald's face fell. "But, what if I tell you what I just caught Penis doing?"

"I do not care of your penis. It is small and soft. I saw ze tapes."

Ronald turned red, glad Put-in couldn't see him. "No, I mean Penis, the Vice President."

"Oh. Zat. Tell me."

"He was fucking my daughter. With Betty DeVoid!"

"Do ju have pictures?"

"Well, no." Ronald Rump wondered if he could go back and get some.

"Zen dis information is useless to me. I only vant pictures."

"Okay."

"Do not be calling me again. I am busy man. Maybe ju should be busy to, yes? You have country to fix. We agree communism is only true way, and ju must work to teach your spoiled country zis."

"But only if I can keep my money."

"Yes, of course. Only poor and ze middle people pay. We keep what we have."

"Okay! 'Bye!" He disconnected the call with renewed determination in his step as he made his way to his next meeting. He was going to make the people love him, no matter what it took.

"Rump!"

Ronald turned to see Penis rushing after him. Crap. Why wasn't he with Ivana Put-in-Rump and Betty DeVoid.

"I saw you pop in. Come back. Me and Betty are done with Ivana. She's got a tight asshole. But I want yours."

Ronald half turned away, pointing back the way he'd been going. "I have meetings."

Penis shrugged, but there was a fire in his eyes. "You can be late. You're the President. You can do whatever you want!"

"Okay." Rump followed Penis back to Ivana's room.

Betty snapped a belt when he walked in, and Penis closed the door.

"Bend over." Penis ordered.

"No. I want Betty between us this time." He saw the strap-on Betty had used on Ivana, and he didn't want that anywhere near his ass when he had meetings to attend!

Penis thought about that a moment then nodded his agreement. "Okay."

Betty sneered, but got on all fours in the middle of the bed. Penis and Rump climbed onto the bed, with Penis at her face, and Rump near her ass. It was old, with wrinkles and dimples, but it was a solid six. He only liked tens, but he was getting older, and those tens were fewer between these days unless he insisted. Then they would let him, they'd let him do whatever he wanted. He was a star, and the President. But they didn't come to his hotel unannounced as often anymore.

He slapped her ass, and watched the wrinkles turn into a wave that rippled across her butt cheek as he stroked his limp dick. It was tiny in his huge hands.

He watched as Penis stuck his cock in Betty's mouth. He wondered how it was still hard, but then remembered how much Penis loved those little blue pills.

Ronald's cock was starting to come alive, but it was taking forever. Betty was moaning around Penis's cock, and Penis was groaning like he was going to finish soon.

"Give me a blue pill." Rump stood.

"In my pants pocket." Penis didn't stop, and kept fucking DeVoid's face.

Rump searched the pile of clothing and found the bottle. He popped one of the little pills. "Trade me places until this kicks in."

Penis shrugged. "Fine." He moved to Betty's ass, and Rump took his place near her face.

"What the hell. You aren't even hard. How am I supposed to suck that?"

He grabbed the back of her head and shoved his soft dick in her face. "Make it hard, you cunt."

He rubbed his flaccid dick on her lips but she wouldn't open up. He grabbed a handful of her hair and pulled.

"Don't make my spank you, whore," Penis said.

"Do it," she shot back.

While her mouth was open, Rump put the tip of his soft cock between her lips. She blew a raspberry as she spit it out, and he felt a tingle in his cock. The pills were starting to kick in.

Penis leaned over to grab the belt. He slammed his cock into her, hard. She moved forward, and her face smacked into his cock. It tingled again, this time stronger. The tingle started in his balls, but was making its way to his dick.

Penis pulled out, and stood. He snapped the belt once, then laid it across her ass. The sound of the belt as it hit her ass filled the room.

"Ouch!" Betty looked back and glared at Penis, and used a hand to adjust the dominatrix harness she was wearing.

Rump reached under her and grabbed her tit. It was as soft as his cock, and dangled down with her hard nipples pointing straight out. He reached a little further and pinched her nipple. Her tits felt like deflated balloons.

"Why you son of a…" She couldn't finish the sentence.

Rumps cock had finally gotten hard enough to shove in her mouth.

Penis smacked her with the belt again before he climbed onto the bed behind her once more.

She moaned around his cock, but pushed at it with her tongue. "Suck, bitch. Not push. No wonder your husband doesn't fuck you."

Penis began fucking her again. He tossed one end of the long belt to Rump, who wrapped it under Betty's chin and handed the end back. Penis used the belt like a set of reins, and fucked the shit out of Betty.

Ronald Rump grabbed a handful of her hair and held her face still while he fucked her mouth. She didn't object.

"Yee haw!" Penis shouted, wiggling his hips in a circular motion. "Prepare your anus!" He pulled his cock back, and adjusted it, holding his make shift reins in one hand, his cock in the other. Once he'd positioned himself over her asshole, he grabbed the reins with both hands and pulled, driving his cock into her.

Rump fucked her face faster. If Penis was almost done, he needed to be also. He felt her lips tighten around his cock, and he shoved it into the back of her throat. She pushed with her tongue again and her teeth started to bite down as Rump's splooge shot into the back of her throat.

She swallowed, but her teeth were still trying to bite down. He quickly pulled his cock out of her mouth.

Penis cried out. "Oh, praise Jesus yes."

Rump and Penis climbed off the bed at the same time.

She collapsed on to her side, her body shuddering.

"Damn she really liked it." Penis pulled his clothes on, but left his cock out.

Rump did the same.

Betty lay in the center of the bed, almost lifeless from pleasure, her tits strapped into the weird harness she liked to use, and her ass being hugged by the ass-less chaps she always wore under her pant suit. Only now, she wasn't wearing her suit.

Rump grabbed a wet wipe from the night stand and cleaned himself off, tossing the package to Penis before zipping his pants back up.

"Thanks." Penis cleaned himself off. "Don't you have a meeting you're late for?"

"Shit." Rump rushed from the room. He was late.

Chapter Five:

R ump was upset. The media polls had him at the lowest approval rating ever. But there was no way that was true. He's the President! O'Humper was the most hated President ever, not Ronald Rump!

He stood in front of a full-length mirror with a towel around his waist. He held his hands close to the mirror. "Your hands are huge! Everyone loves you! You are the best. The greatest! And way better than President O'Humper ever was!" He nodded at his reflection. That's right. He really was the best.

Penis burst through his bedroom door. He was panting and out of breath. "Get dressed."

Rump was outraged. He was the President! "Get out!" He pointed a finger at the door.

"There's no time. Get dressed."

Rump put his hands on his hips. "You can't order me around. I told Put-in what you did with Ivana!"

Penis gasped. "How could you! Now he has even more against us!"

Rump hadn't thought of that.

"Whatever. Get dressed! There's no time! Betty's dead!"

Rumps hands fell to his side. "What? When? How?"

Penis was rooting around in the dresser, and pulled out an undershirt and boxers. He held up a two-foot-long, double sided, pink dildo that was easily four inches across and looked at it thoughtfully before putting it back in the drawer. He threw the clothes at Rump.

Rump caught them and dressed while Penis pulled a suit from the closet.

"I don't know." Penis tossed the suit onto the bed. "Secret service found her in Ivana Put-in-Rump's room, and they said she'd been having sex with multiple partners when she died."

Rump gasped, pulling his pants on. "That whore!"

"I know." Penis closed the closet door. "Can you image the scandal if this gets out?"

Rump quickly dressed and followed Penis to the state room, where most of the secret service had already gathered.

"Gentlemen." Rod Boner stood at the head of the table.

Tony Weiner stood next to him. "Take a seat."

Rump and Penis exchanged a glance, but took their seats.

"This is a big mess," Tony said, taking his seat.

Rod took a seat as well. "Huge. Massive. We need to keep this information locked down."

Rump nodded and tried to look interested. Where they talking about Betty?

Penis hit the table with his fist. "How could this happen? She was a good, Christian woman! And for her to be found like that is a travesty. Think about what it would do to her family if they found out." He shook his head sadly.

Rump was proud of Penis. He was spouting falsities as if they were truths. And, as everyone knew, if you say it enough times it *becomes* the truth.

He pulled out his phone and posted a tweet. *RIP Betty Devoid. Good Christian woman. Sad.*

"What are you doing?!" Rod was staring at him.

"Nothing." Rump put his phone away.

"I swear to god," Penis began, shaking a finger at him angrily.

"What? It's nothing. How are we going to keep this under wraps and hidden? I watched a show one time, and the government just printed a fake autopsy and lab reports, and no one figured it out until the body was exhumed decades later, and by then they couldn't tell what a whore she'd been. She was a total eight, by the way. The actress. She came to my room one time, and I had to turn her away. I already had two tens. That's twenty. Like the number of followers I lost since this morning. We need to do something to fix this."

Everyone in the room was staring at him. He knew he was the smartest, and preened. They never would have thought to lie on official documents. Good thing he was here.

Penis shook his head. "You fucking moron."

"Don't speak to our President like that!" It was one of the secret service members.

"Oh yeah? Or what." Penis stood, and leaned across the table.

The secret serviceman undid his belt and unzipped his pants. They dropped to his knees and he stroked his huge cock.

The other secret service members stood as well, all of them dropped their pants and pulled out their cocks.

Even Rod and Tony dropped their pants. Tony's cock looked just like it did in the email's he got in trouble for sending. Idiot. He got caught. Rod's cock was smaller than Rumps.

Penis, flustered, pulled out his own cock. They all started stroking their hard cocks.

Rump didn't want to be left out. He dropped his pants and stroked his cock. He hoped the little blue pill was still in his system from a few hours ago. He thought of Betty. At least her last moments were pleasure filled. He'd seen the way she was twitching and shuddering. Sure, she shit herself, but that's because Penis had cum in her ass. Nothing to be ashamed of there.

His cock grew in his hands as he stared at the cocks around the table. Soon, everyone had clenched their thighs, and thrust their hips forward. Rump did the same, and he felt it. A familiar tingle that started in his balls.

They all came, covering the table with their cum. The smell of sex filled the air, and Rump wrinkled his nose. He didn't like the smell of sex unless it was his.

Everyone collapsed into their seats, spent.

"What were you saying?" Tony broke the silence first.

Everyone looked around the table, but no one could remember why they were there.

"Whatever." Penis scowled. "We'll take a break. Let someone clean this mess up. We'll meet back here in an hour."

Nods of agreement circled the table. Rump stood, and his stomach growled. He needed to smoke a bowl and find something to eat.

Chapter Six:

R ump made his way back to the meeting room. Now he remembered why they'd called the meeting in the first place. Betty DeVoid was dead. And they needed to cover it up. He pushed open the door and stopped short.

Killary Clits was seated at the table.

"What do you want," he snarled. Killary had lost to him, and he had won the election. People liked him more!

"I heard about Betty."

Rump's jaw dropped. "How did you find out? That's a secret."

Killary glared at him. "You tweeted it, you incompetent ass."

Rump glared back, and took a seat. "Doesn't explain what you want, you cum guzzling whore."

They sat there, and glared at each other.

Penis, Boner, and Weiner joined them, followed by the secret service members. No one spoke. They all just stared at Killary.

"Get on the table and lay down," Penis said, breaking the silence.

"Why?"

"Because you weren't here last time. And I know how much you love the cock." He thrust his hips in her direction.

Ronald Rump laughed.

She rolled her eyes. "Did you guys have a circle jerk again? Nasty."

"You're nasty," Rump shot back.

They were all sitting around the table and arguing. Rump wanted to end it the way they had earlier, and just pull his cock out. But he didn't want Killary to make fun of it again. Besides, the blue pill had probably worn off by now.

He pulled out his phone and posted a tweet. *Killary email still not found. FBI useless. Only good for wire taps during election. Stupid.*

For good measure, he sent out a second, and typed *Bengazi was Killary's fault.*

He looked up from his phone and everyone was staring at him.

"What? She's a stupid head." He folded his arms over his chest.

At that moment, the earth shook. Everyone stood, arms out to keep their balance. It was like an earthquake, but worse.

The doorframe cracked, and bent in the center before shattering into a million pieces. Everyone turned and looked at the gaping hole in the wall where the door had been.

There stood a majestic white unicorn, with a sharp horn. And on its back, was none other than...

"Berdie Sander!" They all spoke together.

Berdie's hair was sticking out at odd angles, and his glasses had fallen low on his nose. He rode without a saddle, and gripped the unicorn's mane with both hands.

"That's right." Berdie spoke with a firm voice, heavy with an old Boston accent. "I'm here to drain your swamp!"

As if on que, everyone in the room wet their pants, the wet stain spreading on their pants.

"And now—" he ducked under the wall as his unicorn carried him into the room "—it's time to get rid of the swamp monsters!"

The unicorn reared back, and crushed one of the secret service members under its hooves. Others pulled their side arms, and fired at

Berdie and the unicorn. But it was no use. The bullets bounced off an invisible forcefield.

The unicorn swiped its head to the side, and cut three of the secret service members in half before impaling Boner and Weiner like a human shish kabob.

Rump backed away, stopping when his back hit the far wall. Where is his hero now? Where is Put-In to rescue him this time.

Penis tried to duck under the unicorn and escape, but he was too slow. The unicorn's horn caught him in the ass.

Penis grabbed his injured rear, and howled in pain.

But the unicorn didn't care. It backed up a step, and impaled him on its now-bloody horn. The unicorn looked at Rump, the sun glinting off its horn, the blood a dark red against the white pearlescent horn.

Rump clutched his throat. Put-in would appear at any moment, and rescue him. This had to be a dream. He was going to wake up for his three am tweet any minute now!

The unicorn pawed the ground with its hoof, and spread the blood around. It dropped its head, and charged.

Rump was impaled through the heart, and pinned to the wall.

"Come on, boy." Berdie patted the unicorn on the neck. "We have more social injustice and inequality to combat."

Berdie rode off on his unicorn into the sunset, in search of truth, justice, and the American way.

The End.

President Obanger and Vice President Bite'm Pound Asses Without Lube: Anal Tearing is Inevitable

By Lonely Woman

Contributing Author: Richard Longfellow

Lonely Woman

Chapter One:

Brock Obanger was the President of the greatest nation on earth. The States of United Americans. He looked in the mirror and fixed his tie with his dark hands. He was almost seventy years old. His hair was grey, and he hadn't been present for long enough. His face was riddled with lines and wrinkles.

His dad left when he was young, a boy who tried to survive in Kenya. His mama had taught him all about image and how important it was. So he'd faked a Hawaiian birth certificate.

A knock on the door to the oval office startled him, and he jumped. The door opened, and his second in command, his Vice President Bite'm, entered the room.

"Looking good, Obanger!" Bite'm smiled. He walked to where Obanger stood in front of the mirror and slapped his ass.

"I'm going to hit that." Brock said, turning around.

"No, not right now, we have a meeting with a couple of the heads of state soon!" Bite'm growled, a sound that rumbled in his chest.

Obanger spun Bite'm around, trading places with him. "I didn't ask." He shook a finger in Bite'm's face.

Bite'm gave a resigned sighed, and unbuttoned his pants.

"Did you you're your erectile dysfunction pill today?" Brock turned Bite'm around to face the wall.

"I did." Bite'm undid his belt and unzipped his pants. His hard cock was proof positive he'd taken it.

Bite'm shuddered with anticipation, and splayed his hands on the wall in front of him.

Brock pushed his trousers down to his knees, and pressed his cock into Bite'm's ass.

"I want to be inside you," Obanger said.

He reached around and stroked Bite'm's giant cock, sliding his own cock between his ass cheeks.

"Beg me," Bite'm whispered.

Brock whimpered. "Please, Bite'm. Let me put my massive cock in your asshole! I need you! Please!"

Bite'm smiled at him in the mirror.

Obanger guided his cock into Joel's ass. He put his hands on Joel Bite'm's shoulders, and slammed his cock into him, hitting as deep as he could.

Bite'm groaned, and pushed his hips out, turned his toes inward, and gave Brock easier access.

Obanger pumped into him several times, and slapped Joel's ass. "Call me daddy," he whispered into Joel's ear.

Bite'm groaned again, and practically yelled, "Fuck me harder, daddy!"

"Damn right." Obanger flexed his cock, and came, filling Joel's ass with his cum. Obanger pulled out, and grabbed a tissue from his desk to wipe off with. "Pull your pants up, son. We have a meeting."

Bite'm did as he was told.

Brock adjusted his clothes, and watched as Bite'm did the same. They hooked their elbows together, and left the oval office. They had a meeting to attend.

Chapter Two:

"**B**ut, Brock, I don't understand!" Bite'm whined to Obanger during dinner.

Brock's wife, Chell, sat at the head of the table, her fork laying on her plate. They'd already finished eating, and Bite'm wanted to join Brock and Chell in their bedroom.

"Now, Joel," Brock Obanger said, leaning back in his seat. "We've had this conversation before. Now. You can either take no for an answer, or keep arguing and get your privileges taken away. It's your choice. And what you choose is yours alone. But you need to remember. That. That all actions. All actions have consequences." He waggled a finger at Bite'm.

Bite'm hung his head. "Okay." He stood and left, looking downtrodden with his shoulders slumped and his head hanging low.

Brock felt bad for his good friend and second in command, Joel Bite'm. Maybe he would take them on Air Force Five to the Bahamas. Sun, waves, and lots of fun.

Chell sighed. She was starting to lose patience with him. "You can't invite him to our bed every night, Brock." She shook her head.

"He needs to learn how to be on his own. He's a grown ass man, after all."

"Okay." Brock hung his head. "But I'm the President! Why can't I invite him every night if I want?"

She shook her head. "I don't know."

"Fine." He pushed back in his chair, and changed the subject. "I tapped that ass before our meetings today. He thought being late was going to be a bad thing."

She rolled her eyes. "You need to tell him to lay off the blue pill. The two of you going at it like dogs in heat. Have you said your evening prayers?"

"But, he can be a top now! Not just a bottom!"

She laughed, a cold, hard sound. "I am not having this conversation with you."

He slammed his hand on the table and sat up straight. "You need to stop, just stop, nagging me about my prayers. You know we can't have people knowing I'm a... a... a Muslim." He shook his head. "What if, just what if the wait staff had been in here. It would end up all over national television. You need to be more careful. We have a code, remember?"

Chell raised a brow, and spoke softer than she had. "You're right. I'm sorry."

"Alright. Let's just, enjoy each other's company. And we can say our prayers after the table's been cleared."

Chell nodded.

He pushed away from the table and rebuttoned his jacket. "I might still have Joel come by here later." Without waiting for a response, he pushed away from the table left the room.

He made his way through the winding corridors to his room. He was upset with Chell. She didn't mean any harm, but golly, that woman sure could wear a man's nerves down. But she was a firecracker between the sheets. He groaned and his gigantic cock started to swell.

In his room, he pulled out his prayer rug. He laid it out on the ground, and kneeled, facing the proper direction.

He said his chants, and did his bows. Over and over. He needed to pray to Allah and beg his forgiveness. It is against his

202

religious laws to speak to his wife with a mean heart. Especially when she'd done nothing wo warrant it.

When he'd finished praying, and felt a little bit better, he folded his prayer rug and tucked it carefully behind the dresser. It would not be good if the house keeper found it while performing their duties.

Brock Obanger stripped naked and flexed. Clothes were so confining. He admired himself in the mirror. His gut was starting to hang, and Chell would verbally chastise him if she knew he'd skipped the gym this week. She was crazy about health and fitness.

He sucked in his gut, and put his hands on his hips. "You have the biggest cock," he told his reflection. He thrust his hips for good measure, and watched his cock swing with the motion.

He lay on his massive bed— the biggest, most comfortable bed in the world, —and spread his legs. Cell would be here soon, and he wanted to be ready for her. He lay spread eagled, and slowly began rubbing his limp dick.

His fingers moved furiously across the screen as he typed in his favorite porn website using the nifty incognito browser on his phone. He started watching a video of gay men, but wasn't enjoying it. Obanger browsed the selection of videos before settling on one.

The video was a big breasted woman, easily triple D tits, who was sitting on her knees. The black man holding the camera had a big hard cock, but it wasn't as big as Obanger's cock.

He watched, the cock in his hand slowly coming to life, as the man slapped the woman in the face with his cock. She sucked him, but then he sat down, and she started rubbing her giant tits over his cock, and Obanger watched, enthralled, as the cock slid into her cleavage and he titty fucked her. The guy came, and Brock felt tingles in his own balls.

Chell came in the room. She looked good in her pale green, fitted, floor length dress. He squinted at her and rose from the bed. "Remind me tomorrow to work on the executive order that would call for martial law. I'm not ready to give up my throne just yet."

"My husband," she said, her voice husky. She ran her hands up his chest. "I will take care of you." She smiled at him.

He sat on the edge of the bed, and spread his legs. His dick looked so gigantic and massive right now. He beckoned her to come forward, and she did as she was told.

Chell got on her knees in front of him. She lowered her mouth to his limp dick, and he leaned back on the bed. He rested on one hand, and held her head down with the other.

He could feel blood flowing to his cock. Her mouth could work wonders. Small miracles even. His cock filled her mouth, and he shoved her head down, making sure she took in as much as possible.

She reached up and fondled his balls while she sucked, and he groaned. His cock was so hard he thought it might explode. He tilted his hips, and pushed on her head, as he fucked her mouth, her spit soaking his cock and balls, as she deep throated him. A moment later, he came. He shuddered as he rammed his cock into the back of her throat. He wanted her to swallow on his cum.

As soon as he was finished, he took his hand off the back of her head and she pulled off his cock. She was panting, and smiled at him, then licked a drop of cum off her lip while looking at him.

She stood, and put her hands behind her to take off her dress.

He stopped her. "Don't bother right now. I'm done. I want to sleep. I have meetings tomorrow." He stood, grabbed a towel from the side of the bed, and cleaned himself off before laying down to sleep.

She still stood at the foot of the bed.

He rolled his eyes. "Go visit Bite'm or something. Hell, go visit Killary Clit for all I care. But go away. I'm tired."

"Fine!" She turned from him and left the room as he drifted peacefully into sleep, with thoughts of being the ruler of all for now and all eternity.

Chapter Three:

B rock Obanger stood on a balcony overlooking the white house's rear lawn. A crowd had gathered. The crowd was so large, they spilled out into the streets and covered the entire area within a mile of his house. They were chanting his name, and he waved. He felt benevolent.

"King Obanger! King Obanger! King Obanger!" They chanted, over and over.

Someone handed him a large, heavy book and disappeared. The cover was blue, and it was bound with thin metal bolts. It had *How To Rule the World and Convert Everyone To Islam* written in fancy gold letters on the front. This book would have all the answers.

He opened it to the first page, but the words swam in front of his face, making them hard to decipher. The crowd below grew impatient, and clouds rolled in overhead.

He frantically thumbed through the pages, desperate to find one that was legible. He looked up as he reached the final page. It was blank. The crowd had stopped chanting, and all looked like his father, with scowls of disappointed on their faces.

The crowd rushed his balcony and climbed up, making a human ladder to reach him. He backed away from the edge, and threw the book into the crowd. He needed more time! He backed into something, stopped, and turned slowly around, afraid of what he would see.

It was his hero, the grand prophet Muhammed! His hero wrapped Brock in his arms.

Muhammed had pulled him to safety when he woke up, alone in his bed. Sweat had beaded on his neck and chest, and his sheets were damp.

Cursing, he climbed from bed. "Well, well." He shook his head. "This just, no, this just won't do. No, it won't do at all."

The red numbers on his clock radio illuminated the dark room. Six am. He sighed. Every damn morning.

He pulled his sheets back so they could air dry, and sat naked in the chair by his closet while he scrolled his wiretap recordings. He laughed, and heard the distinct sound of popcorn being made. He would have to tell Killary to move the recording devices to someone other than the microwave.

Obanger had ordered his service agents to wiretap Rump when Rump had announced his bid for presidency. He needed to make sure Killary didn't win. And if that meant making sure Rump didn't say anything that would drive away or alienate the important voters. Of course, even if he did, the delegates would make sure he won the primaries. But that was only if he couldn't get a martial law executive order signed, thereby truly becoming the king.

Obanger smiled to himself, and listened as Rump had sex with an intern. From the sound of it, they were having their bang fest on the copier machine. His alarm went off a moment later, and Brock shut off the recordings. He'd have to check them later. Right now he needed to get ready for work.

Chapter Four:

Brock Obanger made his way to Joel Bite'm's room. Chell and Joel were on the bed. Killary stood in the corner, and was adjusting the straps of her strap on.

He quickly backed away and shut the door, shaking his head. Why didn't they call him to join?

He wandered off, contemplating the possible ways he could use what he'd seen to his advantage. He pulled out his phone and dialed up his hero, and now good friend, Osama Bin Laden.

"Hallo," the voice answered, his accent heavy.

"Hi, Laden!"

"You do not to call me dat. You call me only Osama."

"Sorry."

"Good boy. Now, vut do ju want. I am a very busy man."

"Want to come back to life now? We faked your death really well, but I'm not any closer to making my stay in the white house permanent. I could use someone like you."

Bin Laden laughed. "Not any way possible no. You have not given me everything I want. But I may to allow you to come to my country and enjoy all the virgins you want."

"But I am faithful to Allah! Why won't you just do me this favor and I'll owe you one."

"Do not be calling me again. I am busy man. Maybe ju should be busy to, yes? You have country to fix. We agree you are to be dictator and benevolent ruler of all, and I will get my Muslim laws passed."

"But only if I can keep my money, and having sex."

"Yes, of course. You will be chosen by God, the mighty Allah."

"Okay! 'Bye!" He disconnected the call with renewed determination in his step as he made his way to his next meeting. He was going to make the people love him, no matter what it took.

"Obanger!"

Ronald turned to see Bite'm rushing after him. Crap. Why wasn't he with Chell and Killary still.

"I saw you pop in. Come back. Me and Killary are fucking Chell. She's got a tight asshole. But I want yours."

Brock Obanger half turned away, pointing back the way he'd been going. "I have meetings."

Bite'm shrugged, but there was a fire in his eyes. "You can be late. You're the President! You can do whatever you want!"

"Okay." Brock didn't need any more convincing. He followed Bite'm back the way they'd come.

Killary snapped a belt when he walked in, and Bite'm closed the door.

"Bend over." Brock ordered Bite'm.

"No. I want Chell between us this time."

Brock thought about that a moment then nodded his agreement. "Okay."

Killary laughed, and Chell sneered, but she got on all fours in the middle of the bed, facing Killary Clit's clit, covered by the strap on.

Obanger and Bite'm climbed onto the bed together. Brock smacked Joel's dick when he tried to put it in Chell's ass.

"Only I get to do that when I'm here."

208

Bite'm hung his head, but moved his dick down an inch to her pussy.

Brock slapped Chell's ass, and watched the wave that rippled across her butt cheek as he stroked his enormous cock. It was so massive and huge.

He watched as Killary put the strap on dildo in Chell's mouth. Chell was moaning, and pinched her nipples with one hand.

"Wait. Killary, I want you in the middle."

Killary scowled.

"Don't make my spank you, whore," Brock said.

"Do it," she shot back.

Chell got up, and slapped Killary, hard enough her head snapped back.

Killary glared, but got on all fours, taking Chell's place.

Chell got in front of Killary, and spread her pussy lips apart. "Lick it, you washed up old hag."

Killary wanted to argue, but did as she was told.

Bite'm lay on his back. "Ride me, you cunt."

Killary looked to Chell, who nodded. With a sigh, Killary climbed onto Joel's hard cock, but leaned forward to rest on her hands.

Chell sat on Joel's face, and Killary leaned down to lick her click while Bite'm licked Chell's asshold.

"Yee haw!" Brock shouted, wiggling his hips in a circular motion. "Prepare your anus!" He pulled his cock back, and adjusted it. Once he'd positioned himself over her asshole, he grabbed Killary's shoulders with both hands and pulled, driving his cock into her as hard as he could without any lube.

Chell was grinding her hips, holding the back of Killary's head to her clit.

"Yeah, I said yes, Chell." He grinned at his wife, with Bite'm and Killary between them.

She smiled back. "I want them to make me cum, baby."

"I'm going to, I said, I'm going to cum in Killary's ass, and cum so hard it shoots past her rectum, into her small intestine."

Chell moaned. "Why don't you fuck her pussy this time."

"Because this bitch's pussy is looser than a mom giving birth. Willy done fucked her shit up good. And I don't want my cock next to Joel's. Not today."

Chell went to nod, but threw her head back instead, her hand holding a fistful of Killary's hair and keeping her from pulling away.

I was so sexy, seeing his wife cum. Obanger couldn't hold back anymore. He pounded into Killary, as hard as he could, and dumped his load into her ass.

Obanger pulled his cock from Killary's ass and Chell let her head go.

"God, damn it. I hate how fucking good you all feel inside me. But I didn't cum yet."

Brock grabbed a wet wipe from the night stand and cleaned himself off.

"Fine." He stroked his cock until it was sort of hard. It was still bigger than Joel's cock. He used his fingers to shove the tip in her dripping pussy.

His cock came all the way hard as it rubbed inside Killary and against Bite'm.

Joel started twitching and Brock felt his hot cum filling up Killary. Brock released another load, his cum shooting deep inside.

Killary moaned, and brock thought he might be feeling her pussy clenching on his cock in orgasm.

Bite'm and Obanger pulled out of Killary, and she collapsed onto her side, twitching and shuddering, her eyes closed.

Obanger cleaned himself off again, and Bite'm did the same. "Chell," Obanger said, zipping his pants back up. "Call housekeeping. Get this bitch out of here."

Chapter Five:

Obanger was upset. He'd missed his morning prayer! He'd gone to a meeting and was back in his room with a towel wrapped around his waist. He had pulled out his prayer rug to say his midday prayers. He kneeled and began chanting and bowing.

Bite'm burst through his bedroom door. He was panting and out of breath. "Get dressed."

Brock was outraged. He was the President! "Get out!" He pointed a finger back at the door.

"There's no time. Get dressed."

Brock put his hands on his hips. "You can't order me around. I will fuck your ass without lube next time if you keep this up."

Bite'm gasped. "How could you!"

Brock glared.

"Whatever. Get dressed! There's no time! Chell's dead!"

Obanger's hands fell to his side. "What? When? How?"

Bite'm was rooting around in the dresser, and pulled out an undershirt and boxers. He held up a two-foot-long, double sided, pink dildo that was easily four inches across and looked at it thoughtfully before putting it back in the drawer. He threw the clothes at Brock Obanger.

Brock caught them and dressed.

"I don't know." Bite'm pulled a suit from the closet and tossed it onto the bed. "Secret service found her after we'd left, and they said she'd been having sex with multiple partners when she died."

Brock gasped, pulling his pants on. "That whore!"

"I know." Bite'm closed the closet door. "Can you image the scandal if this gets out?"

Brock quickly dressed and followed Bite'm to the state room, where most of the secret service had already gathered.

"Gentlemen." Rod Boner stood at the head of the table.

Tony Hotdog stood next to him. "Take a seat."

Obanger and Bite'm exchanged a glance, but took their seats.

"This is a big mess," Killary said, taking a seat.

Rod took a seat as well. "Huge. Massive. We need to keep this information locked down."

Brock nodded and tried to look interested. He needed to call Osama Bin Laden again.

Bite'm hit the table with his fist. "How could this happen? She was a good, Christian woman! And for her to be found like that is a travesty. Think about what it would do to her family if they found out. To our President!" He shook his head sadly.

Brock was proud of Bite'm. He was spouting falsities as if they were truths. And, as everyone knew, if you say it enough times it *becomes* the truth. If he can keep this up, they might get to keep the white house after all.

He reached a hand under the table, stroking his cock through his trousers.

"What are you doing?!" Rod was staring at him.

"Nothing." Obanger put his hand back on top of the table.

"I swear to god," Killary began, shaking a finger at him angrily.

"What? It's nothing. How are we going to keep this under wraps and hidden? We need to do something to fix this. I think you need to pay the coroner to fake the autopsy. Use cash. Then we can kill the coroner, take the cash. Win-win."

Everyone in the room was staring at him. He knew he was the smartest, and preened. They never would have thought to lie on official documents. Good thing he was here.

Killary shook her head. "You fucking moron."

"Don't speak to our President like that!" said one of the secret service members.

"Oh yeah? Or what." Killary stood, and leaned across the table.

The secret serviceman undid his belt and unzipped his pants. They dropped to his knees and he stroked his huge cock.

The other secret service members stood as well, all of them dropped their pants and pulled out their cocks.

Even Rod and Tony dropped their pants. Tony's cock looked just like it did in the email's he got in trouble for sending. Idiot. He got caught. Rod's cock was smaller than Brocks.

Killary, flustered, pulled off her pantsuit, revealing the dominatrix harness she wore at all times. She climbed on the table and lay on her back.

Obanger didn't want to be left out. He dropped his pants and stroked his cock. He thought of Chell. At least her last moments were pleasure filled. He'd seen the way she was twitching and shuddering. Hell, even Killary had gotten an orgasm.

His cock grew even bigger in his hands as he stared at the cocks around the table. Soon, everyone had clenched their thighs, and thrust their hips forward. Bite'm did the same. Brock felt it. A familiar tingle that started in his balls.

They all came, covering Killary with their cum. The smell of sex filled the air, and Brock Obanger wrinkled his nose. He didn't like the smell of sex unless it was his.

Everyone collapsed into their seats, spent.

"What were you saying?" Tony broke the silence first.

Everyone looked around the table, but no one could remember why they were there.

"Whatever." Brock scowled. "We'll take a break. Let someone clean this mess up. We'll meet back here in an hour."

Nods of agreement circled the table. Obanger stood, and his stomach growled. He needed to smoke a bowl, then find something to eat.

Chapter Six:

Back in the meeting room, Killary was standing in a corner. There were weird patches of skin, and Obanger realized they were spots of dried cum. Nasty woman. Bite'm perched on the edge of a chair.

"Now, pay attention." Brock Obanger stood, making sure he had everyone's attention. "I am to become King, and this could be the chance we need. If we can label Chell's death an act of terrorism within the white house, we can stir plenty of fear and terror. The people will be convinced martial law is the only answer."

Nods of agreement circled the table.

"Wait a minute." It was Mick Fuckabee. "What if I don't want you as king."

"Then I'll kill you now, you bitch. In Kenya, we had a way of dealing with softies. And it involved sacrificing them."

Mick Fuckabee looked chastised, and didn't mention it again.

"Anyone else?" Brock looked around the table. There was a thoughtful look on Killary's face. "Killary? Tell me what you're thinking."

"How good your cum tastes. Now Chell is gone, I want to be the one sucking your cock."

"Only if I get to fuck both you and your husband."

"That can be arranged," she said slyly.

At that moment, the earth shook. Everyone stood, arms out to keep their balance. It was like an earthquake, but worse.

The doorframe cracked, and bent in the center before shattering into a million pieces. Everyone turned and looked at the gaping hole in the wall where the door had been.

There stood a majestic white unicorn, with a sharp horn. And on its back was none other than…

"Berdie Sander!" They all spoke together.

Berdie's hair was sticking out at odd angles, and his glasses had fallen low on his nose. He rode without a saddle, and gripped the unicorn's mane with both hands.

"That's right." Berdie spoke with a firm voice, heavy with an old Boston accent. "I'm here to drain your swamp!"

As if on que, everyone in the room wet their pants, the wet stain spreading on their pants.

"And now—" he ducked under the wall as his unicorn carried him into the room "—it's time to get rid of the swamp monsters!"

The unicorn reared back, and crushed one of the secret service members under its hooves. Others pulled their side arms, and fired at Berdie and the unicorn. But it was no use. The bullets bounced off an invisible forcefield.

The unicorn swiped its head to the side, and cut three of the secret service members in half before impaling Boner and Weiner like a human shish kabob.

Brock backed away, stopping when his back hit the far wall. Where is his hero now? Where is Osama to rescue him this time.

Bite'm tried to duck under the unicorn and escape, but he was too slow. The unicorn's horn caught him in the ass.

Bite'm grabbed his injured rear, and howled in pain.

But the unicorn didn't care. It backed up a step, and impaled him on its now-bloody horn. The unicorn looked at Brock, the sun glinting off its horn, the blood a dark red against the white pearlescent horn.

Brock clutched his throat. The prophet Muhammad or the great Osama Bin Laden would appear at any moment, and rescue him. This had to be a dream. He was going to wake up any minute now!

The unicorn pawed the ground with its hoof, and spread the blood around. It dropped its head, and charged.

Brock was impaled through the heart, and pinned to the wall.

"Come on, boy." Berdie patted the unicorn on the neck. "We have more social injustice and inequality to combat."

Berdie rode off on his unicorn into the sunset, in search of truth, justice, and the American way.

The End.

A Pervy Poltergeist: Part One

By Lonely Woman

Prologue:

Lisa glanced at the clock on the night stand. Two am. Her body shuddered, and she closed her eyes. Like clockwork, her ghostly visitor was here. She grabbed the top of her pillow, and threw her head back as far as it would go. Goosebumps formed on her arms, and her nipples tightened with her arousal. She kicked her blankets off with her foot.

"Oh god, don't stop," she moaned.

The cold tongue on her clit made her shiver. It felt amazing against the heat as the blood rushed to her most sensitive parts.

Her toes curled as her body climaxed. By the time she'd come down from the peak, her ghostly visitor was gone. The cold that signified his presence was nothing more than a memory. She pulled her blankets back up and curled onto her side. With a sigh, she drifted back into sleep.

Chapter One:

Lisa wrung the excess water from her long blonde hair, and climbed from the shower. She had been sleeping better than she'd thought possible since she moved into the old house on Sycamore Street. At twenty-three, she was doing well for herself. She was a graphic designer for a publishing company and made more in a month than her parents made in a year.

She dressed wandered to the kitchen. It was her weekend, and that meant sweats, a baggy shirt, and socks. No bra! Today she planned to eat popcorn and watch chick flicks all day. The microwave was over the stove, and she tossed in a bag, listing to the pops with satisfaction.

In the living room, she turned on the TV and put in the first movie for the day.

The movie ended, and the credits had started to roll when the power flickered throughout the house. She groaned. There was no wind, and no storm. She stomped to the circuit breaker in the kitchen, and flipped the master switches off and back on. It didn't work. She pulled her cell phone from the charger on the kitchen counter and rang the power company.

"How may I help today?" A woman answered the phone.

"I have no power. I flipped the power off and back on but there's still nothing."

"May I have the service address?"

Lisa rattled off the address and the woman on the other end put the information into her computer.

"I am not showing any outages in your area."

"Then why don't I have power."

"One moment."

Cheesy elevator music played through the phone while Lisa waited on hold. She tapped her foot impatiently and glanced at the clock on the stove. It was almost five minutes before the woman came back on the line.

"Ma'am. Are you still there?"

Lisa took the phone off speaker. "Yeah."

"Our system shows the service address provided has power currently. If you are experiencing an outage, you need to call an electrician." The woman's nasal voice annoyed Lisa.

"Fine." Lisa ended the call without waiting to hear what else the woman had to say. She closed her eyes and counted to ten. She might make more than everyone she knew, but she spent more than everyone keeping her house repaired.

She opened her eyes and Googled local electricians. She loved her old house, it had been built in the 1700s and had a history Lisa enjoyed learning about. But the cost of repairs really added up. She'd looked into making the property a historical site, but her home didn't qualify yet. She needed to finish making repairs and restorations before the historical society would consider her request.

Over the summer, she'd had to completely replace the plumbing. It had cost a pretty penny, but had been worth it. The plumbing company had been amazing, and even installed the new water heater for no additional cost.

She dialed the number for the electrician and waited on hold. She recounted her problem several times before being transferred to the appropriate department. When she felt a draft, she quickly scheduled the appointment for an hour from now and hung up. Her ghostly roommate was here!

She stood motionless, not wanting to scare it away. But the draft had disappeared. Maybe it had been just a draft. The windows weren't open, but only half had been replaced. The electrician would be here in an hour. And if her ghostly partner wasn't going to join, she would take care of herself.

She reached a hand down and closed her eyes, feeling the slick wetness on her fingers. She shuddered when the tip of her finger brushed her clit directly. She spread her legs slightly, and rolled her head backward. Rubbing and teasing her clit, spreading her juices all over. Her other hand grabbed her breast, and she squeezed gently, brushing her thumb over her nipple.

Her mouth opened and her breathing quickened. Pinching a nipple between her thumb and forefinger, she rolled it around. Applying direct pressure to her clit, she brought herself to climax. Her legs twitched and her knees tried to buckle. She gripped the carpet with her toes and reached an arm out to brace herself against the wall. She slowed her motions, and brought herself down from her orgasm, rubbing around her clit, and sliding a finger inside.

With a sigh, she was done. She pulled her hand up and licked her fingers. She loved the way she tasted. Opening her eyes, she pulled her clothes back on. The electricians would be here soon. They would just have deal with her at-home clothes.

Chapter Two:

The doorbell rang just as she'd lit the last candle. The sun was setting, and she didn't want to sit in complete darkness. Whoever was at the door started knocking. She rushed to answer it.

She pulled open the heavy door. "Hi."

"You called an electrician?" The man was brawny, with wide shoulders, and just enough of a gut to make him look cuddly without being fat.

She unlocked the screen and pushed it open. "Yes, come in."

He removed his work hat with the company logo emblazoned on the front, and stepped inside. "Power's out?"

"Yeah." She led the way to the electrical box in the kitchen. "The power company said I needed to call an electrician. Thank you for coming so quickly." She bit the inside of her cheek to keep from smiling at her little joke. If she had her way, he would be coming later, too.

She opened the box, but not *her* box. "I tried turning it all off and back on again. Didn't work."

He used the flashlight that had been hanging from his waist to peek inside. "Mind if I remove the panel?"

"Not at all." She stepped out of his way and watched him work. He was well over six feet tall, and she like the way his ass moved in his work jeans.

"Your wires are shot."

"Crap. What's that gonna cost me?" She did some mental calculations to see if she could afford to rewire the house now rather than next summer, as she'd planned.

He closed the panel and turned to her. "If the rest of the wiring is as jacked up as the breaker box, you'll be better off paying to rewire the entire house."

"Okay, but what's that gonna cost?"

He picked up the work bag he'd dropped near his feet and pulled out a folder with papers in it. "How big is the house?" He clicked the pen open, and scribbled some notes at the top.

"Thirty-five-hundred square feet."

He wrote the number in a box. "Bedrooms?"

"Yes."

He looked up at her. "I mean, how many?"

"Oh!" She pulled her mind back from the gutter where it'd fallen while she watched him write. "Seven bedrooms. Three bathrooms. I'd say two outlets in each room. If I'm getting it rewired though, I want a bigger breaker box, and more outlets per room."

He scribbled another note and pulled out a calculate. He punched a few keys, scribbled some more, and entered some more numbers. At length, he held the calculator up for her to see.

"That's it? Did you add the cost to upgrade the box itself and add outlets?"

"Yep."

She shrugged, and tucked a strand of her blonde hair behind her ear. "Okay. When can you get started, and how long will it take? You're the one doing the work, right?"

He seemed taken aback, but pulled out a few more forms and handed them to her.

"These are to apply for credit. I want to pay for it upfront."

225

He gaped a moment, but put the forms away and pulled out several more.

She filled in the appropriate information and handed them back.

"I'll call this in. We can get started tomorrow." He picked up his bag to go into the living room.

"Wait." She reached out and put a hand on his shoulder as he passed.

He turned toward her, brow raised.

She smiled at him, and bit her lip. Then reached down to grip the hem of her shirt and pull it off over her head. Her nipples immediately hardened in the cool air, no longer warmed by her shirt.

His mouth fell open.

She took a step toward him, and hooked a thumb in the waistband of her sweats, pulling them down enough to expose the soft rounded part of her belly just above her pelvis.

His eyes followed her hands, his mouth still open. His bag fell from his limp hand, landing ignored at his feet.

She pushed her pants to rest low on her hips, and left one thumb hooked, but brought the other to her breast. She cupped her tit, and gave it a gently squeeze.

He swallowed hard, and slowly raised her eyes to her face. "I cant..." he cleared his throat. "I can't change the prices."

She finished closing the gap between them, and drapped an arm around his neck, running her hands through his hair. Leaning close, she whispered in his ear, "I don't want a discount." She nipped his earlobe. "I want you."

He brought his hands up and nudged her backwards.

She took the step back and pushed her pants the rest of the way off her hips, then stepped out of them, then backed up until her butt was on the edge of the kitchen counter. She reached a hand down, and slid a finger between her pussy lips. She was still wet from earlier. She poked her lower lip in a pout. "Don't you want me?"

"Oh yeah." He took a step toward her, then stopped and shook his head.

He was going to need a little more convincing, she realized. She pushed off the counter, and stepped back toward him.

He took a step back.

She reached out, and started undoing his work belt. He swallowed, but didn't stop her. That was enough encouragement. She unbuttoned his pants, and reached in. She stroked his cock, already hard, and put a hand behind his neck. Still stroking him, slowly but with a firm grip, she pulled his ear with her lips, then trailed kisses along his neck and jaw.

He let out a sigh and closed his eyes.

She led his hand to her breast. He took her direction and teased her nipples.

"Mmm." She moaned. His large hands cupped her full breast, and she pushed into him slightly.

He put a hand at the small of her back and pulled her closer. Her hand on his cock had to stop. He bit her neck, and she let out a yelp of pleasure. She hadn't expected that!

She pulled his shirt off and ran her hands on his chest and belly, curling her fingers in the hair that lead to his cock. He groaned. She pushed his pants down, bending over to get them all the way to his ankles.

She looked up at him, and he was watching her. She closed her eyes and licked his cock, the sucked on each of his balls. Then took him into her mouth. He put his hand on the back of her head, winding his fingers into her hair. She stroked her clit, feeling little waves of pleasure shooting through. She was getting close. She sucked harder, and circled her tongue around the tip of his cock.

He tugged her hair, pulling her off, and spun her around, bending her over the kitchen counter. His cock pushed into her ass cheeks as he reached around, grabbing her tits, and pinching her nipples. He moved a hand down, sliding it along the inside of her pussy lips, and she twitched when he hit her clit. He brought his wet finger to her mouth and she sucked his finger. He groaned. She pulled a condom from the drawer in the kitchen and tore it open, then handed it to him.

He rolled it on, spread her pussy with his fingers. He spread her juices to her asshole, and slid a finger inside her ass before slamming his cock into her tight pussy. She cried out, and he slammed into her a second time, making her cum. Her pussy clenched around his cock as it slid in and out, over and over, hitting deep while he fingered her ass. She came a second time, before the first orgasm ended. He gripped her hips, and pulled her deeper onto his cock, and he grunted as he came. When he'd finished, he slapped her ass.

"Thanks." He pulled his cock out slowly and she twitched with pleasure.

She pushed against the counter, slowly getting back to her feet. She turned and saw him toss the used condom into the trash before grabbing a paper towel and cleaning his cock off.

She grinned at him and pulled her sweats and shirt back on. "Next time? I'll clean your cock off." She winked and sauntered out of the kitchen.

Chapter Three:

The fee for the electrical work had already left her bank account, and the electrician— she really should get his name if she was going to keep fucking him —would be back in the morning to start rewiring the house. For now, she would have to live without electricity. He rigged it enough to power her water heater and the kitchen. But he said if he added anything else to that list, it could catch fire. At least she could bathe.

It was almost two am, and nightly visitor would be there soon, to pleasure her more than she'd ever pleased herself. She shivered in anticipation, wondering what new sensations her visitor would bring this night. The time clicked over to two am, and the cool air of her visitor began moving up her legs, under the covers. Though it wasn't necessary, she bent her knees, opening herself.

She felt the icy kiss of her visitor on her inner thighs, teasing her. Her nipples hardened, and she cupped her breasts. Her belly contracted and her pussy tensed. She kicked off the blankets, her skin warming as her heart beat faster despite the icy chill.

The icy air moved up her body, leaving goosebumps in its wake. She shivered, with both the chill and the sensation. The nightstand wobbled on its legs. She smiled, and opened the drawer. She waited. It didn't take long. The pink sparkle vibrator with the special g-spot stimulator rolled once. She smiled again. That was her favorite one. She pulled it out of the drawer and turned it on.

She got to her hands and knees, and felt the icy air move along her back, sliding between her ass cheeks before moving to her pussy. She slid her fingers inside, enjoying the contrast between her icy visitor and her warm insides. She replaced her fingers with her vibe and closed her eyes.

The vibe turned on to a low setting, and began sliding in and out, slowly, teasing her. Taunting her with the orgasm that was building. It started sliding faster, rubbing her g-spot, and her leg twitched with each pass. She was getting closer. She rubbed her clit, rocking her hips.

"I'm so close," she moaned. She grabbed the pillow, putting it under her breasts, letting the sway of her nipples brush against the fabric. Pleasure warmed her skin. "Harder," she begged, not knowing if her invisible partner would listen. The vibe turned up a notch in speed, and slammed against the back of her pussy. "Oh God," she cried out.

She collapsed face first into the pillow, her ass in the air, as the last tremors passed. The icy air skimmed to her asshole, exploring. "Mmm," she moaned, not ready for another orgasm yet. She pushed the vibe from her pussy, and tried to catch her breath. Her heart was still racing, and her pussy was throbbing from her climax.

The icy air dissipated, and she knew tonight's visit was over. She put her vibe on top of the nightstand. She could clean it tomorrow. For tonight, she needed sleep. She was spent.

Chapter Four:

In the morning, she took a shower and cleaned her toy from the night before. She smiled. This house was the best investment she could have purchased. But if the electricians were going to need a week to rewire the house, she wanted to be around for all of it. Sure, she could ask someone else. But the thought of the electrician's cock was enough to make her wet. She had already talked to her boss and gotten permission to work from home for a month if necessary.

She dressed in her at-home clothes again. Her work week wasn't due to start until tomorrow. She might not be able to watch cheesy movies, but there were other things she could do. She grinned at the thought. If she got her way, she would make sure her electrician collected plenty of overtime pay.

In the kitchen, she heated water on the stove for her morning tea. She loved a good English breakfast tea with her morning yogurt and granola. When the kettle whistled, she made her tea. It was piping hot, so she ate her breakfast first. Scrolling social media and news sites, she sipped her tea. This was the life.

The doorbell rang, and she set her now-empty tea cup in the sink. That should be the electrician. She opened the door and was surprised to see her cuddly electrician wasn't alone. He was with a younger, shorter man. He was lanky, with black hair and the ruddy complexion of a teenager who was still dealing with hormones.

She stepped to the side. "Come on in."

They stepped in. Her electrician cleared his throat and ran his hand through his hair. "This is Damien. He's my apprentice. Hope you don't mind."

Lisa raised an eyebrow. "Did you tell him what all this job... requires?"

Her electrician cleared his throat again, and ran a finger along the inside of his collar. "Um, no. Um. I just briefed him on what we'd be doing."

Lisa suppressed a smile, and stuck out a hand. "Sorry. I'm Lisa. I didn't catch your name last night."

His hand was clammy. "Bill, ma'am."

"Please," she said, "call me Lisa." She grinned, seeing his discomfort. "Can I get you boys anything? Water? Tea?"

"No, thanks." Bill said. "We should be here for about ten or eleven hours today."

She waved a hand dismissively. "No problem. I already made arrangements to be here all day. You have an hour lunch, right?"

Damien nodded.

"Go ahead and get set up. Do whatever it is you need. Don't mind me." She plopped down on the couch.

She watched as Damien and Bill hauled in ladders, tools, and equipment she didn't recognize into the house. The Damien boy was young, but he had some real potential. She smiled to herself, wondering if she would get to be the one who took his innocence.

Damien shut the front door, and the two electricians made their way into the kitchen to begin working.

Lisa followed. "How old are you, Damien?"

"Eighteen."

"Still in school?"

232

"I graduated last spring." He blushed, clearly uncomfortable with the attention.

She nodded and backed away. She didn't want to scare the poor boy away just yet. She went back to the couch, and opened her library app on her phone. There were some books she'd been wanting to read. Now was as good a time as any to read them.

Hours later, Bill came into the living room and cleared his throat.

Lisa looked up from her ebook. "Yes?"

"It's time for us to take our lunch ma'am." His face was red, and he was sweating slightly.

Lisa smiled at him and stood, stepping close to him.

He took a step back.

"And what's on the menu today?"

"Erm," he stammered.

She leaned in, and whispered in his ear, making eye contact with Damien who'd just come out of the kitchen. "Would you like to eat me?" She reached down and grabbed his cock through his pants, the jean material preventing her from doing more. He was already halfway hard. She nipped his earlobe, without taking her eyes off Damien, and watched the boy's eyes widen.

As if she hadn't done anything, she sauntered over to Damien and draped an arm over his shoulder. "Did you bring a lunch?"

"N…no…no ma'am." He stuttered.

She leaned in close as she had to Bill, and whispered, "Would you like to eat me?"

Damien looked over at his boss, who shrugged, as if to say "Why not?"

Taking their silence as acceptance, she pulled her shirt off over her head, and ran her hands over her tits, waist and stomach. Her nipples hardened with excitement. Damien's mouth dropped open, but Bill was taking off his belt.

Lisa grabbed the waist of Bill's pants, and pulled him closer to Damien. Both had their eyes on her perky tits as they bounced with each step. "Come to the bedroom boys. This might take a while." She led the way to the bedroom without checking to see if they followed.

In the room, she sat on the edge of the bed, leaning back on her hands. She watched as Damien came in first, kicking his shoes off and pulling his shirt off over his head as he walked. Bill followed, but didn't disrobe until he had shut the bedroom door behind him.

She scooted further up the bed, and patted next to her.

Damien pulled his pants off his legs, and climbed onto the bed next to her. His cock was hard, and she could see the precum on the tip. She grabbed the back of his neck, pulling him close, and nibbled on his ear.

He fumbled to grab her tit, and she winced. "Gently, Damien," she whispered in his ear. He tried again, this time cupping her tit, and teasing her nipple.

The bed dipped down as Bill climbed on. Bill put her tit in his mouth, nipping and sucking her nipples. She moaned, the pleasure shooting from her breast to her pussy, getting her wet. She guided Damien's hand, using her own hand to show him how to stroke her clit. She was so wet, and Damien was rubbing her clit with the right amount of pressure, making her legs twitch. She lay back, and pushed Damien's head down.

Damien licked her pussy, sucking her clit, and fingering her. She shuddered, and her belly clenched. She moaned, running her fingers through his hair and rocking her hips.

Bill moved to where her head was, his cock one hand, her tit in the other. He straddled her chest and she opened wide, welcoming his hard cock in her mouth as he fucked her face. When she came, it was the most intense orgasm she'd ever had. Damien was teasing her pussy with his mouth and hands, and nipped the inside of her thighs with his teeth. She convulsed, her whole body throbbing and her heart pounding in her chest. She sucked as hard as she could, and felt his cock in the back of her throat. He pulled out, and climbed off the bed as she lay there panting.

Damien and Bill stood on the side of the bed, stroking their cocks, and watching her.

"I want you both inside me," She said, getting onto her hands and knees. "Condoms are in the drawer."

Bill opened the drawer and pulled out two condoms, handing one to Damien.

Once they were wrapped, she got onto her hands and knees, and looked up at them. "Damien, lay down."

He did as he was told, laying flat on his back. She slid up his body, stroking, licking, tasting him, before straddling him.

She looked over her shoulder at Bill. "Come on, big boy. I want you in my ass first."

Bill hurried onto the bed behind her. She leaned over Damien, and he sucked on the tits she'd put in his face. She could feel her pussy getting wetter.

The cold lube hit her ass, and Bill rubbed it around and inside, prepping her. She moaned, and tilted her hips to give him better access. Her pussy was still throbbing from her first orgasm, and she wanted him inside. He slid his cock into her wet pussy first, and she tensed around him. He felt so good.

"Don't pull out yet," she said. Reaching under her, she guided Damien's cock into her pussy as well. She the stretch, and cried out. "Fuck me! Hard!"

They did as she said, both their cocks sliding in and out. Damien lifted his head and bit her nipple, and she came. Oh, god they felt so good. Why had she never had two cocks before!

Bill pulled out, and stopped fingering her ass. She felt the tip of his cock pushing on her asshole and she relaxed. He added more lube, the cold reminding her of her icy visitor. He slid slowly in her ass, and she closed her eyes.

There were so many sensations. Her pussy had Damien's cock, her ass had Bill's cock. All she needed was a cock for her mouth and this moment would be perfect. They began fucking her again, slamming into her at the same time. Bill slapped her ass, and she clenched her pussy and assholes. She rode their cocks, feeling the climax building, getting closer.

She came a third time, her muscles twitching and her toes curling. Her elbows buckled, and she lay on Damien's chest. She heard him groaning as she came, but Bill hadn't cum yet. She lifted herself back up and pushed back against him, clenching her ass on his cock. "Fill me up," she moaned.

He slapped her ass again and gripped her hips, slamming into her. He cried as, his groans filling the room, and came. She rocked her hips, and felt Damien's cock starting to wake up. She leaned down and nipped his neck. "That's all for now," she whispered.

Bill pulled out of her ass, and she climbed off Damien. "You boys ready to get back to work?" She climbed from the bed and made her way to the shower, not bothering to watch them dress.

Chapter Five:

It was the third day of electrical work, and the noise was giving her a headache. The electricians, Bill and Damien, were drilling holes into the walls, and pulling wires. The electric company had been out the day before and upgraded the main line to the house so the box could be upgraded. But her head was killing her.

She closed her laptop, and rubbed her temples. This was getting stupid. A glance at the clocked showed her it was almost time for the workers to take their lunch break. She smiled. The one sure-fire way to get rid of a headache? Sex. She felt her nipples harden at the thought. She'd been working from home, and had dressed in a silk blouse with a knee-length skirt, but she hadn't bothered with a bra. She brushed her hands over her perky nipples, and closed her eyes, feeling the wetness gather in her groin.

She stood, and made her way to the upper rooms where the electricians were working. She leaned against the doorway, watching as they fished a line through the wall to the new outlet they were putting in.

Damien noticed her first. He stood up straight, and she could see his arousal in his jeans.

She licked her lips seductively. "It's lunch time."

Damien dropped his drill and beelined toward her, but Bill didn't move.

"Don't you want to play with me?"

"Yeah, I'll be there in a sec. I gotta clean this up first." He looked at her tits thru her this silk shirt and smiled.

"Ooh, you boys gonna take turns today instead!" She undid the top button of her blouse. "Join us in the room across the hall when you're ready." She turned to Damien, and grabbed the waistband of his jeans, leading him to the room.

Once inside, he quickly took his shoes off and stripped, releasing his cock from his pants. She moaned appreciatively. He stepped toward her, closing the space, and grabbed her tit with one hand, and a hand on her lower back pulling her against him. He leaned forward and nipped her jaw, then trailed kisses and love bites from her jaw, to her ears, then down to her chest. Her back arched, and he undid her buttons, sliding her shirt down to her bent elbows. He flicked a nipple with his tongue and she grabbed the back of his head. The boy was quick learner, and her body was coming awake under his touch.

He pushed her backward, until her back hit the wall, and he hiked her skirt to her waist. He shoved his fingers inside her, groaning at her wetness. She spread her legs apart, and clenched on his fingers. He was knuckle deep, and hitting her g-spot. He took a nipple into his mouth, nipping it when he moved to the other breast, and she moaned out loud.

She reached the edge of climax, and grabbed the back of his head, moving her hips to speed up the pace for maximum enjoyment. Her knees went weak and she trembled, the orgasm clenching her muscles on his fingers, the heat spreading from her groin into her belly and chest. She panted, her pussy throbbing, and pushed him backward.

She kneeled in front of him, watching his face as she fondled his balls, stroking his shaft. She licked the precum from the tip, and he twitched. She took him into her mouth, using her tongue to tease the tip. Her hand wrapped around, grabbing his ass. He put his hands on the back of her head and fucked her face. She stroked her clit, her wetness covering her fingers. She shuddered, and relaxed her throat and mouth, not swallowing the saliva. Her slurps filled the room, and her muscles began to tighten as her climax neared.

Bill walked in, his pants undone and his hard cock hanging out. He stepped next to Damien, and she moved her mouth from one cock to the other, stroking Damien's cock with her hand. She took her hand from her clit, paying attention to both cocks in her face. Bill grabbed the back of her head, locking his fingers in her hair. "Wait your turn, kid," he said, fucking her face and hitting the back of her throat with his cock.

She moaned, before his cock silenced her and she held her breath. Her hips were grinding the air, when she felt a familiar icy presence enter her pussy. She shuddered, and sucked Bill to the back of her throat. His cum shot out and she swallowed every drop, his cock starting to soften. She cleaned it off with her tongue, leaving nothing behind.

Bill left the room, and Damien rubbed the tip of his cock on her lips. She closed her eyes and opened her mouth. His cum shot to the back of her throat as her body shuddered and trembled, the icy visitor making her cum at the same time. She rubbed around her clit, slowly, bringing herself down from the peak, as she sucked the cum off his cock. She sat back on the floor, her muscles giving out on her, and she tossed her head back.

She ran her hands along her chest, belly and legs, loving the feel of her warm, soft skin. She opened an eye to see Damien still standing there. "What? You're done. Don't you need to get back to work?"

He turned red, but left, grabbing his clothes off the floor and shutting the door behind him.

She lay down on the floor, reveling in her post orgasmic relaxation. Goosebumps trailed her body as the icy visitor roamed against her skin before dissipating. She sighed, and sat up, fixing her blouse. She still had work to do, just like she'd told Damien. She stood, and fixed her skirt. Then made her way back downstairs.

The guys were in the kitchen eating their lunch.

"How much longer?" She leaned against the entryway.

Bill looked up. "For what."

She waved a hand to indicate the entire house. "All this. It's giving me a headache."

Bill shrugged and took a bite of his sandwich.

Damien looked between them. "Sir," he said quietly.

"Speak up boy." Bill swallowed his bite.

"We could call in the rest of the team."

"Are you serious?" Bill's mouth dropped open, gaping at Damien.

Damien turned red again, but shut his mouth, and started pushing his food around in its plastic container.

Lisa stood up, and walked the rest of the way into the kitchen. "That is a great idea," she purred, running her fingers down Bills cheek. "Just make sure they want to play with me when you're done working tonight." She winked and sauntered out of the room.

She had work to do, and if she was lucky, a whole crew as well.

To be continued…

A Pervy Poltergeist: Part Two

By: Lonely Woman

Lonely Woman

Chapter One:

Lisa lounged on the sofa, watching as the parade of men came into her house. Bill had come through, and now there were half a dozen men working on her electrics. She'd changed into a bathrobe, her excitement building as she saw the variety of men that had come in. The noise had more than tripled, and her head was throbbing again. She didn't mind if her pussy got to throb, too, at the end of the day.

She curled her toes into the carpet and squeezed her thighs together. She let out an unsteady breath. She'd never dreamed she'd be able to pleasure so many men at the same time. Sure, she'd fantasized about it plenty of times. But her fantasy was finally going to come true.

A tall black man with a shaved head trotted down the stairs. They'd been working all afternoon, and it was almost time for them to finish for the day. She spread her legs on the sofa, her robe opened revealing her upper thighs, and one shoulder of the silk robe hanging down precariously low.

He stopped dead in his tracks when he saw her. His mouth dropped open and he seemed to forget what he'd been doing.

"Yes," she said. She spoke with a husky, sultry voice she knew would start the blood flowing to his cock. She tightened her pussy in anticipation.

"Erm.' He shook his head as if to clear it. "Bill said to tell you we're done for the day." He took a step backward.

She leaned forward, allowing her robe to hang down from her chest, hiding only her nipples. She shivered, the silk material brushing against her taught nipples. "And did Bill tell you what you would be doing after?" she purred.

He put a hand out to brace against the wall of the staircase. He swallowed. "He wasn't joking?"

She shook her head. "Not even a little." She got to her feet, moving like liquid, and undid the tie on her robe. It hung open, revealing her wet pussy, but stopped on her tight nipples. She took slow steps toward him, exaggerating the sway of her hips and the bounce of her tits. Her robe fell open the rest of the way and she shrugged it off.

His eyes roamed her body, and her heart sped up. She was going to have her dream come true! Reaching out, she ran her hands from his belly to his chest, and down his muscular arms. She looked into his eyes, seeing his desire. She reached down and cupped his cock through his pants, feeling it come to life, hardening. She closed the gap between them, and pulled his head down, kissing him deeply, their tongues meeting and sending shivers down her spine.

She pulled back, and licked her lips, then whispered, "Let's get started."

He wrapped his arms around her, his hands exploring her skin, sending shivers of excitement and anticipation through her.

She undid his pants, pulling them down to his ankles, rubbing her tits along his body as she stood back up. His hard cock pushed into her belly, and she took his mouth with hers. Footsteps on the stairs behind her grabbed her attention, and she trailed her mouth to his neck and ear. She locked eyes with the man on the stairs behind them. He'd stopped, as if not believing what he was seeing. She beckoned him with a crooked finger. "Join us."

He descended the rest of the steps unbuttoning his pants.

"Let's get out of the way." She grabbed both of their hands and led them to the center of the living room. The candles flickered, and shadows danced on the walls. "I want you naked," she said, sitting back on the couch.

They exchanged a glance, but quickly did as they were told, abandoning their clothes at the foot of the steps. Side by side, they walked toward her, each holding their cock.

She sat up, and spied another electrician coming down the stairs. She met his eyes, and said, "Strip." Then opened her mouth, and licked the tips of the two cocks in front of her. From the corner of her eye, she could see the new arrival stripping down, and she clenched her tingling pussy. The guy who'd arrived hollered up the stairs for the rest of the guys to come down and get naked. She smiled, and slid off the couch onto the floor.

There were three cocks surrounding her, and she looked up, her pussy dripping onto her foot. She gripped two of the cocks, stroking them, and took the middle cock in her mouth. She rotated which she was sucking and which she was stroking, while grinding her click on her heel. When more than half a dozen cocks fully surrounded her, she sat back on her rear, her knees bent in front of her. She leaned back on her hands, looking up at them. She licked her lips, and slid her fingers into her pussy. She was dripping wet. A well-placed push on her clit was enough to push her over the edge. Her legs twitched, and her head leaned back, riding the waves of pleasure.

She opened her eyes to see the big black cock over her forehead. She stuck out her tongue and licked his balls. Two more cocks were on either side. The rest were near her ankles, watching and stroking their hard members. "Cum on my face," she begged.

She flinched at the waves of hot cum. The sticky heat landed on her face, neck, and chest. She rubbed it in, reveling in the feel of their cum on her skin. The big black cock dropped the biggest load on her face, covering the entire bottom half and filling her mouth. She stuck her tongue out and licked around her lips, eating as much as she could. The three who'd just cum stepped back, and three more replaced them. One straddled her legs, slapping her chin with his cock.

She shuddered and stroked her clit. It wasn't enough. She wanted them inside her, filling her up.

She sat up, and started sucking the cock in front of her, getting onto her hands and knees. Someone slid under her, teasing her taught nipples, the tip of his cock rubbing her clit. She moaned, and tingles shot from her groin to the rest of her. Her belly tightened. She felt the head of a cock between her ass cheeks, spreading her wetness and stroking her.

The man under her slid his cock inside, and another cock joined that one. There must be two men under her, she realized, riding both cocks, careful not to rock her hips too much. She didn't want them to slip out. She sucked the cock in her mouth, praying another cock would fill her ass.

Her prayers were answered, and she stopped riding the two cocks filling her pussy. The cock between her ass cheeks pushed against her tight ass hole. She relaxed, and felt his cock stretching her ass. She sucked harder. She wanted to keep riding the three cocks, but needed to stay still while the one in her ass pushed all the way in.

A hand slapped her ass, and she moaned around the dick in her mouth. Hands twisted her hair back, shoving her face deeper on the cock, and she started moving her hips. The cocks inside her started moving, and she fought to stay still. The hands on the back of her head pushed her further onto the cock in her mouth. She gagged slightly, but didn't let go. His cum hit the back of her throat, and she swallowed, sucking out every last drop.

She felt the icy touch of her nightly visitor on her clit, and the cold was enough to send her over the edge again. She came, her muscles shaking, and pussy and ass clenching on the cocks inside her. She felt hot cum filling her ass, and she threw her head back, screaming aloud. "Give it to me!"

The cocks in her pussy were wrapped in condoms, but she could feel them swelling as they came. She bit the shoulder nearest her mouth, muffling her screams. It felt so amazing. The cock in her ass pulled out, smearing cum on her ass cheeks. She raised her hips, lifting off the cocks in her pussy, panting. She was so satisfied, all she wanted to do was sleep.

She got shakily to her feet, and saw it had been Damien and some guy she didn't recognize in her pussy. Bill had been in her ass. The black guy and two other dudes were off to the side, cleaning up with a pack of baby wipes she'd left on the side table. "Thanks, boys. Next time, I want all of you to come on my tits."

She made her way shakily to the bathroom to clean up. The men could see themselves out.

***

Lisa lay in bed, lazily running her fingers around her clit. She'd had a fantasy come true, and tomorrow she would get to experience her very own bukkake. She wondered if what she'd done could be labeled a gang bang. She turned her head to the side, checking the clock on the nightstand. It was only after two, but her nightly visitor hadn't joined her yet. She was wondering if he'd forgotten.

As if on que, she felt the icy fingers stroking her legs. She spread them wide, and she felt the icy chill brush her clit and move up her body, landing on her nipples, teasing them. She moaned, and felt icy air fill her mouth. She could still breath, but it felt like an invisible cock was in her. She sucked, and stroked her clit, goosebumps covering her skin.

A moment later her mouth was empty, but her ass was full. She gasped, the icy cock surprising her. She rubbed her clit faster. Her ghostly partner stretched her ass wide. She came faster than she'd ever cum before. Her ass twitched from clenching so hard, her pussy dripping and soaking her sheets.

The icy chill dissipated, leaving her alone. She sighed, and pulled up her blankets. Who was her icy visitor, and would she ever see him? Or her? Was it a cock, or a girl ghost's hand? She drifted into sleep, wondering if she would ever find answers.

Chapter Two:

She climbed from her bed, still naked, made her way to the living room. The electrician crew had been there since 8 am, but she'd left the door unlocked. Form the sounds, they'd let themselves in and were hard at work.

It was almost time for their lunch break, and she was looking forward to their attention. She hollered up the stairs. "Come play with me!"

She heard the tools and work noises stop, replaced by the sound of feet rushing to the stairs. She smiled to herself, and sat on her heels in the center of the living room. Tremors of excitement coursed through her body. A finger between her pussy lips confirmed her wetness. She was ready.

The black man made it down the stairs first. His pants were undone, and he had his partly limp cock in his hands. His eyes locked onto her tits, and she cupped one, pinching the hard nipple as she licked her lips.

Three more men came down next, each with their pants undone and their cocks in their hands. She circled her clit with her middle finger, sliding in her wetness. She squeezed her pussy, not wanting to wait.

Soon, the entire crew of electricians surrounded her. She tilted her head back, and hung her tongue out of her mouth, rubbing her clit faster and rocking her hips. It didn't take long until the first hot squirt of cum landed on her chin. She opened her mouth wider, and slid her finger inside her, stroking her g-spot. Her other hand grabbed her tit, teasing the nipple. Hot cum landed on her hand and her tit, and she rubbed it in, moaning. More cum landed, hitting her face, eyes, mouth, and tits. She moaned, riding her own fingers harder, her wetness dripping off her knuckles. She leaned her face to the nearest cock, and licked the cum from the tip. Soon, each cock had been licked, and she began trembling. She came just as the final load landed in her mouth and on her cheeks. She trembled, and quivered, her pussy clenching on her fingers.

Two guys used the tips of their cocks to rub the cum into her face. One stuck he half limp, spent cock into her mouth. She slowed the rhythm of her hips fucking her fingers, and focused on the cock. If he wanted to cum in her mouth, she would help him do it. She cupped his balls, and deep throated his soft cock, sucking as hard as she could. The blood rushed to his dick and it swelled, filling her mouth. She moaned, her mouth full. Hands were pinching and pulling her nipples, and someone stuck a finger in her ass and pussy. She angled her hips, wanting the fingers to go deeper, and stroked the underside of the cock in her mouth with her tongue.

He fucked her face, his hands on the back of her head. Her pussy clenched around the fingers she was riding, and she came, sucking harder as she did so. The waves of pleasure washed over her, and she rode those waves, her skin flushing and her heart pounding in her chest. When she felt the cum start to hit the back of her throat, she swallowed and sucked. Once he had finished, she sucked some cum off his balls, moaning.

Her chest was heaving, and the men had zipped their pants. Most were gone into the kitchen, except Bill, whose cock she'd just cleaned. She looked up into his eyes and wiped a bit of cum from her cheek with her finger, then sucked it off her finger. "Again?"

He sneered, and slapped her mouth with his half limp cock. "I'm gonna fuck your ass later," he murmured. He shoved his cock into his jeans and zipped up.

She shuddered. He wanted to fuck her ass later! She stood, still wobbly from her orgasm, and made her way to her bedroom. She would need to bring out the toys if she wanted to entertain all of them later.

Chapter Three:

She spent the next several hours preparing. She wanted to take turns with every single man in her house. She painstakingly set up the restraint system on the wall of the library. She pulled out her toys, restraints, blindfolds, and gags, laying them out on the desk. When it was almost quitting time, she pulled her silk robe on, tying it loosely, then made her way up the stairs to where they were working.

"Line up," she said from the hall way.

The men came from the various rooms they'd been in and formed a single file line in front of her. "This is the order you may play with me in. I shall in the library, across the hall from the bathroom on the first floor. You—" she pointed to the man in front "—may join me now." She turned and walked down the stairs, knowing he would follow.

In her library, she put her ass on the edge of the desk, and waited for the man to join her. Moments later, he walked in. He had his pants undone and was stroking his cock. He shut the door behind him.

"What do you want to do to me?" she purred.

"Anything?"

She stood and stepped away from the desk, revealing the toys lined up. She walked to the restraint system she'd hooked back up and fingered a leather strap. "Anything."

He stepped toward her, and slid her robe off then turned her to face him. He leaned down and trailed kisses along her neck and chest, sucking on her nipples. "You want to be tied up?"

She grabbed the restraints and hooked her wrist in, the held her other wrist up for him to restrain, which he did. "My ankles, too," she prompted. "Good. Now tighten it. More." Her legs and arms spread until she formed an X.

He walked to the table, and grabbed a red ball gag. He held it to her lips, and she opened wide, biting down on it. She felt her pussy getting wetter, and he went back to the table. She watched him pick up each toy and set it back down, the excitement building as she wondered what he would grab. He finally settled on a thin latex dildo. He brought it toward her. She tried to smile around her gag, but couldn't.

He slapped her tit with the dong then embraced her, biting her neck. He slid the dong along her ass, the pushed it into her asshole. She gasped as she felt her icy visitor join the dildo inside her.

He bent his knees slightly, and bit her shoulder and he rubbed the tip of his cock on her clit. She bit the gag, unable to cry out in pleasure. He aligned the tip of his cock with her pussy, and shoved it in, deep as he could. He held her ass with his hands, squeezing. Her icy visitor held the dildo in her ass. She closed her eyes, her hard nipples rubbing on his shirt. Before she came, he grunted, and swelled inside her, filling his condom with his cum.

Without saying a word, he removed the gag from her mouth and dropped it to the floor. He kissed her, his tongue assaulting hers, and pulled the dildo from her ass slightly before shoving it back in as far as it would go. She moaned. But he didn't finish. He turned and left the room.

She shivered, and her icy visitor began rubbing her clit. She closed her eyes and threw her head back as she started cumming, her wetness dripped to the floor below, her muscles trembling with the release. When she opened her eyes, another man was standing there.

He was stroking his cock and watching her with desire. "I'm yours," she whispered.

He undid her restraints and led her to the desk. He bent her over. Seeing the dildo in his ass, he began fucking her with it.

She moaned, it felt so good. The icy visitor was in her pussy and rubbing her clit, bringing her closer to climax.

He removed the dildo and shoved his dick in, grabbing her hips and pounding into her ass. She cried out, "More!" and he went faster. She felt his cock swell, and his hot cum filled her ass. She gripped the far side of the desk, her muscles tensing with orgasm. He pulled out, leaving her there, and left. She shuddered a final time and felt her icy visitor teasing her nipples. She moaned, and the door opened.

Whoever it was pushed her back down on the desk when she started to move, and slid his cock into her wet pussy. "You're so fucking wet," he said. It was Bill. He held her head down, preventing her from moving, and she lay there.

He moved his cock from her pussy into her ass, and grabbed her wrists, holding them behind her back. He used the silicon handcuffs to keep her hands in place. He gripped her hair, and shoved her head back down. "You like this?"

She moaned. "Oh, god, yes!"

"You want this dick?"

"Fuck me," she begged.

"Damn right, you filthy whore." He slammed his cock into her ass, fucking her hard and fast until he came. His hot cum filled her up. When he was done, he pulled out and slapped her ass. "Don't fucking move. I'm not done." She heard him leave the room. She twitched, her pussy begging for orgasm.

Bill came back in with another guy. "I'm gonna watch," he said. He took a seat in the chair on the other side of the desk. She felt the new guy's fingers sliding over her pussy. "My turn," he whispered.

"Fuck her pussy." Bill said.

She felt the man's cock slide into her and she moaned. He reached around and rubbed her clit while he fucked her.

"Harder," Bill commanded.

The guy stopped rubbing her clit, grabbed her hips, and fucked her harder.

She cried out. This felt so fucking good.

Bill stood, stroking his cock. It had been cleaned, and smelled like soap. He shoved his cock in her face, and she stuck her tongue out to lick it but he pulled away. She felt her climax, and closed her eyes. The guy was pounding into her, so hard and so fast, and she came, clenching her pussy on his cock. He came also, his cum filling her pussy. She realized he wasn't wearing a condom and didn't care. His hot cum made her wetter, and he slid his cock out. She shuddered and trembled, while Bill watched, stroking his cock but not letting her lick it or suck it.

"Next," Bill said. The guy left, and a new one came in.

She felt hands turn her over. His fingers slid to her clit and began rubbing. A moment later, he was wiping her with a towel. "Too wet." He said. "Kneel."

She did as she was told, and opened her mouth. He ran the tip of his cock around her lips, and shoved her head onto it. She sucked, and rubbed her clit. She wanted his cum in her throat. He fucked her face, and grunted as he came, pulling his cock out and dropping hot cum on her mouth and chin. She licked what she could. He shoved his cock back in her mouth, and she cleaned him off, licking and sucking his balls when he pulled back out. Without another word, he turned and left the room.

Bill came around, and grabbed her hair with a fist, pulling her head back. Damien came in the room next, his cock already hard.

"Bend over the desk." Bill said.

She did as she was told. Bill shoved his cock in her mouth, and she sucked, thankful to be allowed to finally taste him. Damien fingered her ass before shoving his cock inside her. She immediately clenched her ass cheeks, and Bill shoved his cock to the back of her throat. She moaned around his cock, and started twitching as she came. She could feel the hot cum of Damien fill her ass at the same time Bill shot his load into the back of her throat. Damien slapped her ass, making her butt jiggle, and he pulled out.

254

They left the room together, and she curled on the floor. She didn't think she could cum again if she wanted to. No other men came in and she closed her eyes. Maybe she could take a nap right here. The icy fingers of her ghostly visitor had other ideas. Her thickest dildo fell off the table. One she never used because it was so big. She felt the icy fingers pinching and pulling at her nipples, arousing her. She was going to cum again.

She grabbed the giant dong and slid it into her pussy. It felt like two cocks inside her, it was so big. The ghost began fucking her with the dildo, slamming it into her and sucking her clit. She teased her nipples, and brought a hand up to her throat. She was so close to cumming. The ghost fucked her faster, and her breathing sped up, her heart pounded. She felt beads of sweat form on her neck and chest. Her belly tightened, and she came. The ghost stopped moving the dong as her pussy clenched around it, spasming in ecstasy. She felt the icy breath on her clit, bringing her down from her climax before dissipating. She tried to catch her breath.

She could hear tools and the workers in the distance, and closed her eyes. She was exhausted, and so satisfied. She ran a hand across her nipples, the orgasms increasing their sensitivity, and she shuddered. Now she wanted a nap.

Chapter Four:

She woke to someone stroking her clit. But it wasn't her ghostly visitor. She moaned, and rolled to her back. She was still on the floor of the library. She cracked open an eye. It was the big black man, and he was naked. She moaned again, and spread her legs.

He climbed on top of her, missionary position, and kissed her. It was a slow, lazy kiss with none of the urgency she'd felt earlier. She met his pace, pushing her hips against his. He brought his head down, taking her nipple into his mouth, stroking her skin with his large hands. He pushed up on his hands, and looked down at her.

His cock flexed, and his angled his hips, stroking the inside of her pussy lips with the tip of his hard dick. He slid the tip in, and rested on his elbows, whispering in her ear, "I wanna fuck you."

She moaned, her pussy getting wetter at the words, a chill of anticipation shooting down her spine. She pushed her hips up, and his dick went the rest of the way inside her.

He started slow, teasing her. As his breathing quickened, he sped up the pace. She met him thrust for thrust, her own breath coming in pants.

She flipped him over onto his back, and straddled him. She guided his hands to her tits, and started riding his cock. When he started teasing her nipples on his own, she moved one hand to his chest, and put the other between them to stroke her clit. She threw her head back, moaning, her legs squeezing his hips.

"Come for me," he said. He moved his hands from her tits to her hips, guiding her, and she stroked her clit to the same rhythm. She felt her muscles clenching and fell forward as the orgasm ripped through her body. As her climax subsided, he lifted her off his cock. She quickly slid down, and wrapped her tits around his cock, sliding on his hard dick.

He helped push her tits together and fucked her titties. His hot cum shot up from her tits onto the underside of her chin, covering her tits. She angled her neck, licking the cum she could reach. He heaved a sigh and his body twitched. She smiled, and took an unsteady breath. "Thanks," she said with a wink.

"Anytime," he said, his voice unsteady. "Could I get your number?"

She sat up straight and climbed off. "Why?"

He shrugged. "I'd like to call you once this is all over."

She shook her head and laughed. "Honey, I don't think you can handle me. In case you didn't notice, I'm not exactly a fan of monogamy."

He stood, and started cleaning her with a wipe. "Me either. But I'd like you to meet my wife. I think you'd be a great addition to our family."

She looked up at him. He was married? "Your wife?" she said, her brain not quite working this out.

"Yeah," he said. He balled the wipe and threw it into the trash then grabbed another and cleaned himself. "We're poly."

She shrugged. She hadn't been with a woman since college, but she'd be down to try. "If you want sure."

"Great. I'll call you after we finish the job."

She sidled up to him, running her hands along his hard abdomen. "Why not tonight? Bring her over. She can join the fun."

He shook his head. "She doesn't like big group sex. Three or four people is her maximum."

"Then I can send away the guys, and you can bring her by." She shrugged. "Might as well see if we're compatible sooner rather than later." She picked her robe from where she'd abandoned it earlier. "I need to get back to work." She pulled her robe on and left the room. If he came back with his wife, she'd figure it out then.

To Be Continued…

A Pervy Poltergeist: Part Three

By: A lonely Woman

Lonely Woman

Dear Reader:

This book is different than the other two. I thought I would try to explore the romance, and the interrelationships a little more. I hope I did a good job. *Kisses*

As always, if you read the book, please leave an honest review on amazon. Thank you.

Chapter One:

Lisa's nightly visitor had made her cum at two am, and again at six. She was feeling motivated. She climbed from her massive bed, and stretched, her breasts moving with her arms. She sighed. Today would be a good day. The electrical crew would be back again, and though she was a little sore, she was ready for them.

Opening the closet, she pushed hangers aside as she tried to decide what to wear. Something easy access, but also something she could work in. She put her finger in her mouth and tapped her foot. Spying a satin number she'd bought a couple years ago, she perked up.

She pulled a red satin nighty from the closet. She pulled it over her head and it slid down her body. Her nipples hardened in excitement. Yes, this was the perfect outfit.

She made her way to the large dresser that matched the bed, and pulled open the top drawer. She dug around a moment before pulling out the matching red lace thong, sliding her smooth legs through the holes. It fit snug against her hips and ass. A pair of sheer red nylons were next. She put her toes in first, and slowly rolled them up her leg, savoring the feel of the nylons against her skin as she rolled.

Last was a red satin and lace garter belt. She hooked her thigh high nylons into the garters, and starred at her reflection in the full-size mirror. Satisfied with her appearance, she grabbed her red satin knee-length robe from the hook on the back of the door, and slid it on, tying the sash loosely around her waist.

She made her way into the dining room and looked around. From the look of things, the workers had already been in her. Everything was covered in a fine layer of white dust from where they'd drilled into the plaster.

Grabbing a dust rag and some cleaner, she set about cleaning all the surfaces. It was easy enough to clean the sides, front and top of the long buffet she'd inherited. But cleaning the top of the china hutch was proving impossible. She sighed, and switched to the table. She leaned across the wooden expanse, and a cold breeze tickled her ass. She shivered, wondering if her ghostly visitor had come to call. But the cold wasn't icy, it was just a draft.

She heard the front door open, and grinned. The workers were here. The draft turned into a breeze as the early morning wind carried from the open door, through the house, and out the window she'd opened in the dining room. She shivered, her nipples brushing against the cool wood of the table, as she closed her eyes.

The workers had become very familiar with her home, and her, and let themselves in. She could hear them tromping up and down the stairs, carrying their tools and anything else they would need to the rooms they'd be finishing today on the second floor.

She was cleaning a stain that seemed to be glued to the center of the table when a pair of large hands gripped her hips. She looked over her shoulder to see the large black man from yesterday. He was standing behind her, fully dressed, and his cock was pushing into her bare ass cheek.

"Hey, big guy." She turned back to the spot on the table, pretending to ignore him. But it was impossible to ignore the wetness in her panties, and her hard nipples brushing against the table through the satin nightgown and robe.

"Call me Al." He pulled away, and moved one hand off her hips.

She groaned, disappointed. "Aww, don't you want to play while the others are busy working?"

He unzipped his pants in answer.

She wiggled her hips, and looked back over her shoulder. She could only see part of his muscular torso. He'd already removed his shirt. She turned, lifting her ass on to the table, and pulled him close with her legs.

His cock pushed against her thighs. He starred at her chest, her nipples prominent against the satin.

She inhaled deeply, and he untied her sash, pulling the robe open and slipping it down her arms. She ran her hands along his muscular arms, enjoying the groves and ridges in the muscle.

He groaned, leaned forward, and kissed her jaw, then traveled his lips to her neck.

She rolled her head back as he nipped the sensitive skin under her jaw. She moaned, and her tits grew heavy with need.

He slid the thin strap of her negligee down her arm, trailing his lips to her shoulder. His hips began a slow rhythm, as he moved his mouth to her chest. He slid the other strap down, kissing her other shoulder.

She inhaled, put a hand on the back of his head, and moaned again. "Yes," she whispered, the smell of his cologne filling her nose.

He pulled the straps down further, and brought his mouth to hers, kissing her deeply. His mouth opened, and she followed his lead, her panties getting wetter when their tongues began to dance. He pushed the front of her satin negligee lower, and her breasts popped over, her perky nipples begging for attention.

He rolled a nipple between his finger and thumb, then cupped the whole breast. He lowed his mouth, sucking her nipple in. His hips moved faster, and she leaned back on the table, wanting more.

Her belly was tight with desire, and her panties felt soaked. He moved his mouth, kissing his way to her other nipple, the skin under him exploding with each kiss. He licked her, tasting her, then took her other nipple in his mouth.

She wrapped her legs tighter around his waist, and pulled him closer. She wanted him inside her, need him to fill her up. She lay on
264

the table, sliding her ass forward, wiggling her hips against his rock-hard cock.

He groaned, and slid a finger between her pussy lips, before penetrating her. He moved the tip of his finger slowly, stroking the sensitive spot near the back.

She slid her arms along the table, raising them above her head. Her hair fanned out behind her, her tits held in place by the satin neckline of her nighty.

He licked her chest between her tits, and traced a path down her belly.

She unwrapped her legs, and set her heels on the tables edge. She moaned, lifting her hips as she tried to get closer. Her body was thrumming with need and desire.

He hooked a thumb in the waist band of her thong, and slid her panting off, his hands caressing her bare thighs. She lifted one foot then the other, and he tossed her panties aside.

He put his mouth on her pussy, and ran his tongue slowly from his fingers still inside, up to her clit. He flicked his tongue, and she shuddered. He opened his mouth, spreading her open, and moved faster. He was sucking, biting, and licking her as he added another finger inside her, stretching her.

She put a hand on the back of his head, her hips rocking to his rhythm. She moaned, and he went even faster. She held his head, not wanting him to pull away as tremors wracked her body. He didn't stop, and she came. Her thighs squeezing the side of his head and her body shook and her pussy clenched on his fingers, making them still. She was panting. "Oh, god. Yes!"

His fingers and tongue stopped, and he sucked before slowly stroking around her clit and bringing her down from her climax. He licked the wetness, and pulled his fingers out, moving tantalizingly slowly.

Her muscles felt like jelly, and she moaned in satisfaction. "Mmmm."

He ran his wet fingers along her lips, and she opened her mouth, sucking her cum off his fingers, exploring his skin with her tongue. He pulled his hand back, and yanked her hips forward. His cock pressed against her pussy.

She rocked her hips, the stirrings of another orgasm started in her belly, and spread to her groin.

He leaned over her, not entering her, and sucked and teased her tits. She moaned in frustration.

He reached his hands under her back, pulling her up, and angled her onto his cock. He thrust once, hard.

She gasped, his cock filling her pussy. She wrapped her legs around him as she tried to ride his cock.

He put his hands under her ass, and lifted her from the table and halfway from his cock.

She put her hands on the sides of his face, and kissed him, teasing his tongue with hers. He turned, and shoved her back to the wall, her legs still wrapped around him. He lowered her ass, and his cock went deeper inside. "You feel so fucking good."

"Your pussy's so fucking wet," he whispered in her ear. He held her pinned to the wall, and began a rapid rhythm, his cock hit deep inside, and she felt her muscles tremble.

She moaned, and he bit her neck, then kissed it, and whispered, "I want you to cum for me."

She shuddered, and matched his rhythm as best she could, the tip of his cock hit her g-spot. "Right there," she panted. "Don't stop. Oh god, I'm… I'm going to… Oh my god." Her thighs squeezed his hips, and her pussy clenched on his cock. She was trembling, the waves of pleasure washing over her.

He didn't stop. He pounded into her, again and again. He put his mouth on a nipple, and bit, then sucked.

She kept coming, her pussy spasming around his cock.

He grunted. "Yeah, baby. Want me to cum."

"Fill me up," she moaned.

He groaned louder, his own thighs clenching as he pushed his cock as deep as it would go. She felt his warm cum filling her, and she shuddered, then reached between them to rub her clit. It was enough to through her over the edge again. He was spent, but his cock was still hard enough for her to cum again. Their fluid mixed, and filled the air with the smell of sex.

He held her up, his hands still under her bare ass, and he slid his cock out.

She felt so empty. She set her feet down, her back still against the wall, and looked up at him with hooded eyes. "Thanks," she panted. Her heart was still racing and she was trying to catch her breath.

He winked, pulled his shirt on over his head and zipped his pants as he sauntered from the room.

Chapter Two:

Lisa finished cleaning the table before pulling her robe on. She searched for her panties and finally found them hanging from the corner of the china cabinet. They were still damp, so she took them to the laundry basket. She'd rather go commando than put on soiled panties.

She thought about going upstairs and checking on the men's progress, but thought better of it. If she kept distracting them while they worked, they'd never get the work done. With a sigh, she made her way to the kitchen. If Al had been serious, today she may get to meet his wife. She cringed. She'd never asked the marital status of any of her partners, ever. She didn't want to know, and truly didn't care.

But it'd been quite some time since she'd gotten to enjoy a woman. And if his lady was as pretty as he was, well, things could be promising. She reached into the top cupboard and pulled down a pitcher to make iced tea and set it on the counter. She turned and eyed the freezer uncertainly. She didn't often cook; it was cheaper to eat out. And cleaner. But, it could be worth it.

Opening the freezer, she was greeted by the sight of freezer burned boxed meals, an old tv dinner, and an ice cube tray with more frost on it than the sides of the freezer. She quickly shut it the freezer door, and shook her head. She would have to run to the store. Which meant getting dressed. She groaned, and stomped toward her bedroom.

Ice and whatever she wanted to cook for dinner. She repeated it over and over as she dressed in a pair of tight jeans and a tank top. She forewent a bra, knowing it would just get in the way later. She like how her tits looked when she constrained them in a bra, but she was not in the mood. Running to the store had put her in a decidedly not-sexy frame of mind.

She pulled on her shoes and grabbed her car keys from the table next to the front door. Normally she would walk, but she didn't want to be gone too long. Heavy footsteps tromped down the stairs behind her, and she turned to see who it was. It was Sam! "Hey, I need to run to the store. You boys need anything while I'm out?"

He gaped at her chest. "Like that?"

She shrugged. "Sure. Why not?"

He shook his head to clear it. "Whatever lady. Want us to wait to take our—" he leered at her and said, "—lunch?"

Goosebumps ran up her arms and she shivered delightfully. "If you wouldn't mind." She peeked up at him from under her lashes. Her gaze hit its mark, and she saw his cock stiffen slightly.

"Okay. I'll just, um, let the guys know."

"Thanks, Sam," she breathed, leaning forward ever so slightly to let her tits hang, and emphasize her cleavage.

He swallowed hard, and rushed back up the stairs.

With a chuckle, the headed off to the store, mentally cursing the necessity of it.

Chapter Three:

By the time she'd returned from the store, it had been over an hour since she'd left. She pushed her front door open, three grocery bags hanging from her arm. She'd picked up a couple meal kits, so she could decide what to make when it was closer to dinner time. She stepped into the house and shut the door behind her before looking up. She almost dropped her bags.

The electricians were already in the living room. Most of them had their pants already down around their knees, cocks in their hands. The few remaining were in the process of joining.

She moaned, her nipples hardening at the sight. "Let me put this away and I'll join you." She winked, and rushed the kitchen where she quickly sorted the groceries. She wiped her hands on the back of her pants, and made her way back into the living room.

Every single man, all six of them, had their pants around their ankles and their cocks in their hands. A couple, including Al, had taken their shirts off as well. She took an unsteady breath, and ran a hand up her belly to cup her firm tit, squeezing gently as she ran her other hand down to her jeans, hooking her thumb in the waist.

Al stepped forward the same time Sam did. Al paused, and let Sam take the lead. Lisa stepped forward to meet him.

She reached down and grabbed his cock firmly, and he froze. She smiled, and stroked it, pulling him closer. He groaned. Al stepped up behind her, wrapping his arms around her waist, and sneaking under her top, and up to her breast. The rough callouses on his hands scraped her nipple as he cupped her tit, then brought his head down to kiss her ear and neck, sending shivers down her spine.

Sam huffed, then grabbed her other tit, squeezing it roughly through her top. He pinched her nipple. She gasped, the contrast between the two men's touch sending shockwaves to her pussy.

Sam gently pulled his hips back, and she let go. He turned, and got to his knees before laying on the floor and turning over to his back. He was stroking his cock, while Al unbuttoned her pants.

She wrapped an arm behind her, and rubbed her hands along Al's smooth back.

"Get on," Sam growled as a bead of precum glistened on the tip of his cock.

She let go of Al. She kept her knees straight, and locked gazes with All. Sticking her ass out, she hooked her thumbs in the waist band and slid her tight jeans over her round ass and down her legs. She stepped out of the flip flops she'd been wearing, and pulled her pants the rest of the way off.

She felt the thrill of excitement bloom in her belly, knowing that every man in the room was watching her, and wanted her. Slowly, she stood back up as she caressed her legs. Never breaking eye contact, she rubbed her hands up her hips, over her belly, and to the bottom on her shirt. She inched it up, teasing them as she slowly lifted it higher before finally pulling it over her head, her tits bouncing. She tossed her shirt to the side, and stepped over Sam while she looked down on him.

She squatted, and hovered over his cock, the tip brushing against her pussy. "You want this?" She teased her nipples, and her lids lowered. Sam was breathing heavy, and her heart was beating quickly in her chest. She held the power.

Al came up behind her once again, and reached down. He replaced her hands with his. She moaned, and reached down. Her pussy was so wet. She spread her pussy lips, and slid onto Sam's cock. Sam's eye's closed, and she lowered the rest of the way to all fours.

All mounted her from the back, rubbing his cock against her ass crack. She moaned, then raised a hand, beckoning one of the other men to come closer. She glanced back at Al. "Put your cock in my pussy," she moaned.

Al slid his cock in with Sam's, and her pussy stretched to accommodate them. Al was almost too big. She moaned, the discomfort turning in to pleasure when she rocked her hips, sliding both cocks part way out before sliding back down.

The man she'd summoned stood at her face, his cock in his hand. A drop of cum fell from the tip of his cock.

She reached out and stroked while Sam and Al fucked her. She was trembling, on the edge of an orgasm that wouldn't come. "Al, put it in my ass," she begged, seeking release.

He pulled out, and rubbed his soaked cock around her asshole.

She moaned, every nerve on fire. The man whose cock she stroked stepped forward, pushing his cock against her parted lips. She looked up at him, and cupped his balls before licking his shaft, from the base to the tip. Opening her mouth, he grabbed the back of her head and shoved his cock to the back of her throat. She gaged momentarily and relaxed her throat.

While one fucked her face, Al worked his cock into her ass. He spit on it, and spread it with the tip of his cock. He stuck his finger in her ass, getting her ready. She moaned around the cock in her mouth.

She moaned, forcing herself to relax, when she felt his cock pushing against her asshole, ready to enter. The man holding the back of her head, grabbed a fist full of hair. She relaxed her jaw, and he fucked her face, filling her throat with his cum at the same time Al got his cock inside her ass. She swallowed, and sucked, cleaning the cum from his dick as he pulled it from her mouth.

She trembled, and her legs were twitching. She was on the edge, ready to come. Sam reached up, pinched and twisted her nipples, then he grabbed and squeezed her tits. Her pussy seemed to explode when her orgasm finally came. Al held her shoulders as he slammed into her ass, and she arched her back. Tremors of pleasure made her toes curl, and she screamed out, "Oh my god, yes!"

Sam and Al increased their pace, fucking her harder and faster as she came. As she came down from the edge, she felt Sam's hot cum fill her pussy. He grunted, and gripped her tits, his fingers digging into the soft flesh. Once he'd finished, he opened his eyes.

He pulled his cock out, and scooted out from under her.

Al spanked her ass, the sting vibrating to her pussy, and she moaned.

Once of the men still standing at the edge of the room walked over, and stuck his cock in her face. She looked up at him, and licked the precum from the tip before taking him into her mouth. One of the other men who'd been standing came to stand beside the other man. She moved her mouth from the first cock to the second, and the first man scrambled to get under her, sliding his smaller cock into her pussy.

She was so wet, and filled with Sam's cum, she almost couldn't tell he was inside.

Al flexed his cock, smacked her ass then gripped her hips, and slammed into her, grunting as he filled her ass with his cum. She sucked harder on the cock in her mouth, feeling the familiar tingles of her orgasm in her pussy.

He slowly pulled his cock out, and the last man who'd been waiting took Al's place.

The new guy had nice sized cock, and stretched her ass. The man under her came, without even playing with her tits.

She pulled her mouth to the edge of the cock in front of her and looked into his eyes. She sucked hard, and followed her mouth down his cock, stroking his balls.

The man under her didn't move, but his cock slipped out.

She reached between her legs, and put pressure on her clit. She closed her eyes. She was getting close.

As the man in her ass came, the man in front of her grabbed the back of her head. He pulled his cock almost all the way out, then slammed it, hard, into the back of her throat, spilling his cum on her tongue and down her throat.

It was enough to push her over the edge again. She screamed, unable to keep quiet, and every muscle in her body convulsed with the intensity.

The man in front of her stepped away, and the man under her scooted out, and stood. The man in her ass pumped a few more times before pulling out.

She collapsed onto the floor, still twitching.

The men wandered off, leaving her alone. She'd just pleased six men. And every single one had gotten off. She swallowed, her throat sticky, as she tried to catch her breath.

After the last man had gone back upstairs, she felt the icy touch of her ghostly visitor. She shuddered, but spread her legs. Her cum, and the men's, dripped down her ass crack, and the cum in her ass dripped out. She shivered as the icy visitor made its way up her body.

She gently teased a nipple, and sighed with pleasure as the ghostly visitor teased her clit.

She was ready to cum when a pressure was put on her throat. She was still able to breathe, but it was hard.

She came, and the pressure on her throat disappeared. She gasped for breath, her legs twitching with every squeeze of her pussy. Her toes were curled, and her fists were gripping the carpet as her heart hammered in her chest. Her ghostly visitor had given her another orgasm.

She lay on the floor, naked, and closed her eyes. She was completely satisfied and drifted off to sleep.

Chapter Four:

L isa woke to see Al crouched over her, gently nudging her.

"Hey. You okay?" She could hear the concern in his voice.

"Mmmm. More than," she mumbled, rolling to her side. Her hip dug into the hard floor and she opened her eyes the rest of the way. She needed to get off the floor. She rolled back onto her back and sighed. "Help me up?"

Al put his hands under her arms and lifted her to her feet. When she wobbled slightly, he wrapped an arm around her waist, and held her steady. "Hey, now."

She leaned her head onto his chest, and listed to his heart. "You sound pretty," she mumbled.

"Hey. Stay awake. What's going on?"

She eyes seemed to have closed again and she opened them. "Hmm?"

"Do we need to call an ambulance?"

"No." She sighed again. "I'm just very satisfied. I want to go to bed now. I didn't sleep well last night."

He didn't look very convinced by her words. He bent over, put an arm under her knees, and lifted her as if she weighed nothing.

Her eyes popped back open. "Oh!"

He carried to her bed, and gently laid her down on top of the blankets. "Can I call someone for you? I don't want to leave you here alone."

She stretched, and felt the dried cum between her legs. She wrinkled her nose, and sat up. "No, I'm fine. Really. Just tired. Haven't you ever masturbated to fall asleep faster? Same thing, but better." She grinned at him.

He looked slightly more relaxed. "Okay. So, hey, do you want to do dinner with me and my wife another night?"

She shook her head. "No. We can do it tonight. I just want to nap for a bit, then take a shower before she gets here."

He raised an eyebrow. "It's already after seven."

She jumped up from the bed. "What?!"

He gently pushed her back into a seated position. "Shh. It's okay. The guys are all gone. I stayed back, because you were sleeping on the floor. But after half an hour you hadn't moved, and I was getting worried." He shrugged.

She shook her head. Had she really slept that long? "Okay. I need a shower. Does your wife still want to come over?"

He sighed. "You're exhausted. Tell you what. I'll help you shower and clean up, and we can come over some other time."

She shrugged. She'd learned long ago, before she'd even finished high school, that when a guy said he'd do it later, he really meant never. "Okay."

She let him lead her into the bathroom. She was already naked, so she sat on the toilet seat while he ran the water, warming it up.

He shook the water from his hand. "Okay. Let's get you in the shower." He helped her stand, even though she wasn't wobbly anymore, and held her hand while she stepped over the side of the tub and into the shower.

She turned, and leaned her head back under the spray. The heat felt so good on her hair and skin. She rolled her head on her neck, letting the water sluice off her face.

276

"Hey!"

She opened an eye and looked at Al. "What? I like to enjoy my showers."

"You looked like you were falling asleep again. Here." He handed her the bottle of shampoo. "Please take a quick shower so I can put you back into bed."

She grinned. "Only if you join me."

"In the shower?" He seemed taken aback by the idea.

"Sure, that too. But I meant in bed."

He chuckled. "Let's get your shower finished, and we'll see."

She sighed as she dumped a dollop of shampoo into her hand. "Fine."

She scrubbed up, with Al watching the entire time. He'd tried to shut the curtain, but she'd insisted he stay and watch. "I might fall asleep again."

He rolled his eyes. "I think you're just trying to get me to join you."

She giggled. That was exactly what she was doing. She rinsed the last of the soap from her body, giving special care to her groin and asshole. Once she'd finshed, she turned off the water.

Al held her hand as she stepped from the tub onto the plush yellow bathmat, then he wrapped her in a large, extra soft towel.

She dried off, and flipped her head over to dry her hair, rubbing the towel along the ends of her hair briskly. When she was satisfied, she hung the towels on the shower curtain rod.

He wrapped his arm around her waist, and led her back to bed.

She sat on the edge of the bed, and looked up at him, pushing her tits together with her arms. "Are you going to stay? You know. Just in case?"

He shook his head. "I cannot leave my wife alone so I can keep you entertained."

"She can come too." She patted the bed beside her.

"Tell you what. Let me call and we'll see, okay?"

She shrugged. It seemed fair to her. "Okay."

Chapter Five:

"She said she wanted to come over anyway," he said, after he'd hung up the phone.

"Good." Lisa crawled to the middle of the bed and lay flat. Her eyes began to drift, but she fought it.

She must have fallen asleep, because it was less than a moment later and he was standing over her, with a woman Lisa didn't recognize. She was shorter, but looked like average height. Her long black hair fell to her ass in a smooth cascade of thick hair that was kept tucked behind an ear. Her face had an almost exotic look, with the upward slant to her eyes, tanned skin, and full lips. She looked good standing next to Al.

They were murmuring to each other.

"—looks sick." The woman said.

Al nodded. "I don't know what's wrong with her."

The woman saw Lisa's eye's open, and spoke a little louder. "Lisa? My name is Natalie. I'm a doctor. Can you tell me what's wrong?"

Lisa struggled to sit up but her muscles weren't working well.

Natalie climbed onto the bed, and wrapped an arm around Lisa's shoulders, and helped her into a sitting position. Natalie brought her other hand up and felt the back of Lisa's neck and her forehead. "Can you sit?" She slowly pulled away the arm that was supporting Lisa.

Lisa wobbled, and fell back into her pillows.

"Okay. Lay there." Natalie examined Lisa, feeling her neck, and making her say ahh. Once she was satisfied, she sat back, and pulled the covers up to Lisa's chin.

"Mmmm," Lisa did her best to snuggle in to the warm blankets.

"You don't have a fever. There doesn't seem to be anything wrong."

"Tired," Lisa murmured, turning her head to the side and letting her pillow engulf her.

"Yes, I can see that. Al has told me about your... Afternoon delight."

Lisa managed a weak smile. Afternoon delight was fun.

"I'm going to make dinner. You sleep for now. But I'm going to wake you up to eat when it's ready."

Lisa groaned. Why?

Natalie sighed. "I bet you haven't eaten. And that should help you get some energy back."

Lisa thought about it, and realized Natalie was right. She didn't know when the last time she'd eaten was. Her stomach growled loudly.

Natalie smiled. "And there you have it. Sleep for now." She turned to Al, and ran her hands up his chest, and Al snaked an arm about her waist, pulling her close. "Stay in here with her, okay? Holler if anything changes."

He nodded, and kissed Natalie's forehead before he let her go.

Lisa watched her go.

Al sat on the side of the bed, and stroked her hair. "Shh. Go to sleep."

Lisa didn't argue. She closed her eyes and drifted off.

Chapter Six:

Lisa was awakened by Al's firm hand on her shoulder, gently shaking her. "Come on," he coaxed, "You need to eat."

When she opened her eyes, he smiled at her. "There you are." He put an arm over her shoulder and helped her up.

Natalie stood in the doorway, concern in her eyes, carrying a soup bowl.

Once Lisa was seated, Natalie brought the food into the room. "Tomato soup and crackers." She set the bowl on the nightstand.

Al propped the pillows behind her, helping her stay seated, and Natalie took his place by her side. Al moved around to the other side of the bed.

Natalie handed her a cracker.

Lisa's stomach growled, and she reached out a shaky hand to take it. She chewed carefully, her jaw muscles aching like the rest of her.

"Good," Natalie murmured, and handed her another cracker.

Once Lisa had finished most of the food, Natalie stood, and looked down at her. "Go back to sleep."

Lisa was feeling a touch better. "What time is it?" Her throat felt dry, despite the soup, and she wondered if someone would get her some water.

Natalie checked her watch before answering. "Almost two."

Lisa almost sat up at that, but her muscles were still ignoring her commands. Her ghostly visitor would be by soon. They needed to leave.

Natalie sat next to her, and held her steady. "Shh," she murmured. "It's alright. Al says the house will be finished tomorrow, and I have tomorrow off. It's okay." She didn't understand Lisa's distress.

Lisa tried to explain without sounding crazy. "I appreciate that. You should go. I'll be okay. I'm feeling much better already."

Natalie exchanged a worried glance with Al. "If you're sure." She spoke slowly.

Lisa had an idea. "If you want, I have a spare bedroom you can use for the night. Clean linens are in the closet at the top of the stairs."

Natalie's brow furrowed. "I don't want to impose."

"No, it's fine!" Lisa waved a hand dismissively. "I don't often have guests. It would be nice for the room to get used. Besides. Tomorrow you're off. We can hang out. Get to know each other."

Natalie beamed at her. "I would like that."

Lisa felt the icy hands of her visitor on her ankles, and they began working their way up. She shuddered.

Natalie turned to her husband. "Al, go get the room set up please?"

"What about tomorrows lunch break." He put finger quotes around the words 'lunch break'.

Lisa's eyes closed as her ghostly visitor began paying special attention to her clit. She moaned.

"Go," Natalie said.

Lisa could hear him leave, and he closed the bedroom door behind him. Her breath was coming faster, and her heart sped up. Her ghostly visitor knew how to please.

"Are you—" Natalie checked that her hands were still beside her. "Hmm."

"Oh, god," Lisa breathed. Natalie was going to watch her orgasm, hands free.

"What the hell?" Natalie jumped up, and Lisa opened her eyes in time to see Natalie shudder, and her nipples harden.

Lisa smiled. Natalie was getting first-hand experience with the ghostly visitor.

The icy chill of the visitor was teasing Lisa's nipples, while pressing against her clit.

Lisa closed her eyes, feeling the tingles of excitement spreading through her pussy.

The bed sank in next to Lisa as Natalie sat.

Lisa moaned at the same time as Natalie. The visitor had increased the pace, rubbing faster. It felt like an ice cube in her pussy, and her muscles clenched around it.

Natalie grabbed Lisa's hand, and held on tight.

About the same time, they both began shuddering and climaxing. Lisa rode the wave of pleasure, and gripped Natalie's hand and her blanket.

"My god," Natalie panted.

"I know," Lisa agreed.

"That was amazing."

"I know."

"Is that why you were worried earlier? This happens every night?"

"Yup. Two am."

"My god." Natalie lay back on the bed, her head next to Lisa's.

"You can still stay the night though."

"Oh, good. That was intense. Where's Al. I'm not finished."

Lisa chuckled. "And now you understand my afternoon delight."

As if summoned, Al came in the room. "The beds ready —." He stopped short. "Oh. Should I—," he motioned toward the door with a thumb.

"Join us," Natalie purred.

Al didn't need to be told twice. He walked toward the bed as he pulled his shirt off over his head, revealing his hard chest.

Lisa watched as he undid his pants and slid them off. His cock was hard, and Natalie moaned in appreciation. He walked to the bed, and Natalie reached out, stroking his cock.

"We should go upstairs," Natalie said with a worried glance to Lisa.

"Stay," Lisa said. "I might want to join you before going back to sleep."

Al grinned, and climbed onto the bed, straddling his fully dressed wife. He reached down and teased Natalie's nipple. "Get naked," he growled, and moved between Lisa and his wife.

Natalie stood, and met Lisa's gaze as she slowly unbuttoned her silk blouse. The thin bra underneath showed off her perky nipples, and Lisa shivered with anticipation as Natalie dropped her blouse to the floor. She hooked a thumb in her slacks, and unhooked them, letting them fall down her shapely legs.

Al teased Lisa's nipple as he watched his wife undress.

Natalie reached behind her, and unhooked her bra, letting it fall like her blouse and pants. Her tits were only a 'B' cup, but looked firm and ripe. She slipped her white panties next, and stood a moment, letting Lisa appreciate her firm, tight little body.

She crawled on to the bed, and leaned her face down. She paused, a breath away from Lisa's lips, then kissed her. Slow at first, then deeper, their tongues brushed in a tantalizing dance.

Al pulled the blanket down, and Lisa gasped as the cold air hit her warm body.

Natalie pulled her mouth away, and trailed kisses to her ear, and down her neck before stopping on her tits. She used her mouth to tease Lisa's hard nipples, and Lisa spread her legs.

Al slid a finger along her pussy before sliding a finger inside her.

Lisa reached out and pinched Natalie's nipple, then cupped it, squeezing it gently and teasing her firm tit.

Al lowered his face to her pussy, and licked Lisa's clit as Natalie brought her mouth back to Lisa's, kissing her once more.

Lisa moaned into Natalie's mouth, grinding her hips against Al's tongue.

Natalie pulled away, and kissed her neck, her chest, her tits, teasing the nipples once more. When she moved her mouth to trail down Lisa's belly, the cool air on her wet nipple hardened it back up.

Al lifted his face from her pussy, and ran his hands along her belly, near where Natalie was kissing. He made his own trail with his mouth, and stopped at her tits. He pinched her nipple before putting it in his mouth.

Lisa stroked his hard cock, and gasped as Lisa's mouth covered her pussy, licking and teasing her clit while she stroked Lisa's g-spot with her fingers.

Al flexed his cock, and Lisa opened her mouth, running her tongue along her bottom lip. Al took the unspoken invitation, and sat up on his knees.

Lisa stroked his cock, then licked the shaft and sucked his balls. She ran her tongue from his balls to the tip, tasting his precum before she opened her mouth wide and started sucking his dick.

He groaned, and grabbed the back of her head, guiding her mouth.

Lisa moaned around his cock as Natalie brought her to the edge of climax. She sucked harder as she rocked her hips. She cupped Al's balls with one hand, and fisted Natalie's hair with the other.

Natalie moved her fingers from Lisa's pussy and slid one into her asshole, and one into her pussy. Lisa gasped, then sucked harder as her body trembled, her muscles clenching as she came. Natalie used her tongue on Lisa's clit a final time, and Lisa's legs twitched, then Natalie circled around her clit with her tongue, licking Lisa's juices and bringing Lisa down from her climax.

Al pulled Lisa's mouth off his cock, his breathing labored as he murmured, "Not yet."

Lisa groaned in frustration, and Natalie smiled at her as she pulled her fingers out, teasing Lisa with the slowness.

"I want to sit on your face," Natalie purred, and crawled up Lisa's body, kissing and licking. She kissed Lisa. "Mm, my husband's cock tastes so good on you."

Al made his way down Lisa's body, and kneeled between her legs, stroking her pussy as he watched Lisa and Natalie kissing and teasing each other.

"I want you," Lisa whispered to Natalie.

Natalie straddled Lisa's face, then lowered her pussy to Lisa's waiting mouth. Natalie tasted so good.

Al lifted Lisa's legs to his shoulder, and slid his cock into her waiting pussy. She moaned, and wrapped her arms around Natalie's thighs as Natalie rocked her hips.

Natalie ran her hands along her body, and cupped her breasts, teasing her nipples, while Al slammed into Lisa's pussy. Lisa wanted to scream out, but Natalie's pussy was there. She licked, and put pressure on Natalie's clit with her tongue. Natalie cried out, "oh, god, don't stop," as tremors shook through her entire body as she came.

Lisa took the pressure from her clit and licked her entire pussy, not wanting to miss a drop of Natalie's tasty cum.

Al reached between Lisa's legs, and rubbed her clit as he fucked her, and Lisa's legs twitched.

Natalie climbed off Lisa's face, and lay next to her, teasing her nupples and rubbing her clit while Al fucked her.

"Yes, yes, yeesss," she cried out, her stomach clenching, her legs twitching and her pussy squeezing Al's cock.

He groaned, and his hot cum filled her up.

Spent, they all lay next to each other on the large bed, with Lisa in the middle of their spoon.

She sighed. This was something she could definitely get used to, she thought as she drifted off to sleep.

Chapter Seven:

She woke briefly when Al climbed out of bed, needing to work in the morning, and didn't stir again until Natalie woke her with a kiss.

"Hey sleepy head," Natalie said, smiling down at her.

Lisa rubbed the sleep from her eyes. "Hey."

"I brought you lunch. Can you sit up?"

Lisa pushed herself up, and smiled in satisfaction when she'd managed to do it without help. "Looks like."

"Good." Natalie smiled back and handed her a sandwich on a plate. "I had a great time last night."

Lisa took a grateful bite and nodded. After she'd swallowed she said, "So did I. You guys should stay tonight again."

Natalie beamed. "I'd like that. I have to work tomorrow, but we can play a little after the crew leaves if you want."

Lisa grinned, and swallowed another bite. "Why not now?"

Natalie chuckled. "They're cleaning up right now so they can leave. They seemed upset when I told them you wouldn't be available today. One even asked if I was your replacement." She shook her head, still chuckling.

Lisa smiled, and finished her sandwich. Once it was all gone, Natalie handed her a glass of water.

"Drink this. I'm glad you're feeling better."

Lisa hadn't realized how thirsty she was until she'd drank the entire glass of water. "Thank you," she gasped, catching her breath.

"Come on. Let's get you dressed. You can say goodbye to the crew."

Lisa reached out and tweaked Natalie's nipple. "I'd rather say hello to you."

Natalie grinned, and kissed her. When she pulled away, she looked pensive. "Are we rushing things a little?"

Lisa laughed. "No. I have a ghost who pleasures me every night at two am. And now I have the chance to add the two of you to my home. No, we aren't rushing things. In my opinion, we aren't moving fast enough. You and Al are exactly what I need."

Natalie smiles, and kissed Lisa gently. "That's what I wanted to hear," she whispered. Natalie sat up and tapped her chin thoughtfully. "But I don't think we're moving in just yet. Let's give it a month, and then see."

"Ugh," Lisa groaned. "I guess." She smacked her hands on the top of the blanket, clearly frustrated.

Natalie laughed. "We'll be here as often as possible. Your home is closer to the hospital than ours is." She shrugged. "But I want you to understand how important communication is. We want a relationship with you. But that means talking to both of us if something is bothering you. It's almost twice as much work as a monogamous relationship."

Lisa raised an eyebrow. "Fine. But no priests. I like my poltergeist."

Natalie sighed, and stroked Lisa's cheek. "Me, too. Let's not tell Al." She grinned mischievously. "Let him find out for himself."

Lisa grinned back. "Agreed."

Natalie lowered her mouth to Lisa's, and kissed her deeply, and their tongues brushed. Natalie's hands roamed Lisa's body as Lisa unbuttoned the blouse Natalie had been wearing the day before.

Natalie hadn't put her bra back on, and Lisa trailed her mouth to Natalie's perky nipples.

Natalie pulled away, and Lisa moaned, but watched as Natalie pushed her pants off her hips without undoing them and step out of them. She hadn't put her panties back on, either. Natalie pulled the blanket down, and straddled Lisa. "Is this what you want?" She led Lisa's hands to her tits.

Lisa teased her nipples, and moaned. Natalie slid her hand between them, and slid her finger along their touching pussies.

With Natalie straddling her, Lisa reached between them, and teased Natalie's wet pussy. "I want you to cum for me," Lisa murmured.

Natalie tossed her head back, and slid her finger over Lisa's clit.

They rubbed each other's clits, their hips grinding as they teased each other to climax and came together.

They snuggled on the bed until Al came in, smiling when he saw them cuddled together, naked, on the bed.

"Can I keep you?" Lisa asked softly, stroking Natalie's hair.

"You can now. The crew is gone."

Natalie patted the bed on the other side of Lisa. "Come on, honey," she said. "Join us. Looks like we might be staying here." She kissed Lisa's neck.

"Come on, Al," Lisa patted the spot on the bed beside her, mimicking Natalie's words and actions from a moment ago. "I want to keep you. And my new wife says I have to communicate if something's bothering me, but with both of you."

Al sat on the side of the bed, and ran the tips of his fingers up Lisa's arm, then Natalie's. "Are you sure?"

Lisa giggled. "I'm sure. But you might be in for a few surprises."

Al shook his head when Natalie giggled. He stood, and stripped naked and lay beside them, draping an arm over both of them.

***

The ghost made an appearance that night at 2am, and the three of them enjoyed a simultaneous, hands-free orgasm, courtesy of the ghostly visitor. He laughed once they'd explained what happened, and they all drifted into sleep, to live happily ever after.

The End... For now.

Printed in Great Britain
by Amazon